D1566181

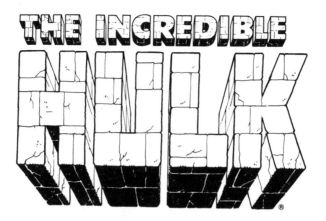

THE INCREDIBLE HULK

WHAT

SAVAGE

BEAST

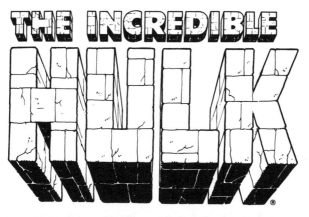

THE INCREDIBLE HULK

WHAT

SAVAGE

BEAST

BY PETER DAVID

ILLUSTRATIONS BY GEORGE PÉREZ

BYRON PREISS MULTIMEDIA COMPANY, INC.
New York

A Boulevard/Putnam Book

A Boulevard/Putnam Book
Published by G. P. Putnam's Sons
Publishers Since 1838
200 Madison Avenue
New York, NY 10016

Byron Preiss Multimedia Company, Inc.
24 West 25th Street
New York, NY 10010

Special thanks to Lou Aronica, Ginjer Buchanan, Lucia Raatma, Julia Molino, Bobbie Chase, Ken Grobe, and the gang at Marvel Creative Services

Edited by Keith R. A. DeCandido
Interior design by Heidi North

Byron Preiss Multimedia Company, Inc.
24 West 25th Street
New York, NY 10010

Library of Congress Cataloging-in-Publication Data

David, Peter (Peter Allen)
    The Incredible Hulk : what savage beast / Peter David ;
  illustrations by George Pérez.
        p.   cm.
    ISBN 0-399-14104-9 (alk. paper)
    1. Hulk (Comic strip)—Adaptations.   2. Heroes—Fiction.
  I. Title.
  PS3554.A92144I5   1995   95-20019 CIP
  813'.54—dc20

Printed in the United States of America
10 9 8 7 6 5 4 3 2 1

This book is printed on acid-free paper. ∞

To All Who Have Gone Before,
But Most Particularly

Stan Lee
Jack Kirby
Steve Ditko
Bill Mantlo

And also to my wife, Myra
Who has charms to soothe savage beasts*

* Yes, I know that's not the quote. But we couldn't very well call the book *What Savage Breast*, now could we. So save the letters and let's move on, okay?—*The Author*

PROLOGUE

Predictions were for a storm, but he had lucked out. It was *such* a nice night.

Thus lulled into a false sense of security, the trucker was not anticipating any problems whatsoever. He certainly wasn't expecting the sunburst of light to flare into existence directly in his path. Then again, he wasn't expecting to die either, so clearly it was a night made for the unexpected.

His name was Jack Marciano—Marsh, to his friends—and he was in the middle of a run driving a delivery of gasoline to Detroit. Marsh wasn't feeling the least bit tired; his stamina was somewhat legendary. The road ahead of him was clear, his gaze was unblinking, and there was a full moon so that—even though this stretch of highway was unlit by anything other than his headlights—he had fairly good visibility. Nothing was coming his way.

Which was why the sudden flare of lights about fifty feet directly in front of him caught Marsh so completely by surprise.

Marsh had three thoughts in fairly short order.

His first thought, out of long experience, was that an oncoming vehicle was heading straight toward him with headlights on full brights. But there were no other trucks or cars on the road. Just him.

His second thought was that he was suddenly being confronted by a UFO. He had never believed in such things, but on this night just about anything seemed possible.

He slammed on his brakes, but the truck had been shooting along at a fairly brisk clip of seventy miles an hour, his fuzzbuster serenely informing him that there was no hint of a speed trap around. There was absolutely no way that he was going to stop in time.

The brakes locked, the tires screeched, the air became thick with burning rubber.

The corona of light was holding steady, shimmering on the road, and then a massive form seemed to just step right out of the air. Human in shape, but mammoth in size.

There was too much glare for Marsh to make out any more details than that, and then there was no more time for anything except for Marsh to have his third thought. As it happened it was also his last, and unfortunately wasn't especially profound or memorable. In fact, it consisted of exactly one word, a slang term relating to human bodily waste.

The human-shaped obstruction turned and saw the truck barreling toward it. Rather than make any endeavor to get out of the way, the new arrival merely braced itself.

The irresistible force collided with the immovable object.

The object remained immovable.

As for the truck, it was as if it had slammed into a brick wall, or the side of a mountain. The trailer shoved against the back of the cab, while the front of it crushed in against the roadblock. The cab was waffled in between the two, Marsh never having a prayer or even a full comprehension of what happened to him. He was crushed flat, never even hearing the deafening screech of metal. The truck twisted back in on itself, the rear of the trailer skidding around, bending and jackknifing with a roar that sounded almost human.

The vehicle flipped over, continued its skid, and gasoline now poured from the cracked-open trailer. An instant later, metal crunched against pavement, sparks flew, and fuel ignited. Within seconds the sound of torn metal was replaced by a Vesuvian roar as the entire truck erupted in flame. It hurtled upward and outward, enveloping the newly arrived being who had been responsible for the crash. The tar of the highway melted into black rivulets, fire ripping outward and consuming shrubbery that lined either side of the road. Heat belched in all directions in waves. Stenches competed to see which could be the most noxious—the burning rubber battling the tar, the odor of bubbling human flesh, or the smell of death.

The truck had finally stopped all motion, lying in the pyre of its own creation. Black smoke swirled heavenward.

And standing there, watching it all, was the immovable object.

The smell didn't bother it, nor did the suffocating heat. It was not in the midst of the conflagration, but had merely stood its ground as the truck momentarily wrapped around it and then flew off, continuing on its way to its final resting place. It watched the black smoke curling, obscuring the light.

Obscuring the light. Yes, that certainly had a nice feel to it.

The figure parted from the shadows, and only then was it apparent that it was carrying something. In the large right fist there was a large briefcase. It was a bizarre apparition—a mammoth individual, walking away from an inferno utterly unperturbed, toting a briefcase as if heading for a meeting.

Behind him was death, destruction, and calamity.

Far in the distance was his destination. He could have gotten there relatively quickly, but he was in no hurry, for he had all the time in the world.

And so he started walking.

Because it seemed like *such* a nice night.

PART ONE

HOPE

Chapter 1

"Incredible."

Major Talbot was not one given to casual exclamations of amazement, but in this instance he simply couldn't help himself. What he was watching on the video screen defied all belief or attempt at rationalization. The rest of the sparsely furnished conference room was fairly dark, making the illumination of the screen that much clearer.

There was a battery of heavy-duty combat equipment converging on one lone being. On the face of it, it was a woefully uneven match. Granted, the creature opposing the assembled hardware was massively, powerfully built. Beyond powerfully built, actually. His muscles seemed to defy all known rules of human anatomy. They were huge tracks of cable, flexing and pulsing beneath skin that was, bizarrely enough, emerald green.

It was easy enough to get a view of them, for the creature was wearing a simple white tank-top shirt and dark pants. His hair was short, but not cut or brushed into any style; it just sat there atop his relatively small head. His furrowed brow ridge was ever so slightly distended, his jaw a bit elongated.

His smile was unnerving.

Talbot shook his head in wonderment. He was a handsome

enough fellow, with wiry black hair and a face that was normally tanned but, just at this moment, had gone a shade or so paler. His voice was deep and carefully modulated. By far his most striking feature was his eyes, which were a cobalt blue and seemed to be fired with an inner light.

"Freeze it," said Talbot, and the picture obediently paused on the screen. The creature was in motion and so his features were a slight blur. But they were still easy to discern.

"You can tell. You can tell he's no longer a simple, mindless brute. You can see that Banner's mind is running the whole show. A half a ton of muscle, with the brain of a genius in charge. Not enough that he can outmuscle us. Now he can outthink us." He paused and then, looking slightly embarrassed, added, "You have to understand," as if not wanting to seem unduly disconcerted, "I've seen him in action before. . . . God knows, I saw enough films of it. But nothing this recent and nothing this . . . disturbing."

"Disturbing in what way?" came the question.

Talbot rose from behind the table and came around to the screen. He tapped the arrested image on it. "Look at the smile. I've never seen that before."

"You've never seen a smile?"

Talbot let a flash of impatience creep into his voice. "Don't play games with me, Doctor. You know damned well what I mean. When I've viewed tapes of his destructive rampages in the past, I'd see rage in his face. Anger, fury. Like a deer caught in headlights, presuming that the deer could take a direct hit from a cruise missile or bench press a hundred tons. An animal . . ."

"Hunted animal, Major," said the man he'd addressed as "Doctor." "It might behoove us to keep that foremost in mind. Hunted by *your* people."

The major let it pass, instead continuing, ". . . a rampaging beast, Doctor. That's what he was. But in all my years, I never saw anything like that smile. Look at that. He was going up against heavy-duty, S.H.I.E.L.D.-issued armament. He was about to embark on a course of destruction and mayhem, violating national and international laws. And he was pleased about it. Look at that grin, Doctor. He was *pleased* about what he was going to do. Thrilled about it. The bastard was positively reveling in it."

"And you find this a surprise?"

The major paused a moment, blowing air impatiently through his lips. "You know, I feel constrained to say that I don't entirely like your attitude, Dr. Samson."

Dr. Leonard Samson regarded Major Talbot in the same manner as a child might study a bug, deciding whether or not to pluck off the helpless insect's legs. Apparently determining that it was more politic to leave the major in one piece for the moment, Samson nevertheless concluded that a small show of nonverbal intimidation might be in order.

He got up from his chair. The chair creaked gratefully, thrilled to be relieved of the weight.

When Samson rose, it was in a manner reminiscent of a mushroom cloud rising from the detonation of a nuclear warhead. He just seemed to keep going, up and up, towering well over six feet (not to mention well over the major). Plus there was more than just the simple matter of his height to consider: There was his width as well, which seemed to the casual viewer roughly on par with that of a tractor trailer. He was wearing a dark blue suit, tailored to accommodate his massive proportions, but it did nothing to downplay or diminish the raw power and size of the man.

Most striking of all was his hair. It was long and green, hanging to below his shoulder and tied off in a ponytail. When he scowled, it was like a storm cloud hovering. "Tell me, Major, just between you and me: Did you have a rough time potty training?"

Talbot did not seem particularly amused by the question. He

stepped forward slowly and looked Samson in the eye, although it did require craning his neck to do so. "Do you have a problem with me, Doctor?"

"Well, I guess it's what you would call your continual shirking of responsibility, Major." He gestured toward the creature's image, still unmoving on the screen. "That smile you're so obsessed about? You say he's enjoying it. Perhaps you're right. Perhaps he feels some measure of satisfaction in paying the military back."

"This wasn't payback!" said Talbot, slightly alarmed at the sympathy that Samson seemed to be displaying for such displays of unrepentant destruction. "This was a deliberate strike against the government of a small country called Trans-Sabal. A strike that he apparently spearheaded, with the assist of some mysterious rogue organization called the Parthenon, operating out of God knows where."

"Greece."

Talbot's eyes narrowed. "They're based in Greece? And how would you know that, Doctor?"

Samson smiled thinly. "The Parthenon is there, Major, and has been for a couple thousand years. It's a building. The name of the group is the Pantheon."

"Fine, whatever," said Talbot with a dismissive wave. "Pantheon, Parthenon, you know who I mean. The point is that they took it upon themselves to go in and overthrow the ruling government. A government that, I might add, was an ally of the United States."

"A government repeatedly criticized by Amnesty International as barbaric, a fact that we were more than willing to overlook in exchange for extraneous considerations, such as oil exports or even just plain political cronyism." He fought to keep the annoyance out of his voice and was not entirely successful.

"That's not the point," said Talbot.

"Well, perhaps to him," replied Samson, tapping the screen with a large knuckle, "it was indeed the point. Maybe he was smiling because, after so many years of the U.S. government making his life a living hell, he was reveling in the opportunity to send a message to the government telling it exactly what he thought of it and its policies. The policies that harassed him and—"

"Harass *that?*" Talbot spun on his heel, shouted to the unseen technician who was running the video, "Roll it forward!"

There followed five minutes of inconceivable destruction. The green-skinned behemoth stormed through whatever was tossed at him. Gleaming futuristic tanks with pulse cannons, ground pounders, infantry, even human-operated robots . . . all of it met the same quick, painful end. Oh, there were moments when the green creature seemed slightly staggered, even thrown for a loop once. But he would simply come back for more, and more, and what might have slowed him moments earlier didn't even faze him on the subsequent go-around.

"Are you telling me," said Talbot in a quavering tone, "that the government—and the military, Doctor, let's not mince words. It was our responsibility to bring him down, our responsibility to get the job done. So are you telling me that . . . that nuclear warhead on legs *wasn't,* and *isn't,* something that we have to contain? *Harass?* That isn't some shrinking violet, Doctor. That isn't some frustrated employee, or helpless individual caught up in the cogs of an 'uncaring' government machine. That's the incredible Hulk, a danger to everyone and everything we hold dear!"

Samson stared at him, and then made no effort to stifle his laugh. " 'Everything we hold dear'? Oh, good God, Major, save it for the next military appropriations hearing, okay? Don't waste perfectly good rhetoric on me. I've seen it and heard it all."

Leonard Samson walked slowly around the screen, never taking his eyes off it. "Look, Major . . . I don't mean to demean your efforts, and those of good soldiers before you. But in the old days, whenever the tanks would come rolling out in force to try and drag the Hulk away, so you could study him or imprison him or dissect him or in some other way deprive him of every single right ranging from due process to the pursuit of happiness, in those old days," and he kept going even as Talbot tried to interrupt him, "there would be the Hulk, smashing, destroying. And shouting. Always shouting the same thing." He turned to face Talbot and bent over slightly, bringing his face very close to that of the major's. " 'Leave . . . me . . . alone.' That's what he'd say, every time." He straightened up. " 'Leave Hulk alone. Leave me alone. Hulk just wants to be left alone.' With all due respect, Major, this should have been a no-brainer. When you've got all that destructive power in one package and all it wants to do is be left to its own devices, then it doesn't require any of history's great minds to figure out how to proceed. To be specific: You leave him alone. Send memos, write letters, go on TV, have the President call a press conference. And the message is the same to everyone: Leave the Hulk alone. That's all. Just leave him be. Don't get within a mile of him. Three miles, if you want to stay outside of his jumping range."

"And if America's enemies ever got their hands on him?" demanded Talbot.

"In that event, I'd suggest sending condolence cards to America's enemies."

Talbot waved a finger at Samson. "That's easy for you to say, Doctor. But I have to consider all the worst-case scenarios . . . particularly those created by well-meaning but boneheaded psychiatrists. Because, unless my latest information is woefully incorrect, we have *you* to thank for the Hulk's current condition. He's no longer a brainless brute, thanks to you. That's why we're having this meeting today, Doctor, in case I need to remind you. So that you can explain to me personally what happened."

"It was in my report.".

"A very sparse, very carefully worded report. You opted to tamper with a being who has been classified a military priority. The only reason you're not in jail now is because some high-powered people covered your ass. Now bring me up to speed, Doctor, if it's not too much trouble."

Their gazes locked for a long moment. Talbot was the first to look down, covering himself by picking up a pen and making some quick notes.

Samson sighed. "Dr. Robert Bruce Banner was . . . is . . . was a brilliant nuclear scientist who developed weapons for the military. Some years back, during the testing of his latest weapon, which he called a gamma bomb, Dr. Banner ran out onto the testing range to rescue a teenager named Rick Jones who had driven onto the field. For reasons involving sabotage, the gamma bomb was detonated while Banner was still on the field. . . ."

Talbot looked annoyed and impatient. "And the rays of the gamma bomb affected Banner and changed him into the Hulk. Old news, Doctor."

"New news, Major, because it wasn't until years later that we fully understood what had happened. Banner was an MPD . . . suffering from Multiple Personality Disorder. He had that condition long before he was struck by the gamma radiation. The savage aspect of his personality was already in place, although strongly repressed. Plus other . . . aspects, as well, all buried deep within his psyche. The gamma bomb didn't 'create' the Hulk so much as it gave form to that which already existed within him."

Talbot stroked his chin thoughtfully. "From what I've read, MPD comes about because of childhood abuse. Is that what happened with Banner?"

For a long moment Samson regarded him with a cold glare. "Now, Major, we're moving away from that which has been documented into the realm of doctor-patient privilege. To answer your question would be a breach of medical ethics."

"Ethics would seem to be a fairly flexible commodity as far as you're concerned, wouldn't it, Doctor?"

"No. They are not flexible," said Samson, the warning clear in his voice.

Talbot seemed to consider making an issue of it, but then clearly thought better of it. "So what happened?"

"I endeavored to, through the use of hypnosis, merge the different aspects of Banner's personality. There were three," he said, rubbing the bridge of his nose, suddenly feeling much older. "The green, rampaging one . . . a gray-skinned version which was weaker, but far more intelligent and crafty . . . and the core personality, which was the repressed, ostensibly 'normal' scientist. Through hypnotherapy, I managed to blend the three personalities together, to create a 'whole' Bruce Banner . . . something that he had never been in all the years I'd known him. The result was a powerful being with the strength of the green Hulk, the craftiness of the gray, and the intelligence and humanity of Bruce Banner.

"It was supposed to be the first step on the road to recovery for him . . . a long road that, theoretically, I was going to be accompanying him on. I didn't anticipate that he'd first be abducted by, and then wind up leading, the Pantheon . . . or Parthenon, if you will," he added, expecting (and being rewarded with) an annoyed glance from Talbot. "Still . . . progress was made, although on something of a catch-as-catch-can basis. Even had a breakthrough or two. . . ."

"Like what?"

Samson didn't answer at first. Instead, he remembered that moment when Bruce Banner, all one thousand emerald-green pounds of him, had crumbled at Samson's feet after coming back from a particularly traumatic adventure in the future. The events had frightened him, held up a mirror to a very possible, very undesirable destiny that he had wanted no part of.

And then it had started to unravel. Bruce talking of how he felt his old, raging impulses pushing at him. How he was becoming more and more afraid that he was going to lose control completely, perhaps irreparably. The fear in his face, as if something were eating away at him, consuming his sanity, his soul. And then . . .

"Well?" prodded Talbot.

"Doctor-patient privilege applies, Major. I'm sure you understand."

Talbot thudded his fist in irritation, thudded it so hard that he jammed a knuckle. Grabbing the sore hand, he snapped at Samson, "Look what you made me do!"

Tiring of the major's attitude, Samson's hand whipped around and thudded the table. It promptly collapsed, snapping in two with a sound like a rifle shot. Talbot had had files and a clipboard on top of the table. It all spilled to the floor. He made no move to pick it up.

"Look what you made *me* do," Samson said evenly.

Talbot said nothing for a moment, and then carefully asked, "Can you at least tell me what happened with the Pantheon?"

"I wish I could," said Samson. "Lord, I wish I knew. All I know is that there was some sort of massive blowup. When the dust settled, Banner's wife, Betty, was critically injured . . . almost fatally so. And Bruce himself . . . well, he developed a new wrinkle. His mind was savage, berserk . . . as bad as the old Hulk, even worse. But his body was its old, helpless human self. I believe what happened is that he reached a point where he felt himself losing control completely. Rather than let that occur, his mind activated a sort of psychic failsafe. He re-created for himself the harmless human shell of Bruce Banner. Shapeshifted himself, as it were, and shoved his out-of-control psyche into a place where it could do no harm. The last time I saw him, he was being kidnapped by your people. . . ."

Talbot waggled a finger as if scolding a child. "Now now, Doctor. I've put up with all your complaints about the army's terrible, awful, mean old treatment of this time bomb on legs you call a patient. But I feel constrained to point out that *we* didn't take him. S.H.I.E.L.D. did that. They are their own agency, connected with the UN, and are not a military organization."

"My mistake. They're paramilitary. I don't know *how* I could have gotten so confused. In any event, Major . . . he escaped. Sometime after that, his wife, Betty, vanished from the hospital where she was recuperating. I don't know where they are now."

"And what have you been doing about it, Doctor?"

"Doing?" Samson looked amused. "Major, I have a private practice that was going down the toilet. I have a life, and people besides Bruce Banner who depend on me. I've gotten on with my life, Major, just as I assume Bruce has done with his."

Talbot stared at him incredulously. "Gotten . . . *on with his life?* You're not serious."

"Why wouldn't I be serious? Is it that shocking a concept?"

"Doctor . . ." His mouth moved with no words emerging for a moment. It was as if he had stepped out of a silent film. "Doctor . . . the Hulk is a monster! He doesn't *have* a life."

Samson circled him, keeping a distance as if Talbot were a new strain of bacteria. "Haven't you heard anything I said? Hasn't any of it gotten through to you? This isn't a Godzilla movie. This isn't simply some rampaging berserker that the army comes in and wipes out in the final reel of the movie. This is a human being we're discussing. A human being who was dealt what is, quite simply, the lousiest hand it has ever been my misfortune to witness. We get to wear our demons inside us, Major, keep them locked away neatly. We display them or we don't, depending on our choices. Not Bruce. He spent years with the entire world a witness to the creatures that exist within him. That he didn't just open his wrists or blow his brains out ages ago is one of the greatest testimonies to the strength of the human spirit I've ever known." His voice had gotten louder and louder, and he thudded an outstretched finger against Talbot's chest. He barely tapped Talbot, and yet the major was nearly knocked off his feet. "So don't you stand there and tell me that he's a monster undeserving of a shot at simple happiness. He's shown more nobility of spirit and character than anyone I know. More determination in the face of hardship than you or I will ever be called upon to display in our lifetimes. Leave him . . . the hell . . . *alone*."

For a long moment they stared at each other. This time Talbot did not lower his gaze. "You know where he is, don't you?"

"No," said Samson quietly.

"Would you care to be hooked up to a polygraph?"

"That depends. Would you care to have one crammed up a bodily orifice?"

Talbot actually seemed curious. "You're no different than the Hulk in many ways. Is it the gamma radiation? Is that it? When you were transformed by gamma rays into your current incarnation, did you—like the Hulk—decide that the laws of the United States are for lesser mortals?"

"Your words, Major. Your characterization. Not mine."

"Do you approve of what the Hulk did in Trans-Sabal? Do you approve of his leading a fugitive life? Well, Samson?"

Samson chuckled softly. It sounded like a race car revving. "My biblical namesake was a judge. It would seem you have me mixed up with him. I try not to judge, Major. Merely to help."

"Well, now there you go," said the major. "You see there, Doctor? We have something in common. I'm not trying to judge, either. Merely to do my job. And my job is to try and bring in the Hulk."

"A job that you will do with an inordinate amount of pleasure, isn't that right, Major?"

Talbot shrugged. "I take pleasure in doing my job. That's hardly a crime."

"Oh, but it's personal for you, isn't it?" Samson took a step forward. Power seemed to crackle around him. "So tell me . . . just precisely how are you related to the late Major Glen Talbot? Brother? Cousin?"

"My uncle," said Talbot.

"And the fact that Betty Banner was once married to your uncle . . . why, that wouldn't have anything to do with your vehemence regarding Bruce Banner, would it? The fact that your uncle is six feet under while his widow is married to the man that Glen Talbot considered his greatest rival . . . that wouldn't have *anything* to do with your rather zealous view of whatever endeavor this is you're embarking upon?"

Talbot didn't deign to respond at first. Then he said, "My uncle was a great man. A *great* man. His career—his life—was ruined by the . . . person . . . about whom you are so concerned. So when I was approached about heading up this—"

"What? This what?" asked Samson quickly. "What, precisely, are you heading up, Major? The army didn't bother with the time and expense to bring me out here to brief you, just for your health . . . and certainly not for mine. What's going on? What are you fellows up to? Are you going after him again, is that it? He's struggled to keep a low profile, to keep out of harm's way . . . and you can't leave well enough alone?"

"And all past sins forgiven? Is that what you would like to see happen, Doctor?" Talbot said in a voice heavy with sarcasm.

Samson nodded. "Yes, Major. Believe it or not, that is exactly what I would like to see happen. What I've been saying—and you would understand this, had you been listening—is that neither side has been without blame in this entire sordid, sorry affair. What I've been saying is that Bruce Banner never asked for any of this to happen to him. He would have been perfectly happy to lead a long, quiet life of repressed anxiety, and who knows? Maybe his MPD condition might never have seen the light of day. It happens, you know. There's many people out there remaining undiagnosed, making it from one day to the next. Sometimes by the skin of their teeth, granted, but they make it. If Bruce Banner had not been persecuted, hounded—"

"Pardoned," Talbot cut him off. "He was pardoned as well," and now his voice was rising angrily. "The President of the United States—in a move I freely admit would have killed my uncle had he still been alive to see it—pardoned your pal for all his past crimes. He was given a clean slate, Doctor. He was given a chance to live that normal life you keep crying he was deprived of. And he still blew it . . . and that's where we're going to come in."

And Samson understood. He had suspected already, but this was the confirmation. "My God," he said. "You're reactivating Project Hulkbuster, aren't you?" Talbot cleared his throat, but when he didn't say anything, Samson continued, "That's it, isn't it? You crazy sons of—"

"Keep your insults to yourself, Doctor."

"Don't you understand? Hasn't it penetrated that military mind of yours?" Samson said, his voice thick with urgency. "You can't stop him that way. You can't deal with him that way. No one on this planet can. He's the mightiest mortal on the face of the globe. All you do when you come at him with your tanks and armament and all of it . . . it just results in bigger and greater destruction, which you then turn around and blame on him!"

Talbot continued as if Samson had never spoke. "Besides

which, Doctor, we actually have hope of stopping him this time. Stopping him for good."

"Oh, really?"

"Yes. You said it yourself. He was in a situation where he became so angry, so berserk, that he transformed into his helpless human incarnation of Bruce Banner. The answer is therefore simple. All we have to do is provoke him, push him, hound him sufficiently . . . and it will trigger the change. And once he's changed back to human, we've got him. It's over."

" 'Got him'? What do you mean, 'got him'? What do you mean, 'It's over'? What, you wouldn't just shoot him down in cold . . ." His voice trailed off and he sighed heavily. "But why am I surprised? That's exactly what you mean, isn't it? If you have the opportunity, you'll put a bullet in his brain."

"Why do you sound so horrified, Doctor? We spent years lobbing artillery and missiles at the Hulk; it wasn't because we were out to show him a good time. We were hoping that one of those rounds would do the job, end the destruction. And no one heard word one from you about that."

Talbot knelt down and gathered his files and clipboard. Then he rose and headed for the door, the hard heels of his shoes clacking on the floor. But he paused at the door, unable to resist getting in one final comment.

"You're not upset because we're going to try and kill the Hulk, Doctor," said Major Talbot with grim satisfaction. "You're upset because you think, for once . . . we might actually have a shot at succeeding."

He walked out of the room, leaving Doc Samson with the truth of those words ringing in his ears.

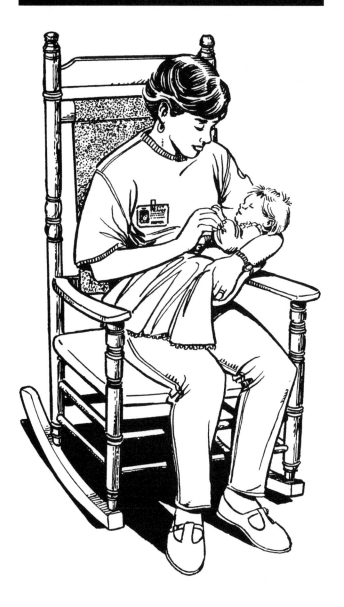

lk Ridge was a bustling suburb just outside Chicago. Although there were stores and such that serviced the residents, there wasn't really much of a sense of community spirit beyond those actions taken under simple necessity of keeping Elk Ridge going. Pretty much all of the residents were Chicago commuters. They'd be up in the morning, off to work during the day, collapse in their homes at night, and for the weekend—if they were looking to relax—would head off to larger communities in the vicinity for superior shopping and partying opportunities. Elk Ridge, in short, existed to provide housing for people while they were busy going to, and coming from, other places.

This suited Mr. and Mrs. Tanner just fine.

Bruce and Betty Tanner lived a fairly quiet life in a nondescript, very small rented house (since they valued their privacy quite highly) in one of the less affluent sections of town. Betty commuted to her job at a large software company called Multitech, situated in the heart of Chicago. Betty was as close to computer illiterate as someone could be. She swore that all she had to do was touch a keyboard and the entire thing would crash. She remained resolutely terrified of the machines, although she had pretty much resigned herself to the notion that, sooner or later, she was going to have to learn how to operate one of the things.

Betty was an attractive woman, with a round face and soft, sympathetic eyes. Her hair was red and cut short. If one watched carefully, one would see that she walked with a slight limp. Once she had needed a cane to facilitate her getting around, but that was no longer necessary. She was one of those people whose inner calm instantly made her likable. This was particularly useful in light of her job at Multitech, which was working—not in any of the research and development areas—but rather in the child-care department. Multitech was one of the more progressive companies around, and had instituted on-site child care several years before. The short-term cost had been considerable, but the long-term benefits of cutting down on absenteeism and promoting overall employee morale were considered well worth it.

Ironically, Betty was filling in for a caregiver who was out on maternity leave. The hours were long and the pay wasn't sensational, but Betty accepted both with happiness bordering on glee. She was well-liked by her co-workers, the children's parents, and, most important, the children themselves. So well liked, in fact, that there was talk about trying to keep her on even after the woman she replaced made her return.

This particular day, Betty was seated in a rocking chair, gently swaying back and forth with an infant in her arms. Sylvia, an older woman who was one of her co-workers, glided over to her and looked on approvingly. "Finally got him to sleep, I see," she whispered to Betty.

"Oh, it was no trouble," Betty said dismissively. "He's a sweetheart." As if the baby heard her, he made a gentle cooing noise in his sleep.

"Have any of your own, Betty?" Sylvia asked.

"No," said Betty after a moment. "I was . . . I had a miscarriage once."

"Ohhh." Sylvia clucked sympathetically. "My first pregnancy ended in miscarriage. But I had two kids since then. I know it sounds trite, but it's not the end of the world. Have you and your husband discussed trying again?"

"Not really. Now doesn't seem to be a real good time."

"Oh, there's never a real 'good' time when it comes to starting a family," Sylvia said. "Believe me, there's always reasons to put off having children. Maybe it's money. Or maybe you want to refurnish the house first. Or go on that trip that you've been planning. There's always reasons not to have children. The only reason *to* have children is because . . . well . . . just because."

"Just because." Betty smiled. "Well, that certainly sounds like reason enough to me. I'll discuss it with my husband, see if he's interested."

"What's your husband like?" asked Sylvia. "You should bring him around sometime. I'd love to meet him."

"Ohhh, I don't know about that," said Betty. "He's something of a homebody. Doesn't get out much."

"What does he do for a living? Don't tell me you're the sole means of income. Not on what you're being paid around here . . ."

"No, no. He works out of the house," Betty said. The baby was starting to stir, so she bounced him slightly in her arms, immediately calming him back down. "Computer stuff. I don't even pretend to understand it. But he makes enough of a living at it, so I have no cause for complaint, certainly."

"What's his name?"

"Bruce."

"Bruce." Sylvia smiled. "How nice that name's coming back."

Betty looked at her quizzically. "I'm sorry . . . I don't follow. . . ."

"Well, yooouuuu know," said Sylvia. "Years ago, the name Bruce wasn't considered . . . you know, masculine. They'd just mention the name on game shows and audiences would laugh. On television, you couldn't even have a hero named Bruce; you'd have to call him David or something."

"I wouldn't know," Betty told her. "I never watched much TV."

"It doesn't matter much now, anyway. It's not like that anymore. I hope your husband didn't have to put up with too much ribbing during that time."

"Oh, I'm sure he didn't," Betty said confidently. "If there's one thing that people don't generally accuse Bruce of, it's lack of masculinity. He's about as masculine as they come."

Sylvia nodded approvingly in response to Betty's obvious pride in her husband. "Let me guess. Is he able to leap tall buildings in a single bound?"

"No challenge at all."

"Bend steel in his bare hands?"

"In his bare hands?" Betty sniffed derisively. "My dear Sylvia . . . he could bend steel in his sleep."

"He sounds like quite a man."

The baby started to whimper. Betty turned him around and placed him on her shoulder, patting the infant on the back. "Sylvia," she said with pained awareness, "you don't know the half of it."

Bruce Tanner, a.k.a. Danner, a.k.a. Banner, sat in front of his computer terminal and cracked his knuckles. The reverberation of the sound shook the shelves, and a couple of knickknacks fell off in response. Bruce made a mental note to pick them up and restore them to their proper places.

The keyboard was an ergonomic one, angled upward with

slightly larger-than-normal keys, which accommodated—although not perfectly—his larger-than-normal fingers. To his right was a scanner, into which he had completed feeding a sheet with equations on it that he had finished scribbling an hour ago. He sat there, staring at the computer screen, waiting for an on-line response.

His enormous arms were folded across his equally copious torso. He was bare-chested, since he felt more comfortable that way. The house was warm anyway, although extremes of temperature didn't bother him one way or the other.

His arms were green, as was the rest of him.

He reached up with his huge right hand and, with incongruous delicacy, adjusted the black-rimmed glasses poised on his face. He wore them out of habit for close-up work. A pipe was tightly clenched between his teeth, a small trail of smoke winding lazily toward the ceiling. He tapped the finger of his left hand impatiently on the desk.

The computer beeped at him, and a message flickered onto the screen.

You've done it again, Braintrust.

Bruce laughed to himself and promptly typed in a response: *It was no problem.*

No problem? came back the reply moments later. *Your equations got us over the hump. Standard payment method okay?*

Bruce nodded once, and then mentally kicked himself as he remembered such gestures weren't exactly visible through monitors. He typed briskly, *That will do just fine, thanks.*

You're the best consultant we've got, Braintrust. Don't ever bail on us.

Not to worry. Can't beat the hours.

Even as they communicated with each other, Bruce knew that a direct money transfer was already under way, pumping up the Tanners' bank account. He felt almost guilty about it. It really had been no effort for him at all to solve the snag the firm had gotten into. It was like taking money under false pretenses. But it was silly for him to feel that way. There was nothing false about his knowledge, and he had certainly labored long and hard for the opportunity to generate an income in some sort of calm, rational manner.

And besides, it beat making bombs.

He checked the time on the small clock next to his computer, typed in quickly, *Gotta go,* and logged off the direct connection to his customer. He switched over to another computer service, worked his way to a private chat room, and waited.

For some time nothing happened. This was fine by him. He checked in there once a day, and if there was no one waiting for him, then that was—

Bruce suddenly popped onto the screen.

He stared at the hail for a long moment. So there was going to be news of some sort. Somehow he had the feeling that it wasn't going to be news that he wanted to hear. Nevertheless, he gamely typed in, *I'm here.*

You got a problem. I just came from a charming little discussion with an old/new friend of yours: Major Talbot.

Bruce blinked several times, not quite sure he was reading that correctly. Then he typed, *I don't suppose the fact that he's dead slowed him down.*

Different Major Talbot.

Evil twin?

Cranky nephew.

Bruce shook his head, sighing. "Perfect," he said. *And what's the dear boy got planned?*

They're reviving the Hulkbusters.

Oh dear, typed Bruce. *Tons of armament created for the express pur-*

pose of wiping me off the face of the earth. That's your tax dollars at work for you.

They pumped me for information. Fortunately, I don't know where you are.

Fortunately. And we should do nothing to change that.

Bruce . . . I'm worried. What if they find you?

I'll handle it.

Bruce's response sat there a long moment, unchallenged. And then Samson replied, *What if you can't? Bruce . . . if you come to me, voluntarily . . . we can continue your therapy. We can help you deal with this situation.*

Bruce shook his head even as he typed, *I've been dealing with it for years, Leonard. I've gotten somewhat used to it. Don't worry. After all this time, I doubt there's anything they can toss at me I can't handle.*

I hope you're right.

He heard the key in the front door and quickly wrote, *Betty's coming. I have to go.*

Wait! I want to

But that was all Bruce saw, because he had logged off the service and shut down the computer. The screen promptly flicked out.

Bruce turned in his specially reinforced chair as Betty entered. She kissed him firmly but pleasantly on the lips and said, "How was your day?"

"Solved some folks' problems. Made us some money. Same old same old. You?"

"Played with babies. It was fun."

She let the statement hang there for a bit, and Bruce regarded her with curiosity. "Betty . . . something on your mind?"

"No. No, not at all." She paused. "Yours?"

"My mind's a complete blank," said the Hulk.

"That's what I hear," said Betty. She turned and headed toward the kitchen. "Okay if I nuke some frozen dinners tonight? I'm not much in the mood right now to do a lot."

"You sure everything is okay?"

She stood in the doorway of the kitchen for a moment, then turned and said to him evenly, "What's not to be fine? I'm married to the incredible Hulk. We live with one eye over our shoulders at all times to make sure no one is after us. We're . . . tentative . . . in our physical interaction. We can't ever make friends, go out to eat or to a movie, or do anything else that vaguely resembles normality. What's not to be okay?"

"Betty . . ."

"Never mind!" she said, far angrier, far less patient than she wanted to be. She reined herself in and repeated, this time more in control, "Never mind. It's nothing important."

He rose to face her. "Obviously it is."

"Obviously," she said in a tone that would brook absolutely no disagreement, "it's none of your damned business." And with that she went into the kitchen, the door swinging noisily behind her.

"Obviously." He sighed, knowing that this was going to be one of those days in which—for no reason he could easily discern—he was suddenly in Dutch with the wife.

The house was a small but nicely stylish town house. The occupant was an older gentleman by the name of Amos Trotter. Dr. Trotter was in his early sixties, with a swatch of curly white hair that clung to his otherwise balding head like a halo. He was slightly stoop-shouldered and very soft-spoken.

Trotter had made something of a name for himself in his field of psychiatry. Whereas his brethren tried to treat diseases of the mind via a combination of therapy and drugs, Trotter was heavily involved with the development and creation of devices that could accomplish what the therapy and drugs could not: Provide cures.

His work had caused occasional gasps of outrage from some associates, and words of overwhelming praise from others.

It had all come to a head at a psychiatric convention several years previously, when Trotter—making a keynote address—wound up getting into an argument with a belligerent audience member.

"Problems of the mind stem from deeply profound causes," the audience member had said. "You suggest using microchips, processors, surgical procedures to operate as a shortcut! Not caring about the reasons for the problems, but instead only about quick and easy solutions."

"Oh God forbid, in the lofty world of psychiatry, any solution should ever be quick and easy," he had replied sharply. "God further forbid that maybe we should do away with years of treatment and therapy which go no place except into our heavily lined pockets. How could we, as men of science, possibly contemplate anything less than long, drawn-out agonies for patients and family members?"

The argument had gotten louder and more boisterous and, in a moment that the media had made sure to play up for all it was worth, Trotter and several audience members almost came to blows.

It was shortly after that that Trotter had gone into semiretirement. He'd been getting up in years, but his overall sense of disdain and impatience for his own profession had begun to color all of his day-to-day dealings with people. He still did research, and he was available for the occasional consultation . . . but beyond that, he kept pretty much to himself.

Which was why he was extremely surprised to hear a knock on his door one evening. Visitors were something of a rarity.

The fireplace was flickering, and so inviting that for a moment

he considered simply ignoring the knock and continuing to read
his book by the fireside. But his curiosity got the better of him. He
placed a bookmark carefully between the pages of the book, set it
down, and walked over to the door.

"Yes?" he called through the door.

"Dr. Trotter?" came a voice, deep and rough. "I'd like to talk
with you, if I may?"

"And you would be . . . ?"

"I'm a doctor, sir, like yourself. And I'd like to talk to you about
your advances and theories. I think we're on the same wavelength,
and I think I can be of tremendous importance to all your future
plans."

"Is that a fact?" said Trotter, bemused, not having any clue
what the fellow wanted.

"Yes, sir. That is a definite fact."

Trotter shrugged. No reason not to pursue matters. It was a
slow evening anyway, and who knew where this encounter might
lead? He was, after all, a man of medicine. An investigator. What
sort of investigator would he be if he didn't explore the mysteries
that awaited him on his own porch?

He opened the door and looked out at the individual standing
there, smile glinting in the moonlight, a briefcase looking small in
his huge hand.

"Dr. Trotter," he said. "I've come a long way to meet you. And
I'm confident in saying that we are going to do a great deal for
each other. A *great* deal."

Dr. Trotter stared, and didn't stop staring for quite some time.

Chapter 3

There was no warning.

The commuters on the Chicago elevated train were caught completely off guard. One moment they were reading their newspapers, or dozing slightly, rocked into security by the gentle motions of the train. The next moment, the world had suddenly been tilted at a forty-five-degree angle. The screams of the people were drowned out by the screeching of metal as the support beams and struts twisted, as if being trashed by an earthquake. They grabbed for support and found none.

The track beneath them angled downward. The train lurched toward the ground, cars twisting back and on themselves. There were prayers, there were curses, there were released bladders. And then, within seconds, there was a crash as the tracks, the supports, and the train all collapsed to the ground. The train sat there for a moment, some cars still caught in the upper reaches of the tracks. People skidded, trying to haul themselves upward as more people slid down atop them.

And then there was a roar.

It was a sound like a herd of rogue bull elephants. But, even more frightening, it had something of a furious human quality to it.

The ground beneath them shook, as if a giant were approaching. But it was not, in fact, a giant at all. Instead it was a green-skinned behemoth, slamming the street with his fists with seismic force.

He was bare-chested, clad only in purple pants with torn-up knees. His hair was wild. His eyes were insane.

He raised his arms overhead once more, howled defiance, people trembling at his fury. Then his legs coiled and he leaped skyward, leaving a wrecked train, a trashed section of elevated rail, and several hundred commuters who would wake up screaming for the rest of their lives.

Screaming with visions of the incredible Hulk in their minds.

At Fort Meade, Maryland, Major Bill Talbot put down the phone. He couldn't contain the excitement in his voice as he came from around his desk and yelled, "Chafin!"

His aide dashed in. "Yessir?"

"The bastard's on the rampage on Chicago. We've got him. Scramble the team." As Chafin ran out, Talbot murmured, "Just leave him alone, eh, Samson? Just leave him be. Let him get on with his life." He smirked. "So much for that, Samson. So much for you. And so much for the Hulk."

Sylvia ran into the child-care room as Betty was busy cleaning up some spit-up off of a nonplussed toddler. Betty glanced up and saw that the older woman was deathly white. "What's wrong?"

"Everyone's talking about it!" she said. "Have you heard? About where all the police cars and ambulances are going?"

Betty had heard the passing sirens far below, but hadn't given it much thought. "No. What's wrong?"

"It's that monster! The Hulk! He's tearing up downtown!"

Betty felt her throat constrict, and fought off the haze that danced in front of her eyes for a moment. "The . . . the Hulk? Is he . . . he's fighting someone?"

"No! No! He's just berserk!"

"Oh my God!" Betty suddenly stood, her fingers to her mouth. "My husband! He was . . . heading downtown today! I've got to call him! Tell him not to go! Sylvia, cover for me!"

Sylvia made no attempt to hide her confusion as Betty pushed past her. "I thought you said that he stayed at home. . . ."

"Well, he was . . . he was trying to get out for once! Just *cover for me!*" and she dashed out the door.

She ran down a hallway, arms pumping, and found an empty office. She dashed in, kicking the door shut behind her, grabbed up a phone and quickly dialed, trying to hold back the pounding in her temple.

"Be home," she whispered. "Be home and pick up. Please don't have gone berserk. Please . . . please let it be a hideous mistake." The phone rang twice, a third time. She repeated it steadily, like a mantra, "Please please please . . ."

A fourth time, and there was a click. She held her breath . . . and heard her own voice speaking to her.

"Hello, this is the Tanner residence. Please leave your name and number, and we'll get back to you as soon as possible."

The beep sounded, and Betty practically screamed into the phone, *"Bruce, if you're there . . . if you're not busy reverting into a destructive monster . . . then pick up the damned phone!"*

Downtown looked like a war zone.

The Hulk had been busy stampeding through the Chicago Museum of Modern Art. Statuary lay in shattered ruins, large areas of the building had been destroyed. As the Hulk's rampage continued in the museum, the entire area had been evacuated. Police had set up barricades, not that they had any particular hope of containing the Hulk. If he could smash through concrete, large orange and white boards were not going to pose much of a problem.

Police had their riot guns and equipment out. They faced the situation with a sort of bleak desperation. They knew they didn't have a hope in hell of keeping the Hulk at bay. But they had to do *something*. They were heavily armed, helmeted, wearing flak jackets. And they were praying that maybe, just maybe, the Hulk was overrated.

The front of the museum—what remained of it—exploded outward. In the shower of rubble and debris, the Hulk howled with fury. He looked completely out of control, an unstoppable engine of destruction.

What he did not look was overrated.

"*Open fire!*" shouted the S.W.A.T. captain.

They did so, with everything they had. For a full minute, there was nothing except the rapid fire of high-caliber bullets. The Hulk staggered under the assault. Gas shells exploded at his feet, sending up huge, billowing clouds. The Hulk went to his knees as the haze enveloped him, and for one moment there was actually hope that they were going to bring him down.

Then, pistonlike, his legs started to drive him forward. He picked up steam, an emerald locomotive, bearing down on the forces of the Chicago Police Department and moving faster with each passing second.

The cops held for as long as they could, and then they broke ranks as the Hulk bore down on them. The Hulk plowed into them and through them. He knocked aside gas canisters, sending more smoke billowing through the air. Then he grabbed police cars, one in each hand, and smashed them together over his head, creating one huge ball of metal. Cops ran in all directions to get the hell out of his way as he shot-putted the massive metal ball into the air, sending it crashing to the ground.

And finally he spoke, not that there was anyone hanging around to hear. "You think you can hurt Hulk!" he bellowed. "Fools! *Fools!* Hulk is *strongest one there is!*"

"So I've always been led to understand."

The Hulk spun to face the newcomer, and found himself staring into the angry face of Dr. Robert Bruce Banner. He was barefoot, wearing a tank top and a large pair of blue jeans.

The Hulk roared his contempt, a battle cry.

Banner let the echo die down, and then slowly, sarcastically, applauded. "Very good," he said. "You've certainly got the attitude down. Now would you mind telling me precisely who or what you are?"

The Hulk charged forward and slammed into Banner, driving him back. He lifted Banner clear off his feet. The Hulk's massive arms were wrapped around his rib cage, trying to shut off his air. Banner furiously pounded on the Hulk's back, but was helpless to stop the forward motion as they plowed into a small, and now deserted, coffee shop. The glass exterior shattered, their huge feet crunching the shards. Normally packed at that time of day, this time there was no waiting for a table. Indeed, within seconds there was no finding a table as the Hulk hurled Banner upward through the ceiling, bringing plaster and debris raining down.

Within seconds Banner had crashed back down to the street. "Okay!" he bellowed. "I've had enough of this! More than enough of this! Come on, you two-bit terror! *Come on!*"

The Hulk came at him again. Banner dug in and, when the Hulk slammed into him, was driven back about a yard. His feet chewed up the asphalt, and then he slowed and stopped, not budging another inch. The two of them struggled, power against power, muscle pitted against brute muscle, grunting and snarling and angling for leverage.

"Who . . . *are* you?" demanded Banner.

"Hulk is strongest one there is!" the Hulk replied in a deafening voice.

"Been there, done that," Banner shot back. He was doing everything he could not to blow his temper, not to let himself get too overexcited or caught up in the sheer thrill of battle. And it *was* a thrill, as much as he hated to admit it. He'd been cooped up in the house, trying to keep a low profile, telling himself that if he spent the rest of his life just that way, he'd be happy. But there had been some days, some very long days when he had paced, a caged animal, his muscles growing stiff with inactivity. A violent streak in him, looking to be satisfied, to pit himself against a stronger adversary and to grow stronger himself in turn. To be the powerful, unstoppable juggernaut that he could become when the situation demanded it.

All this, which he had never dared discuss with Betty. She wouldn't have understood. No, cancel that. She might have understood only too well. She might even have left him if she'd heard such ruminations from him.

So he'd kept it to himself, buried as deep as he possibly could. Unfortunately, that hadn't been all that deep, and it had continued to percolate dangerously near the surface.

They were like two powerful dinosaurs locked in combat, from a time when creatures walked the earth possessing greater power and ferocity than anything people in a civilized era had experienced.

And then Banner hoisted the Hulk over his head. His heart was racing, his head swirling, and for one panic-stricken second he thought that he felt a change rattling around inside him. A change that would prove instantly and irrevocably fatal if it got too far. The

Hulk poured out invective in his savagery, and deep within Banner a voice tried to reply in kind. Banner shoved it down and away and, with all his strength, smashed the Hulk to the ground.

The power of the move packed more force than anything that the police's collective armament had carried. Not waiting to gauge the effectiveness, Banner lifted him and brought him crashing down again, this time headfirst. The Hulk struggled in his grasp but seemed to be slowing down.

Banner leaped atop him, jamming one knee into the Hulk's chest. He swung his massive fists, delivering blow after blow to the Hulk's head, concentrating all his power there, leaving the monster too rattled to move, not giving him a chance to think or react or collect himself.

The Hulk started slowing down.

That's when Banner knew he had him. More than that, that was when the Hulk's counterfeit status was made even more painfully clear to Banner (not that he was ever confused as to precisely who was who, or had any question as to who was the facsimile). The real Hulk would not have slowed down, or gotten tired or confused. The real Hulk, fed by his rage, would have become stronger, would have fought back with greater intensity, the fury serving as fuel to stoke the fire of his rage.

Banner struck again and again, and then he heard a significant crack.

The Hulk's head flew off.

It was not, as one might expect, accompanied by a fountaining of blood and gore. Rather, there was a crackling of electricity, the sound of metal being torn, of sparks flying, and there was a sizzling and frying of circuitry.

"I knew it! I *knew it!* Another damned robot!" snarled Banner as he reached in through the top of the Hulk's now-exposed neck and ripped out greater heaping hunks of the mechanoid's innards.

The robot's arms flailed about a moment, and then dropped life-lessly to its sides.

Within seconds, like a berserk surgeon, Banner had ripped open the machine's chest. It lay there helpless and unmoving as Banner stared down at it.

The rage that had been building within him faded, to be replaced by scientific interest. He whistled softly.

He had encountered more than his share of robots, including several previous impostors. And as a genius technician, he was no slouch when it came to being conversant with the latest technology.

But this . . . this was like nothing he'd ever seen. There were things in the robot that he'd never encountered before. Machinery of a sophistication that surpassed even the robotic genius of Dr. Doom. The fuel source seemed to be some sort of blue gem, filled with an odd liquid that was glowing softly in the chest of the machine. But what was it, and how was it powering the robot?

"What in the world—?" he murmured to himself.

Then the blue gem suddenly started to radiate heat. Although it posed no threat to Banner, reflexively he stepped back.

The air filled with a sharp hissing, and the liquid burst through the containment of the gem. It spread quickly throughout the unmoving metal "corpse," devouring it every place it touched. Within seconds the entire robot had melted down into a puddle of blue liquid, unidentifiable as anything other than slag. "At least he's tidy," murmured Banner, but it was a tossed-off comment that covered his intense disappointment. He'd dearly wanted a shot at studying the robot closely. Who knew what he might have learned? The origin of the thing, for starters . . . and perhaps, beyond that, advancement in robot technology that could in turn have had all sorts of applications.

There, in the middle of a trashed city block of Chicago, Banner was actually lost in thought—so much so that it took him long moments to realize that the air was churning around him . . . and even longer to look up and see the reason.

"Well? Was he home?" Sylvia asked urgently.

"No," Betty said, chewing her lower lip as she always did when she wasn't telling the truth.

The truth had been that Bruce was indeed home, and had picked up the phone in response to her desperate shouting. When she'd breathed a sigh of relief, her voice had almost choked in doing so. She told him quickly what she'd heard.

"You didn't really think it was me?" he had demanded, sounding hurt.

"Of course not," she had replied, chewing her lower lip furiously. "Bruce . . . stay put. Don't go out. Let the authorities handle it, whatever it is."

"Someone is going around impersonating me, causing destruction, danger to life and limb . . . and you want me to stay put? Betty . . . I can't. It would be wrong. You *know* it would be wrong."

She had tried to argue, but there wasn't much point, since he had already hung up.

"I'm so worried about him," Betty said now to Sylvia.

"Is he the helpless type?"

"No . . . no, hardly that . . . but . . . sometimes . . ."

And suddenly an image flashed into her mind. A mental picture of Bruce totally losing control and transforming into his helpless mortal form. Of being at the mercy of whoever or whatever was tearing up Chicago.

Betty had been able to calm him during his "seizures," for want of a better word. Restore him to his rational, thinking state, albeit huge and green. It was one of the links between the two of them; somehow she was always able to reach his calm, loving center and bring it out. The shape and form didn't matter . . . he was still her Bruce, no matter what.

And he might be in trouble now.

Her first instinct was to go to him. To be by his side. It was an instinct that had badly betrayed her during the end of their time with the Pantheon. Determined to see matters through when matters came to a head with that super-secret organization, she'd gone charging in like Rambette. Betty did not want for confidence in a combat situation; she was an army brat, born and bred. She was comfortable with guns, she didn't back down from a fight, and—after spending all these years in the company of the Hulk, and all the bizarre occurrences that that association entailed—she was not easily fazed.

That confidence had nearly gotten her killed. The slight limp in her walk was her souvenir of that.

But, knowing that her husband was in a battle, could she just cower at work, listen for a news report or word of mouth, and pray that he came out of it okay? If something went wrong—if he didn't survive—wouldn't she then spend the rest of her life wondering if she shouldn't have done more somehow? Even if she was being unreasonably hard on herself. Even if she was making impossible demands. Still . . . still, wasn't she honor bound to do whatever she could, whenever she could, to help her husband?

Still she hesitated, fearful of almost having died the last time she took that notion into her head.

Her gut instinct was to help.

Her fear was the repercussions such a decision could bring.

But if she stayed away . . . if she hid . . . if she cowered . . .

And Bruce's words echoed in her head . . . *It would be wrong. You* know *it would be wrong . . . .*

She turned quickly and said, "Sylvia, you drive in to work, right?"

"Uhm . . . well . . . yes."

"Give me your keys."

"What?"

"I said give me the keys! Bruce is out there somewhere and I have to go find him!"

"But . . . but my car could get damaged! And you could be killed!"

"Thank God your priorities are in order," Betty said icily.

Sylvia winced, started to stammer some more. But then, under Betty's steady gaze, she simply grabbed her purse, dug out the keys, and tossed them to her. "It's parked on level two, row twenty-three. The station wagon."

"Thanks, Sylvia." She kissed her quickly on the cheek and ran out.

And Sylvia was unable to refrain from calling after her, "The *white* station wagon! The one without so much as a scratch on it!"

Chapter 4

The incredible Hulk looked heavenward and knew immediately that not only was he in deep trouble, but that there was going to be no way of getting out of it except by battling his way out.

They descended from the sky, the helicarriers stirring up great clouds of dust. Even as the Hulk looked up at them, his lips drawing back into a snarl of contempt, the bomb bay doors slid open, clacking into place so noisily that the sound reverberated even above the beating of the chopper blades.

The first of the armored figures hurtled outward. Even from down below, the Hulk could see that it was massive. It blotted out the sun as it dove toward him.

Its arms were huge, outfitted with onboard cannons that shot who-knew-what. It had similarly proportioned legs, jets flaring out of its boot thrusters. There was no head; the armor was simply flat at the shoulders. But as they got closer, the Hulk quickly became convinced that there were human operators inside. The armor was evocative of the "Mandroids," weapons created by the Strategic Hazard Intervention, Espionage, and Logistics Directorate (S.H.I.E.L.D.).

"Not these things again," he said with intense annoyance. "How many of them do I have to trash before they realize—"

A second appeared, and a third. Then a fourth.

His eyes widened. An even dozen was coming toward him, the first one almost upon him before the last had even emerged from the helicarriers. The sun glinted off their gleaming silver hides.

"C'mon, then!" the Hulk bellowed. At that moment he didn't care how many they threw at him. His rage was towering, overwhelming.

The armored figures surrounded him but did not descend. Instead they remained about fifty feet above the Hulk, the roar of their jets filling the air. Each of them was about twenty feet tall. A voice blasted from one of the robots, although it was impossible to tell which one.

"Attention, Hulk!" it said. "This is Major William Talbot!"

The Hulk blinked a moment, amusement penetrating his anger. He shouted back, "Oooh. Another Talbot. My fear knows no bounds!"

Apparently unmoved by the Hulk's sarcasm, Talbot barked, "We are the unit designated 'Hulkbusters.' . . ."

At that, the Hulk actually laughed. "Not you people again! Haven't you realized yet when something is a bad idea?" Then his voice grew angry again. "I don't suppose it would interest you to know that I've been set up! That some sort of mechanical construct, impersonating me, was tearing up Chicago. That I stepped in and stopped it before it did any more damage." He turned in place, glancing balefully at each of the robots floating before him. "I'm the aggrieved party here, Talbot! I'm the hero! And I'm the one who has to tolerate petty garbage from brainless army bureaucrats like you!"

"You expect us to care about your excuses, Hulk? To believe your lies?" The voice rebounded from all over. It sounded like the wrath of God unleashed. Obviously Talbot had notched it upward a bit for effect. "You've committed more destruction, more atrocities, ruined more lives than any being on the face of the earth. Save your stories, Hulk. Save yourself, through the one means left open to you: surrender."

"So that you can what? Stick me in a box somewhere? Or are you just going to kill me outright? Try and dissect me, perhaps?"

"Surrender, Hulk."

"*Go to hell!*" The shout was defiant, a buildup of years of persecution, frustration, and a continued sense of feeling that he was the most powerful creature on earth, and yet utterly helpless to have any control over his own destiny or life.

And there was this guy, this Talbot, nephew of the late, unlamented Glen Talbot, according to Samson. Ghosts of the past, haunting him, not leaving him in peace.

The Hulk had been spit out into the world a newborn creature, as angry and confused and full of trepidation as any other infant, with a bomb for a mother and an explosion for a midwife. His earliest memory was fury. Persecution. Soldiers, tanks, heavy artillery, anything and everything that they could throw at him. And they did, without letup, without remorse, hounding him and tracking him. . . .

They had treated him with nothing but inhumanity . . . and *he* was accused of being the monster? *He* was?

All of this went through his mind in a second. His heart racing, his breath curling in his chest and building up to an earsplitting howl of wrath as he picked a robot at random and charged toward it.

Two steps, three, and then his powerful legs propelled him upward. The armor's plasma cannons flared to life, bolts smashing into the Hulk, knocking him back down toward the street. He didn't even feel the impact as he struck the ground, and in an instant was back on his feet, leaping once more toward the armored entity. This time the plasma blasts didn't even slow him down and he plowed into the armor, grabbing it around one of its legs. For a moment the armor managed to resist the pressure of his powerful arms, but only for a moment. Then the right boot jet began to crumble, skewing the robot, causing it to spiral almost out of control.

"Converge! Converge!" came the voice of Major Talbot, and more Hulkbusters moved toward him. Two grabbed the Hulk by the arms, and—to the Hulk's astonishment—actually managed to pry him off of the damaged soldier. Two more grabbed him by the legs, and now the Hulk struggled furiously in their grasp, unable to achieve any leverage. "You're done, Banner!" came Talbot's voice. "You're done, and we barely had to exert the smallest part of our weaponry! Our new Hulkbuster units are impossible to defeat. The kinetic energy you expend against them is simply redirected against you. The madder you get . . . the stronger we get."

The Hulk twisted in their grip. His legs coiled, shoved against the warriors who were holding them. For a split second he was braced against them, and then, in a dazzling display of strength, he whipped his arms around, smashing one set of Hulkbusters against the other.

Talbot, hovering ten yards off to the right, couldn't believe it. The armor had been subjected to unimaginable stress in the laboratory. So many tons per square inch that Talbot had about figured they could take the entire moon and rest it upon one of the suits of armor, and the armor would show no significant stress.

And here was the Hulk, ripping free of constrictions, not backing down, not falling back. Instead, he landed atop one of the fallen warriors, pounding furiously, methodically, like a slave master in an old sailing galley, drumming and keeping the oar pullers in synch. The armor began to buckle under the hammering. Other warriors started to move forward, and then the Hulk spun and howled at them.

And the Hulkbusters saw, truly saw for the first time, the face of just what it was that had laid waste to battalions those many years ago. He was, at this point, beyond words, perhaps even on the way to moving beyond coherent thought. If the Hulkbusters had decided to send in robots, then the robots at least wouldn't have known to be intimidated. They would have kept on coming, kept on trying to wear him down, heedless of their own welfare or even their own likelihood for longevity.

The Hulkbusters were not cowards, by any means. All of them were hardened combat veterans, handpicked by Talbot. All of them were willing and able to lay down their lives in the service of their country. All of them had run training maneuvers, watched tapes, developed strategies, worked up a dazzling assortment of possible scenarios.

But all of them, ultimately, were only human.

And so they hesitated, taken aback for a moment by the in-the-flesh reality of a berserk Hulk. The Hulk wanted to take that moment to lay into them. To unleash his full fury, to tear them apart, to shred them as a child would pick apart a fly.

But from deep within him, there was a warning, a whispered voice, penetrating the haze of resentment. And the voice said, *Get out of there! Now! Now, before it's too late!*

He listened. All within a matter of seconds, the Hulkbusters had temporarily fallen back to regroup in the face of the Hulk's assault, and that was when the Hulk leaped skyward. One of the warriors was starting to move to intercept, and the Hulk simply shouldered him out of the way with a sound like a mammoth gong.

"Sonics!" bellowed Talbot, rallying himself and determined not to let the Hulk get away. Even as he snapped the order, he was the first to implement it. Deep within the heart of the robot warrior, Talbot manipulated the controls of his armored shell. The robot's arm stretched out, tips snapping off at the fingers. Other warriors followed suit, and wave upon wave of tightly focused, high-powered sonics blasted forward from the hands of the warriors.

Two hundred feet in the air it caught up with the Hulk, lancing through his head. He clapped his hands to his ears, but that didn't even begin to keep the devastating sound out of his head. As powerful and impenetrable as his body was, there was nothing particularly invulnerable about his ears, or his brain, for that matter.

The Hulk's trajectory was completely thrown as he twisted and writhed in midair. He plunged toward a small row of evacuated buildings, crashing down and through, rubble caving in atop him.

In pursuit were the Hulkbusters, angling down, not needing to see their target to use the sonics. All they needed was the general area and they were able to do the job.

The Hulk staggered out of the rubble, his head threatening to break apart from within.

Fight fair, damn you! Toe to toe with an enemy, he could beat him. Get something in his hands, he could crush it. But this assault with nothing . . . with sound waves, invisible, sinister . . . it was cowardly, underhanded. Not worthy of the Hulk.

And, worst of all, it was working.

It wasn't fair, it *was not fair*.

He slammed his hands together, generating a wave of concussive force. It was a devastating and reliable tactic, but in this instance it had little effect. The Hulkbusters were blown slightly back, but they swung around and continued the assault.

They were there in force now, the nine suits that were still functioning sufficiently to be a part of the attack. From all sides the sound pounded at him. He staggered left and right, trying to find surcease, trying to lash out. But every few steps he took in the direction of the armored Hulkbusters, he was driven back by the pure power of the sound waves.

The unfairness, the injustice of the situation started to drive him completely over the edge. Drive him berserk.

And that was when he knew. That was when he realized.

That's the purpose of this! came the inner voice. *They know! They know what'll happen if you lose control!*

They were trying to force him to revert to his helpless mortal form. And if they succeeded in that, then he would last perhaps half a second before they . . .

Before they killed him.

There was no question in his mind at all. If they had him powerless, they would have to be insane to wait for some future time when he might revert to the Hulk once more.

This wasn't about imprisonment, or even dissection. This was an execution, pure and simple.

But the realization came too late.

He felt the telltale sensations in his body, felt his intellect starting to shut down and be overwhelmed by the uncontrolled savage mind that inhabited the defenseless human shell of Bruce Banner.

The change was coming. He tried to beat back the savage consciousness, but it would not be stopped. It knew nothing of its vulnerability, of how easily it could be damaged or destroyed. Its vision of itself was as an unyielding, unbeatable juggernaut of strength, and there was no way to gainsay it.

Which meant that, in the seconds before the savage mind's arrival, he had to do *something* to get out of this hellish situation, while dealing with the unceasing assault from the Hulkbusters.

Once again the Hulk slammed his hands together, but this

time he did not aim the tactic at the hovering armored forms. Instead it was designed to strike a nearby burned-out building, about ten stories tall. The Hulk backed the strike with all the power at his command, and for a brief moment he thought it might not besufficient.

It was, however. The shock wave generated by the Hulk's powerful hands smashed into the building, bricks and beams collapsing, plaster and wood exploding. And the entire building falling precisely where the Hulk intended it to fall.

On himself.

Before the armored figures could converge, the building crashed in and down on him. Their vision of him was obscured, and for a moment they lost track of him.

"Keep on him!" shouted Talbot.

Although they couldn't see him, they knew where he had fallen. They came together, continuing to blast with the sonic waves for long seconds.

From beneath the rubble, nothing stirred.

"Cut off sonics!" Talbot ordered. They promptly did so, albeit it with just a slight degree of trepidation. There was, after all, the slightest possibility that this was some sort of trick. That the moment they halted their frontal assault, the Hulk would leap out at them, fists poised and ready to crush them into oblivion.

As if reading his men's minds, Talbot made it clear that he expected none of his men to take a chance that he himself was unwilling to take. "Cover me!" he ordered as he descended toward the pile of rubble.

The armor landed on the street with a loud thud. It started toward the pile of debris that the Hulk had brought crashing down upon himself. Each step of the armor's foot crunched rubble beneath it. His weapons were on full auto-standby. The slightest hint of the Hulk playing dead—the merest twitching of the monster's corpse—would be enough to bring the full might of the armor to bear upon him.

He started shoveling the rubble aside, eagerly burrowing to get to the bottom of it. He tried not to let his excitement get the better of him, but there was part of him that simply couldn't wait to see the unmoving body of his personal demon. It would be glorious, so glorious to look upon. . . .

He wasn't finding the body.

He started to shovel rubble around, faster and faster, with greater urgency. "Where are you?" he muttered under his breath. "Where *are* you?"

He got to the bottom of the rubble, and it started to fall downward. . . .

Downward?

Where in hell was downward? They were at street level. There was no downward for the ruins to . . .

"No. *No!*" bellowed Talbot as he suddenly realized.

The last of the debris was pushed aside, and below him now was a hole that had been torn through the street. Below Talbot, his audio equipment detected rushing water.

The sewer.

"The sewer! He escaped into the sewer!" shouted Talbot.

His mass was far greater than the Hulk's, but nevertheless it took Talbot only seconds to punch a hole large enough for him to drop through. But he was too tall, too tall by far. His twenty feet of height, while impressive as anything in the open arenas of the street, was a major handicap in the cramped quarters of the sewer system. He couldn't fit his entire bulk into the tunnel.

With a howl of indignation that was not dissimilar from the

infuriated sentiments expressed by his target, the frustrated Major Talbot slammed his metal fists on the street.

Bruce Banner staggered through the foul stench of the sewer, growling furiously and muttering to himself, occasionally shouting a few words before lapsing back into a steady monologue notable for its animal fury and its relatively empty threats.

"Hulk will smash them . . . kill them all . . . kill soldiers . . . kill Samson . . . everyone who has ever hurt Hulk . . . *everyone who has ever hurt Hulk,*" that last reverberating through the sewer tunnels.

The smell had become unbearable to him. He grabbed a ladder and hauled himself up to street level. Above him was a sewer plate. He shoved at it with one hand, which should have been enough to send it flipping like a poker chip.

It sat there resolutely, not the slightest bit impressed with the force he was placing against it.

He shoved again, this time with both hands. The sewer lid moved slightly, but then Banner's bare feet lost their grip on the rungs of the ladder. He slid off and plunged heavily back down into the filthy sewer water. He came up gasping, shaking it off his body like a mastiff. At that moment, he weighed one hundred and twenty-two pounds, soaking wet. He had no clue that his immeasurable power was gone. He had no idea that he wasn't green anymore. If he chanced to looked down at himself, his mind told him that he was exactly the way he had always been. A look in a mirror would not have revealed to him the pale face of Bruce Banner, but instead the fearsome visage of the snarling, savage Hulk.

Determined and angry, he climbed back up the ladder, shoved at the sewer plate, and pushed it out of the way. It slid bit by bit under the steady pressure, until enough space had been cleared for him to worm his way out.

He stood upon a street, the mightiest weakling on the face of the earth.

The streets around him were chaotic. Police were still trying to clear out the area, unaware that the battle—and the emergency—was pretty much over. Talbot had not alerted the authorities to any sort of "all clear," because he was still holding out hope of getting his hands on the Hulk.

Consequently no one was paying attention to Banner, which under ordinary circumstances would have suited him just fine. But he was wet, and he was angry, and nothing suited his savage personality better at that moment than to send frightened, puny mortals screaming on their way, terrified of his wrath.

"Puny humans!" he shouted at people clearing the area under police instruction. "Hulk will smash!"

They barely afforded him a glance. Those who did looked at him as if he were out of his mind. He wasn't, really. He was just out of his body.

He lurched down the street, still smelling of the sewer and still bellowing defiance. There was no telling how long he might have gone on like that, had he not had the remarkably bad misfortune to run squarely into the police. . . .

A homeless man sifted through the rubble, barely affording a glance at the armored figures arcing up toward the helicarriers. It was of no interest to him whatsoever.

Instead, what he did find somewhat curious was a head. A green head to be precise, staring up at him with lifeless mechanical eyes. He shoved the head in his shopping bag and shuffled away.

Chapter 5

Betty threaded the station wagon through the running hordes, trying to get as close to the scene of the action as possible. But she was swimming upstream, getting nowhere at it, and then she could get no further as a policeman in riot gear suddenly stepped in front of her car, blocking her way.

She rolled down the window as he made firm gestures indicating she should turn around and back away. Ahead of her, cars had been abandoned, the owners fleeing on foot as traffic had jammed to a halt. "I'm . . . I'm trying to find . . ."

The cop looked to be about twenty-three. "Turn around, ma'am!" he said, which made Betty feel rather old in comparison. *Ma'am? I'm a "ma'am" now?*

"But I'm looking for—"

"Turn it around, ma'am! Now!" His hand was hovering around the butt of his gun, and it was trembling. He was scared. He was petrified, and Betty knew it.

"Officer," she said as softly as she could, "I'm looking for my . . ."

Then, suddenly, she saw him.

"Ma'am, for the last ti—"

She shoved open the car door, uncaring of what the cop might do. "There he is!" she cried out. "There! Officer . . ." she glanced at the ID tag, "Beddeker! Please, Officer Beddeker, you've got to help me! That's my husband there! Right there!"

He turned to see where she was pointing. About thirty yards off, there was a large police van that was rounding up looters. As always, whenever there is some sort of emergency, there are those who are more than happy to cash in on the mishaps of others. Looters had been going from store to abandoned store, grabbing whatever they found of interest. Fortunately enough the police had, in turn, grabbed the looters.

But there was one who was unquestionably not a looter. He was, quite clearly, a nutcase.

He was struggling furiously in the hands of the police, his arms pinned back and put into handcuffs. He was dressed in tattered slacks and a ripped shirt, both of which looked rather loose on him. His hair was dirty and matted, and he was shouting at the cops who were endeavoring to shove him into the van. Even the looters were complaining about him, considering that he was somewhat pungent. He smelled, in point of fact, like a sewer.

"That's my husband!" Betty said urgently to the cop.

Beddeker looked back to Betty and chucked a thumb. "That guy? *That's* your husband? Ma'am, are you sure?"

She felt that if he called her "ma'am" once more, she was going to pop him one. "Yes, I'm sure, for crying out loud!"

"Okay, okay." He ran in the direction of the police wagon. The subject they were trying to subdue was endeavoring to kick his way to freedom. Since he was relatively scrawny, the thrusts were not doing any particular damage to anyone.

Beddeker spotted the ranking cop. "Hey, Sarge," he said. "You ain't gonna believe this."

The man he'd addressed as "Sarge," an angular man with graying hair and fraying temper, turned. "What?"

"She says this guy's her husband."

"Let him go . . . please," Betty begged. "I'll take full responsibility for him. . . ."

At her voice, Bruce turned and spotted her. There was still the brutal personality of the savage Hulk in charge, but even that persona—as wretched and as bestial as it was—was capable of recognizing in Betty the one ally it had in the world.

"*Betty!*" roared Bruce. "You tell them! Tell them I'll smash them all!"

"You gotta be kidding," said the sergeant. "Lady, the guy's a mental case."

She figured "lady" sounded better than "ma'am." "He's under a doctor's care," she said desperately and, embellishing the lie, said, "I . . . I was supposed to pick him up . . . and then with all this confusion and . . . he's having one of his 'episodes' . . . I swear, I can handle him."

"I wouldn't bet on that, lady."

"Has he hurt anyone?"

"Nooo," the sergeant admitted. "He was just running around scaring the crap out of people . . . plus stinking to high heaven."

"Body odor isn't illegal, Sergeant," Betty pointed out, trying to sound calmer than she felt. "If he didn't attack anybody . . . Come on, you know none of those people he 'scared' are going to bother to show up and press charges. You'll go to all this trouble to arrest him, do the paperwork, and for what? The 'victims' won't show up, and the judge will release him into my custody anyway. So save everyone some time and effort . . . please . . ."

"*I'll smash them all! All!*"

Betty did her level best to ignore him, instead focusing those large, puppy-dog eyes of hers on the sergeant.

"That your car down there?" he asked.

"Yes, sir."

"Beddeker," the sergeant sighed after a moment. "Help the

lady with her package. Keep the cuffs, lady," and he tossed her the keys, "until you get him all settled down. But I'm telling you right now . . . you might want to consider a stay at a mental institution."

Beddeker moved past them, dragging the angry Bruce with him. "You will see! I'll smash you all!" he threatened as Beddeker dragged him in the direction of the station wagon.

Betty appeared to consider the mental institution suggestion. "For me or him?" she asked after a moment.

"I meant for him."

"Oh. Pity," she said, heading toward the car. "I could have used the rest."

Major Talbot was taking what small bit of pleasure he could in this entire fiasco.

The Hulk had, quite simply, vanished. It had been Talbot's inclination to scour the entire city, flying everywhere in the Hulk-buster armor, trying to flush him out (so to speak).

But the plan had immediately been nixed by Talbot's superiors, who feared that the entire operation might blossom completely out of control. As far as they were concerned, the maneuver had been successful. The Hulk had been stopped in his rampage, been beaten back. He'd gone back into hiding, where he might stay for weeks, months . . . even years, if they were lucky. And the next time he surfaced, they might be lucky and it would be in some fairly desolate area where there were no extraneous considerations such as civilians or property. At such a time, they could completely cut loose with whatever they had and whatever it took. At that time, they would finally be able to put a stop to the rampaging Hulk.

That attitude infuriated Talbot. He was interested in heading off danger *before* it happened, not reacting to it afterward. A pre-emptive strike, not one that cleaned up after the mess that the

Hulk left behind him. Talbot felt frustrated, his hands tied, and he said as much to his superiors.

"Your recommendation is noted, Major," was all they said, which was the official military way of saying, "Go screw yourself."

Talbot entertained the notion of disregarding, or at least playing fast and loose with, the orders. Of making a few sweeps over Chicago just in case. Of doing whatever it took.

But Talbot was a good soldier, a proud soldier, one who respected the chain of command. Disobedience represented anarchy. And he had seen the face of anarchy, bellowing in fury and arrogant in its strength.

So he had obeyed, recalling the Hulkbusters and retiring to the helicarriers that were whisking them back to their headquarters at Fort Meade.

But just because he was following orders didn't mean that he couldn't take some small comfort in rubbing *someone's* nose in the events of the day. So, from the carrier, he had contacted Dr. Leonard Samson. Samson had no screen on his end, so Talbot had to settle for Samson's voice instead of a visual. It was a pity. He'd have liked to see Samson squirm as well as hear him.

"You said to leave him alone, Doctor," Talbot reminded him smugly. "Let him go on with his life, I believe you suggested. And look what happened."

"You said he claimed it was a robot impostor?"

"Some such farfetched nonsense. I suppose that's the aspect of his great intellect now in control, eh? In the old days, he destroyed things merely for the pure animal, monstrous joy of doing so. Now . . . now he's got to make up excuses."

"I don't suppose you entertained the notion that he might have been telling the truth."

"Not for a minute, no. I mean, that's a staggering coincidence, wouldn't you say? Monster shows up in the Hulk's general vicinity, trashes the place, and conveniently disappears. That's something of a stretch."

"Oh, I don't know about that. We live in something of a far-fetched world, Major. You should learn to expand your thinking."

"And you should learn, *Doctor*, when to realize that you were off the mark. Your patient, your pal, is back to his old destructive ways. And if he hadn't escaped into the sewer, we might have been able to put a stop to him once and for all."

"The sewer, huh?" Samson sounded amused.

"Yes, Doctor, the sewer. May I ask what's striking you as so funny about that?"

"Are you, by any chance, familiar with *Les Misérables*?"

"I don't get out to Broadway shows much, Doctor. I'm too concerned about the real world."

"Well, it did happen to be one of the great works of literature for a century before it was set to music, but that's neither here nor there. I just thought I'd mention that, at the climax of the story, the hunted man—Jean Valjean—escapes into the sewers of Paris, there to confront his longtime pursuer, police Inspector Javert. And in that showdown, Javert realizes the emptiness of a life spent in pursuit of the letter of the law, without mercy to temper it. The revelation destroys him, and he winds up committing suicide."

"That was a damned fool thing of him to do," said Talbot sharply. "What's the point you're getting at, Doctor?"

Samson's sigh was audible. "I would have thought it would be self-evident. Good-bye, Major." And the connection clicked off.

Talbot tilted back in his chair and shook his head. The cop kills himself? What kind of crap was that? Now he was glad he'd saved the price of a ticket by not bothering to see the show.

Samson's attitude was utterly pigheaded . . . and yet, Talbot figured that he shouldn't have been surprised. Some people simply could not even entertain the notion that they might be wrong about something.

"Let Hulk go! Or Hulk will smash!"

Betty had Bruce securely belted in the backseat. Beddeker had expressed genuine concern over the wisdom of the move, saying, "Lady, are you *sure* about this?"

In truth, she wasn't. The demented, bellowing creature in the back bore no resemblance whatsoever to the intelligent, soft-spoken, civilized man with whom she had fallen in love.

She kept her eyes fixed on the road, desperately trying to ignore the thrashing about. She kept trying to speak soothingly to him, to calm him down, to help him find the stable core of his personality that would trigger the transformation back into his calm intellect. There were moments when she thought she was in the throes of success. When he seemed actually to be paying attention to the steady stream of calm, loving words flowing from her lips. And then, without warning, he would suddenly start to twist and struggle.

At one point Bruce kicked forward so violently that he struck the back of the driver's seat, jolting Betty so that she almost lost control of the car. She banged her forehead against the wheel and cursed loudly, then quickly and reflexively crossed herself. "Knock it off, Bruce!" she admonished, rubbing her forehead.

"Hulk thought you cared about him! But *you* make Hulk a prisoner too! Hulk will smash you too!"

Her patience exhausted, Betty pulled over, slammed the car into *park*, and twisted around in her seat to face him. He glared at her balefully.

"Look!" she said, her air of calm completely crumbling. "In case you haven't realized it yet, I saved your butt from the police! If they'd gotten you to the police station and realized who you were, that would have been all for you! You'd be finished! *We'd* be finished! The only reason you've got any measure of freedom at all is because of me! Is any of this getting through to you?"

He roared at her, but there was something in his eyes that seemed to indicate that her words were indeed penetrating. Either that or it was just a major case of wishful thinking.

"I'd take the handcuffs off you if I thought you could be trusted not to jump at me, or out of the car, or try to show that you're the strongest one there is by pounding the snot out of this car, which is borrowed, by the way. But I don't think that, and the cuffs are staying on until *you learn how to behave yourself! Understand that?*"

This time he said nothing. There was fury in his eyes. They were hard and burning cold, like dry ice, and Betty shuddered slightly to feel that malevolent gaze upon her.

She turned back around in the seat, but could still feel that stare on the nape of her neck, burrowing into her. She shoved the car back into *drive* and rolled back out onto the street.

The remainder of the drive passed in silence, punctuated only by the occasional low snarl from the peanut gallery.

Desperate, frantic thoughts about the gravity of the predicament tumbled through her head. She felt she had to be insane for continuing to allow things to exist as they did. When Bruce, as a result of Doc Samson's hypnotic therapy strategy, had transformed into his gargantuan and permanent self, she had been extremely taken aback. Indeed, it had taken her months to even reconcile herself to the notion that this remarkable being was, in fact, the man she had married. His height and mass, curiously, were the secondary (although considerably daunting) aspect of his condition.

The Bruce Banner that she had known, the scientist she had fallen in love with, had been soft-spoken. Compassionate. He had *needed* her; that was the bottom line. She had a place in his life and understood it, and she drew comfort and security from that.

But his new incarnation seemed utterly self-sufficient. Where the old Bruce had been amenable, this one bordered on recalcitrant. The old Bruce spoke softly; the new one carried a big stick. Every single aspect of the man that had attracted her to him seemed to have been supplanted by this . . . this creature who answered to the name of Bruce Banner, and claimed to *be* Bruce Banner. She felt like a vice-presidential candidate, wanting to say to him, "Sir, I knew Bruce Banner. I was married to Bruce Banner, and you, sir, are no Bruce Banner."

But as time had passed, she had begun to see her husband within him again. The swagger, which he had sported like a shield at first, had slowly begun to give way to the simple humanity that she had long associated with the man she loved. It was as if the "old" Bruce was beginning to reassert himself. All his various personalities had been jockeying for position in his head, trying to find a moderate position for all concerned so that they could exist together harmoniously. Perhaps it had simply taken time for the gentler aspects of Bruce Banner to make themselves known. Once they were there, though, they didn't back down in the face of his stronger sides.

And he had seemed happy, which was something that Bruce never seemed to be even in their "happiest" days. The closest he came to happiness was a sort of melancholy, and when Betty was in a good mood, Bruce would seem merely to watch her with a bit of envy. Or even be studying her, as if he were taking mental notes on happiness, hoping in some way to be able to aspire to such a condition someday.

Betty had taken their vows of marriage very seriously. She had not entered into their wedded state capriciously. She had sworn to be with him for better or worse, and she had known going in that life with Bruce Banner was easily capable of getting worse, with no hint of better in sight. But she had done it, and acted in good faith, and the thought of walking away from her wedding vows was anathema to her.

Still, for a long time she felt as if the man who had stood beside her that day had simply ceased to exist. From that concern had developed her trepidation and hesitancy over the continued status of their marriage. However, as the newly integrated personality of Bruce Banner settled in, Betty felt a strong degree of attraction to him. It was fresh and new, as invigorating and exciting as those earliest days when he'd been the bright, thoughtful young scientist, and she'd been the army brat daughter of a blood-'n'-guts officer known throughout the service as General "Thunderbolt" Ross. Her father had strongly objected to any sort of relationship between the "weak-kneed" Banner and his daughter. Perhaps the "forbidden" aspect of her associating with Banner had been part of what had attracted her to him. She was willing enough to admit that.

Who knew? Perhaps the element of danger in being the wife of a six-and-a-half-foot, green, gamma-irradiated colossus was something of a draw to her as well. Army brats, after all, are accustomed to associating with men who are willing to risk their lives in the heat of combat. That had to have rubbed off on her to some degree. It might even have been that her initial concerns about an ongoing marriage to her newly integrated green goliath of a husband were becoming secondary to . . . what? A need for some danger in her life? A sense of living on the edge?

She had had the normal rebellious nature of a teenager when she'd been that age, but she'd felt totally intimidated by her bellicose father. Could it be that, even though her teen years were long behind her, and her father long dead . . . she was still rebelling? Still pushing? Still seeking a sense of validation through defying convention?

Or could it be something as stupid, and as simple, as that she still loved her husband, and would do whatever was required to continue their relationship for as long as it was possible?

After months apart, she had reconciled with him. He'd actually seemed surprised, as if he'd resigned himself to Betty's telling him that she was planning to leave him for good.

Granted, the physical side of the relationship had been somewhat . . . daunting. They'd both made accommodations as best they could, and both of them were so happy to be together again that everything else had been secondary to the simple pleasure of being in each other's company.

Then everything seemed to have fallen apart once more. Bruce had become leader of the Pantheon, but eventually Bruce's predecessor, and the Pantheon's founder, Agamemnon, returned long enough to unleash "the Endless Knights." Betty never really understood the rationale behind the Knights' attack, but the end result was the Pantheon's headquarters in ruins, Betty almost fatally wounded, Bruce "fired" from the Pantheon, and the pair of them on the run.

But by this point Betty had bound herself to a course of action, and nothing was going to turn her away from it. She had not been expecting the return of the "savage" aspect of Bruce's personality. On the other hand, deep down, she hadn't completely ruled it out, either. It was a possibility, she had always known that.

But there were always possibilities. If one's spouse developed cancer—or Alzheimer's disease—would it be right to simply turn and walk away? No.

And this condition of Bruce's, at least, was controllable. Perhaps, in time, even reversible.

She couldn't walk away. She couldn't turn away.

She had to cope, just as she had been doing her entire life, and would continue to do.

She turned into the driveway of the house, rolled the car into the garage. She rolled down the windows, for the smells of the sewer still clung to Bruce and were stinking up the car something fierce. Sylvia would kill her if she brought the vehicle back in this condition. Betty would have to make sure to take the thing to get washed and cleaned out before returning it.

Bruce roared and started kicking the door again. "Let Hulk out! Let Hulk out *right now!*"

"Hold on, for crying out loud, hold on!" she said in exasperation as she came around and unlocked the door. She grabbed Bruce by the handcuffs and yanked upward, pulling his arms back tighter and more painfully. She hated to do it, but it was like dealing with a mule. The first thing you have to do in a situation like that is get his attention.

"*Arrhhhhhh!*" he growled at her.

"I'm bringing you inside now, Bruce. Do you understand? Bruce, do you understand?"

"Not Bruce! Not puny Banner! I am Hulk! Hulk is strongest one there is!"

"Not in this garage," she said, and she was probably right. In ferocity she couldn't hope to match her husband, but ever since their reconciliation, Betty had been working out—a lot. Lifting weights, running, swimming, trying to tone her body. She had no interest in competing or turning herself into a bodybuilder, but the muscle she did have was solid and effective. She was able to haul Bruce out of the car with minimal exertion. If his hands were free it might have been a different story altogether, but with the handcuffs on he was manageable.

"C'mon," she said tersely, and brought him inside.

He was still growling, still making defiant noises, but he wasn't struggling as much. She took that as a good sign.

"I've got the key to the handcuffs in my pocket," she said as he glared at her. "As soon as I know you're calm, I'll unlock them and everything will be fine."

"Hulk hates you," he said venomously.

She turned him, took his face in her hands, and with all the sincerity she could muster, said, "But Betty loves you," and she kissed him firmly.

She could sense the beginning of it.

In the far-gone days, when Bruce had changed into the Hulk and vice versa, it had taken only a matter of seconds for the transformation to be complete.

But with this new set of circumstances, the rules had changed. It took somewhat longer for the transformation from the "savage Banner" back into the calm and collected "incredible Hulk." Could be several minutes, perhaps as much as fifteen or twenty. It was as if his more benign personality had to be coaxed out from wherever it was hiding deep within his psyche.

Well, she could do that, she was certain. Gentle words, whispering of love, reassurance of acceptance and support . . . these would induce and complete the transformation. But at the moment, her nose wrinkled in disgust as she was unable any longer to ignore the stench of the sewer that hung on him.

"Let's go," she said, pushing him upstairs.

Moments later they were in the bathroom, and she had started the shower. He wasn't saying anything at the moment, merely glaring at the water suspiciously.

"Come on, get in," she said.

He frowned at the water. "Why?" he demanded.

"Because you stink."

"Don't want to."

"Bruce, the smell's really starting to get to me. I'm going to throw up, and if I do, I'll make sure that you're directly in the line of fire."

"*Don't want to!*"

With a grunt of exasperation, Betty stepped fully clothed into the shower, figuring she might as well since the smell was already sticking to her. She dragged Bruce in with her. He stumbled and almost fell, started to push back against her, and nearly knocked both of them to the floor of the shower stall.

This would be a really stupid way to die, thought Betty. *I wonder what they'd make of it when they found our bodies . . . two people in the shower, both with some clothes on, one of them handcuffed, dead of broken necks. Like to see them make heads or tails out of that one.*

"Bruce . . ."

"Water's hot," he grunted, but he had stopped struggling. Now he sounded more sullen than anything else.

"We need the water hot if we're going to get this smell off you," she said firmly. She grabbed soap and started washing him down. She started to work the muscles of his bare back. "You're tense," she said, in a steady and even voice. "That's your problem. You're just tense. Just relax and everything is going to be fine. I promise you."

He started to sway slightly under the ministrations of her fingers, his head rocking a bit in rhythm. "Hulk feels good," he admitted. But then his temper started to flare, all the old suspicions from the many times in the past that he'd been betrayed coming to the forefront. "But maybe you're trying to trick Hulk! Maybe you still hate Hulk!" The muscles beneath his shoulders, which had been starting to loosen, began to coil once more. "*Maybe you want Hulk to go away so you can kill him!*"

She felt as if maybe she was starting to lose him. Blinking the water out of her eyes, Betty said, "Okay . . . okay, look . . . I'll prove it to you. Okay? I'll prove it."

She took the key out of her pocket, jammed it into the handcuffs, and prayed she wasn't making a hell of a mistake. With his hands free, anything was possible. He could strike out at her, make a break for it . . . anything.

The handcuffs snapped open. She pulled them off him, then quickly turned him around so that he was facing her. She held the cuffs up in his face.

"I took them off you, Bruce. See?" She dangled them. "Just so you don't start thinking you broke free. I removed them. Because I trust you. Trust me, Bruce. Okay? We're . . . we're all each of us has."

She could tell that, in his gaze, he was trying to decide whether or not he *could* trust her. He'd known so much hurt and betrayal in his life. He'd been taken advantage of by so many people, exploited for so many ends, many of them nefarious. And here was his wife, Betty, who loved him, who had risked herself for him and would willingly do so again . . . and she was the one paying for those years when he'd known nothing but treachery.

She kissed him again, the water pouring down over them. He growled, but there was something different in it this time. He brought his arms up around behind her and drew her closer to him, his mouth seeking hers hungrily. She ran her fingers the length of his body, and all her concerns for herself, for their future . . . all of it was washed away at that moment, swirling down the drain with the water, replaced by the passion of the moment and the intensity of her husband. Intensity that had been daunting seconds before, but now caused her own heart to race, her own breath to come in short gasps.

What happened in the shower over the next few minutes was many things: a need for communion; a spiritual and physical joining; a golden opportunity; therapy; all that and more.

But most important . . .

. . . it was incredible.

Chapter 6

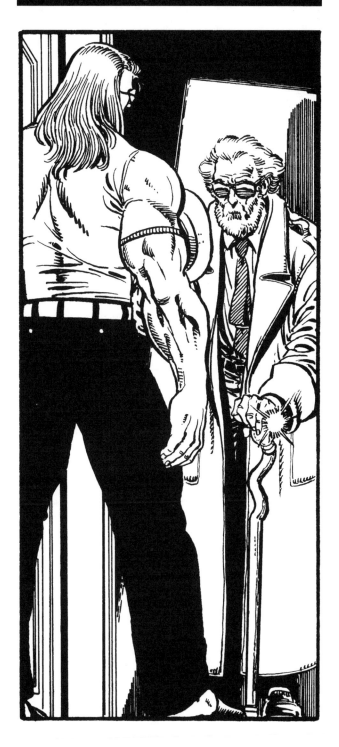

Doc Samson's doorbell rang, several times. He almost ignored it as he glanced at his watch and noted the relative lateness of the hour. He wasn't expecting anyone. It was probably just that idiot Talbot. He'd called several times, and stopped by once, since the entire Chicago debacle of some weeks back, trying to pump Samson for information as to the Hulk's whereabouts. Samson had no idea. Of course, he didn't volunteer the information that he'd been in regular computer contact with Banner, answering questions, counseling as best he could. It was an odd way to advise a patient. Then again, who could say? Perhaps it would catch on.

Meantime, the doorbell continued to ring with growing insistence. Annoyed to the point where he could ignore it no longer, Samson tossed aside the pen he'd been using to jot notes for a forthcoming speech and strode over to the door. At the door, making no attempt to hide the irritation in his voice, he said, "What the hell do you want?"

"Doctor Samson?" came a voice. It definitely wasn't Talbot. It was an older man, sounding about in his sixties. Sounded vaguely familiar, although nothing that Samson could put his finger on.

Frowning, Doc Samson opened the door. Standing there was

a man at least in his sixties. His hair and beard were thick and white, making it hard to get a real feeling for the shape of his face. But he had a pleasant, rather avuncular expression. He wore a heavy coat and a tweedy hat that he doffed as he bowed slightly, revealing a bald spot on the back of his head. He wasn't especially tall, and his hands were thin and bony. He was leaning on a cane that had an impressive diamond-shaped ornament on top. The ornament seemed to flicker in the light from Samson's fireplace.

"Yes?" prompted Samson.

"My name is Amos Trotter."

Samson blinked a bit in surprise. "Doctor Amos Trotter?"

"You were expecting another, maybe?"

"I wasn't expecting any at all. But don't get me wrong. This is an honor, sir."

He gave a soft, self-deprecating laugh. "There are some who would disagree with that. But that's neither here nor there. With you, Doctor Samson, I'd like to speak a little, if you've got the time. I think I might be able to give you a hand . . . with a tricky little problem you've got on your hands involving an individual. The 'Hulk' he's called, yes? And you are familiar with the case, of course."

"Passingly," said Samson dryly. "Wrote a paper or two on it."

"Read them. Nice job, although a little . . . how shall I put it . . . layman-esque."

"Fair enough. There's a lot of general interest in the Hulk. I felt it would help for people to better understand him. That's what he could use, to a very large degree."

"You think maybe I could sit down?" He gestured vaguely toward a chair.

"Oh, of course. By all means." Samson stepped back, allowing Trotter to enter, and gestured for him to take the fairly large (all of the furniture in Samson's home was fairly large) chair facing the television set. "Please excuse my manners, or lack thereof. Can I get you something to drink?"

"You wouldn't have a *bissel* sherry around, would you?"

"I'll see what I can dig up," said Samson. By this point, he was fairly sure he knew why Trotter's voice sounded so familiar. His vaguely Yiddish accent reminded Samson of his uncle Isaac, Samson's favorite uncle from his youth. The one who was always pulling coins from Doc's ear, or telling slightly off-color stories in a booming voice that Samson rarely understood, but liked because it always got his mother saying, "Ike, for crying out loud, not in front of the boy!" and looking utterly mortified in her son's direction.

Moments later, Samson had pulled up a chair and was sitting opposite Trotter, who looked as if he were getting rather comfortable there. Trotter was holding the sherry in a rather genteel manner, and Samson found himself taking an immediate liking to the old man. "I'm familiar with your research, of course," said Samson, "although you've been keeping a low profile for quite a few years now."

"You know the old saying, if you got nothing positive to say, say nothing? Well, I've lived my life by it," Trotter told him. He leaned forward, his fingers interlaced. "May I be honest with you, Doctor? Bluntly so, in fact?"

"Of course."

"I'm a bit tired of laboring in relative obscurity. I'd like recognition for my work as much as the next fellow. I suppose I should feel guilty about that."

"I wouldn't," said Samson.

"Oh, I don't," Trotter assured him. "I said I *should* feel guilty. But if I'm not for me, who's going to be, eh?"

"Indeed. My grandmother often said the same."

"Your grandmother was a genius. This I know, and I never

even met her." He took another sip. "I'm not even looking for fame in my own lifetime, mind you. It can be such an annoyance. Talk shows, book tours, whatever. I'm not looking for a lot of money. Money I got. Health I got," and he rapped the wooden coffee table in front of him. "But real immortality . . . that I haven't got. That, I think, might be nice. When you start to reach my age . . . being remembered becomes important to you. Now, me . . . I've got no family. Barely any friends anymore, and those I do have will probably go before I do. You see, I've dedicated my life to helping the mentally ill, Doctor. I care about them, want to help them. They're so important to me, these people without hope."

"They'll remember you, won't they?"

"Feh. Who wants to be remembered by a bunch of *meshuggeners*?"

He said it with such a straight face that Doc had a hard time figuring out just how serious he was. But Trotter wasn't quite able to hold it, and he smiled, looking a bit like Santa Claus when he did. "You know what I mean, Leonard . . . may I call you Leonard?"

"Of course."

"Good. And you may call me Dr. Trotter. As I was saying, I'd like to be remembered for something big . . . something of major consequence. And I was thinking, wouldn't it be nice if I were . . . say . . . the man who cured the Hulk?"

"It certainly would," said Samson, scratching his chin thoughtfully.

Trotter looked concerned. "You wouldn't be offended, would you? You'd help. Without you, I couldn't do it."

"Not offended at all," Samson assured him. "But curious . . . that I am. What exactly did you have in mind?"

The older doctor leaned forward. "I've had a major break-through. It's rather remarkable, really. Within the last several weeks, as a matter of fact."

"And that would be—?"

Trotter patted Samson on the arm. "Why tell you about it, when I can show you? Get your coat."

"Where are we going?"

"I'm going to introduce you to a small miracle."

"Martians! Martians are landing today! I swear—!"

The therapist tried to calm Mr. Needleman, but it was not easy. Other clinic patients walked past, not even glancing at Needleman. No reason for them to; they all had their own problems.

"Mr. Needleman," said the therapist gently. "Mr. Needleman, you say this every week. And every week, the Martians don't land. Shouldn't that tell you something?"

"It means they're clever," said the rail-thin Needleman. "Very, very clever. But they can't fool me. Not forever. This time I'm onto them."

"Mr. Needleman, this business of little green men—"

"I never said that!" Needleman said aggressively. "Don't you remember? They're big . . . like in *Warlord of Mars.* Big, with huge muscles, and long green hair . . . I've told you this so many times."

"Yes, of course, I'm sorry." The therapist sighed, rubbing the bridge of his nose. "But don't you see, Mr. Needleman? Every single week you talk about this, and you're positive every week, and every week there's no hint of . . ."

But then the therapist's voice trailed off, and his eyes widened. Other patients slowed in their tracks and looked where the therapist was looking. Needleman stared in confusion at the therapist, then turned in his chair to see what was going on.

Striding toward him was a Martian, just as he'd always said. He was huge. He had green hair. And he was brazen as anything, his large arms swinging casually with every step of his long measured stride. There was a shorter man next to him, and the shorter man frightened Needleman even more.

He pointed a trembling finger at Samson and said, "Martian!" and then swung it in the direction of Trotter and said, "Incarnation of evil! You thought you could fool me?"

Samson stopped where he was, smiled at the patient as benevolently as he could. "I'm not a Martian, sir. I know I look odd. But I'm as human as you. And this gentleman is hardly the incarnation of evil."

"Once, I had a fiancée who might actually have agreed with the 'evil' part," Trotter put in.

Needleman recoiled against the wall. Samson shrugged, and he and Trotter kept on going.

"I knew it," said Needleman. "I told you. They're finally here. Now . . . now it begins."

"Uhm . . ." the therapist said, watching Samson and Trotter move on down the hallway. "And . . . and when does it end?"

Needleman looked at the therapist in undisguised amazement. "When it's over, of course. When else *would* it end? What a stupid question. What are you . . . crazy?"

Meantime, Dr. Trotter had stopped outside a private room. He tapped on it gently. "Mrs. Clark?" he called softly. "Are you in there?"

"Dr. Trotter?"

"Yes, my dear."

"By all means, come in."

The door opened and there was a pleasantly sunny, smiling woman in her late forties. She had copious brown hair and a mild British accent. She was wearing a simple blue dressing gown.

Inside the room was a balding man about the same age, wearing street clothes. She gestured toward him and said, "You remember Herbert."

"Yes, of course," said Trotter, shaking Herbert's hand warmly. "So, Herbert, how has Patricia been?"

"You haven't heard the news, then?" asked Herbert.

"I've been out of my office all day. What news?"

Herbert smiled at Patricia. "You tell him, darling."

"I'm getting out tomorrow," she said. "The doctors here are completely satisfied about my condition and, on a trial basis, I'll be going home. My God," and her eyes started to tear slightly. She wiped the wetness away, looking mildly embarrassed. "I'm sorry, I . . . thought I was over that. Getting so emotional, I mean."

"No reason to," Trotter told her. He hugged her warmly. "I'm so happy for you," he whispered. Then he released her from his embrace and said, "Oh, may I introduce you to Dr. Leonard Samson?"

Patricia stared up at him. "You look familiar . . . oh! I saw you on television, didn't I? On a talk show? That young fellow and his wife."

"Yes, that's right," said Samson. He saw that Trotter was looking at him questioningly. "A friend of mine, Rick Jones, has a late-night talk show. He and his wife, Marlo. It's called *Keeping Up with the Joneses*. Maybe you heard of it?"

Trotter shook his head. "A TV person I'm not."

"Oh. Well, Rick likes to have shows with themes to them. He had me on with Dr. Kevorkian. Billed the show as a 'Pair o' Docs.' " Seeing Trotter's blank look, he said, "Pair o' Docs? Paradox? It's a sort of joke."

"A joking person I'm not either," Trotter told him.

Samson sighed, and turned his attention to Patricia Clark. "Mrs. Clark, the good doctor here has been somewhat mysterious as to what this is all about. Might I ask what, precisely, was the nature of your problem that caused you to be a patient here?"

"By all means. I suffered from Multiple Personality Disorder, and acute paranoid schizophrenia." She smiled benignly. "I was quite the mess."

Samson could scarcely believe that this utterly calm, collected woman could have been in such dire straits. "How long had you been here?"

"I was institutionalized in . . . ?" She frowned, trying to remember, and turned to her husband. "Herbert?"

"It was seven years, four months ago," he said.

"Seven years, four months," she affirmed. "Oh, they tried everything. Everything."

"I thought she would never get out," Herbert said with tremendous melancholy.

"Then how . . . ?"

Trotter moved toward her, putting a hand toward the side of her head. "If I may . . . ?"

Patricia nodded and reached up to pull her hair back. Trotter looked closely at an area around the base of her skull, running a finger over it cautiously. He gestured for Samson to come over, and Samson did so. There was a small incision, no wider than a thumbnail, situated just above the nape of her neck.

"Too small for any sort of serious surgery. Some sort of cell scraping? I don't . . ."

"A device."

Samson looked at him, puzzled. "Device? What sort of device?"

Trotter stepped away, draping his hands behind his back. "The human mind," he said, "is a computer. The single most sophisticated, most amazing, fastest processing computer in all of nature, but still a computer. Diseases of the mind are simply examples of that fine device . . . what's the term? Yes . . . 'crashing.' When a computer crashes, you don't simply dispose of it. You fix it, if it's at all possible. My procedure was, to put it mildly, unorthodox. But I received full permission from Mr. Clark to perform it since, to be honest, the poor fellow didn't have much to lose."

"That's for certain," confirmed Herbert.

"So I inserted a bio-chip into Mrs. Clark's skull."

"A what?" asked Samson. "A . . . bio-chip? I never heard of that."

"Since I'm the inventor, and I've told virtually no one about it, I don't doubt that," said Trotter easily. "Without going into the endless and boring details, let's just say that it's a computer chip that functions with a biological entity . . . like, oh, the brain, for instance?"

"You're not serious."

"Oh, but I am."

"I've . . . I've never heard of anything like that."

"As I said, a breakthrough," said Trotter. "I had a bit of . . . inspiration."

There was something just a touch odd in the way Trotter said it, but Samson couldn't quite figure out what it might be. He looked at the point of incision once more.

"Not even major surgery," said Trotter. "Local anesthetic, done right here in the clinic."

"I didn't go to sleep, and never felt a thing," confirmed Patricia.

Trotter reached into his briefcase and pulled out a thick file folder. "Right here I've got the results, Leonard . . . and it's pretty thorough. You'll see the immediate improvements, all the coverage done on her. It's fairly indisputable."

"To say you're in a gray area here, Doctor, is to put it mildly," said Samson. "We're talking procedures, devices not approved by—"

"You want to know what we're talking?" said Trotter forcefully, pointing at the Clarks, his finger trembling slightly. "We're talking a woman who's going home tomorrow. We're talking success."

"We don't know what the long-term results will be."

"We will. We'll observe her, keep a close eye on her. But in the meantime . . . in the meantime, Leonard . . . she gets to live a full life. A real life, not the . . . the shadow that she's inhabited for as long as she can remember. There's no victims here, Leonard. It's all winners. All success stories."

"One success story, Doctor, if I understand this correctly."

"I'm hoping for another." Trotter put up a finger, indicating that he didn't want to speak for the moment. He kissed Patricia lightly on the cheek, shook Harold's hand, and then guided Samson back out into the hallway. The door closed behind him with a click.

He didn't even have to say anything, though, because Samson was one step ahead of him. If his body language was any indicator, however, he wasn't exactly amenable to the idea.

He looked down at Trotter, his arms folded across his massive chest. "You want to try this on the Hulk, don't you?"

"This is a small, private clinic, Leonard. Privately funded. Very discreet. And stop that, Leonard, don't you go start shaking your head at me."

"Dr. Trotter," said Samson, lowering his voice as if someone might be eavesdropping. "You're talking untested, uncertain procedures, that you want to try out on a being of unbelievable power."

"A being who is, so I understand, stuck at nearly seven feet tall, and green as grass. This is right?"

"Yes," admitted Samson.

"Is there any reason he's stuck this way?"

Samson sighed, scratching his head. "He's a shapeshifter. He always has been. His mind is in control . . . but he, himself, is not."

"Which means all we have to do is reprogram his mind to be in charge. Again this is right?"

"It's not that easy."

"With all due respect, Leonard . . . perhaps it is."

They regarded each other for a time. "I can't recommend to the Hulk that he undergo this procedure. There's too many unknowns."

"Recommend, I'm not asking. Here," and he thrust the file folder of papers into Samson's arms. "Look it over. Any questions, call. And understand . . . what I *am* asking is that you tell him about it. That's all. Tell him."

"Dangle some sort of possible magic cure-all in front of him, after all the disappointments he's had in the past?"

"That's exactly right, Leonard. Exactly right. And let him decide. He's entitled to decide his own future, don't you think?" He paused. "*Tell* him. That much, you owe him . . . don't you."

It wasn't a question. And if it had been, it was one to which Doc Samson, reluctantly, knew the answer.

Chapter 7

The Hulk couldn't bring himself to look at his wife.

She sat on the couch, curled up, her legs tucked under her, her head propped up by her elbow. She was staring off into space. She had a book by her hand, but she wasn't reading it.

Finally he brought himself to turn to her. "Is there . . . is there anything I can get you?"

"No," she said very softly. Then, after a long moment, her gazed shifted to him. "Bruce . . . what are we going to do?"

"I don't know."

"What are we going to *do?*"

"Honey, shifting the emphasis of the question isn't going to—"

In anger she tossed the book at him. It bounced off his massive green chest. He barely felt it. "Stop it!" she yelled in anguish. "*Stop it!* Stop talking like a scientist! Stop trying to make me feel inferior.*"

"I wasn't. I swear I wasn't," he told her, feeling completely helpless.

She put her hands to her face, trying to compose herself. But when she spoke again, her voice was still wavery and uneven. "This isn't something that I can discuss in . . . in clinical terms. Damn it,

Bruce, this is our future. This is a situation. This is our lives, and I have no idea what to do or how to handle this."

She rose from the chair and turned to gaze out the window. "I mean, jeez, Bruce, look at us. Always keeping one eye securely riveted behind us. You're the Jolly Green Giant . . . except on those occasions when you become normal sized but a raving maniac. We have no security at all. None. What kind of life can we offer . . . ?" Her voice trailed off.

"You think I haven't thought of that?" Bruce said, trying to keep his voice neutral. "You think I'm not as frightened by the concept as you? I wasn't expecting it, Betty—neither were you— and now we've got to figure out how to deal with it."

"Well, I'm clueless, Bruce," Betty said, sounding more defeated than he'd ever heard her. "I've tried to roll with every punch tossed at me. Tried to deal with everything that an uneven past and an uncertain future has handed me. But now this . . ." Her eyes began to moisten and she stubbornly wiped it away.

He started to speak again, but then caught himself. There was no point to it. Because the fact was that they had had this conversation, or variations on it, about twenty times in the past week. It seemed an eternity since he'd last seen Betty smile. Instead, she just looked at him with . . . what? Disappointment? Frustration? Anger that her ties to him had ruined her life?

What *was* he going to do? What kind of security could he possibly provide when his mere physical presence was a liability? Sooner or later . . .

There was always a sooner or later.

Betty was right. They had no security. Nothing on which to build.

If he'd been any sort of considerate being—if he'd truly loved her—he would have left her long ago, so that she could go back to some sort of sane existence. But no . . . he'd been selfish. He'd wanted to be with her, and cooperated as best he could with her ludicrous desire to try to live a normal life.

Ludicrous. After all, why should Betty—the most gentle, understanding, brave, tolerant woman in the world—why should she be entitled to something that everyone else just took for granted?

He got up and went into his den, closing the door behind him. He went to his computer and logged on.

Moments later, he was being hailed in cyberspace by Doc Samson.

But it quickly became apparent that Doc was not in the mood for a casual chat. *Call me*, said the message, followed by an area code and phone number that Bruce was unfamiliar with.

Where are you? Bruce typed in.

Motel, picked at random about 150 miles from home. I don't trust Talbot. For all I know, my phone line is tapped. I'm on my portable computer. Call me.

Why?

Because this is going to be too clumsy and take too long. I'm in room six. Call me.

The phone number appeared again, and after a moment Bruce reached over to the nearby phone, punched in to the second line, and dialed. When the desk clerk answered, he asked for room six. Samson picked up on the first ring.

"Bruce?"

"Hello, Leonard. You sound well."

"Thanks, Bruce. I'm glad you finally logged on. I've been sitting in cyberspace for hours at a time, waiting for you to show up. Haven't heard much from you lately."

"Yes, well . . . it's been a fairly exciting week."

Samson sounded nervous. "Someone find you? Track you—?"

"No, no, Leonard. Nothing like that. It's . . ."

"What?"

Bruce took a deep breath and tried to sound upbeat about it. "Well . . . there's no other way to put it. . . . Betty is due around the middle of September."

There was dead silence on the other end. "What?" finally came back.

"You heard me."

"She's due in September? You mean . . . you mean *Betty's pregnant*?"

Bruce sighed. "No, she's a library book. Of *course* that's what I mean. She's pregnant."

"Bruce, I . . . I don't know what to say! I suppose congratulations are in order. Aren't they?"

"I'm not too sure myself, Leonard. A baby is high profile. A baby is paperwork, and questions that we're not in a position to answer. A baby is someone who deserves a real life, not this . . . this fugitive existence that we have to offer. Betty's as close to falling apart as I've ever seen her. I'm feeling guilty as sin. So pardon me if I restrain my enthusiasm."

"Bruce . . ."

"Leonard, tell me why you needed to talk to me. What's so important? What's happened?"

In quick, broad strokes, Samson outlined what he'd learned and experienced over the past few days. Banner listened without interrupting. Even when Samson finished speaking, Bruce remained silent for a time.

And in that quiet, he could hear Betty sobbing softly in the next room.

"If you'd called me about this a few weeks ago," said Bruce finally, "I'd've told you to forget it. That it was too risky. All the things you told this Dr. Trotter."

"But now . . . ?"

"Now . . . now there's other considerations. I'd like to talk to him. . . . No. Scratch that. I want to do it."

"Bruce, that's a rather hasty decision."

"I don't see it that way, Leonard. I'm . . . I'm stuck in this behemoth of a body. I've tried everything I could to force myself back to normal size. It's as if my brain refuses to cooperate."

"And I'm sure there are reasons for it. . . ."

"I'm sure there are. But what I'm also sure of is that we don't have the time to figure out what they are anymore. Betty deserves normality. This baby deserves some sort of sane household to arrive in."

"It could possibly make things worse."

"It could make them better. I'm willing to take the chance. I'm anxious to do it."

"Perhaps you should wait until you've consulted with Betty. . . ."

"My mind's made up. I'll consult with her, of course. She deserves to know. But . . . set up a time. A place. And I'll be there."

There was a pause and then Samson said, "All right, Bruce. I understand how priorities can shift at times like this. I'll speak to Dr. Trotter. Call me in an hour and I'll have details for you."

Banner hung up without saying anything further. He sat there for some time, and then he heard a soft rapping on the door. He glanced at the clock. Yes, she was pretty much on time. When they'd had "discussions" in previous days, Betty usually took about this long before she decided that she'd been too hard on him. "Yes?" he called.

The door opened enough for Betty to stick her head in. "I . . . just wanted to say I was sorry. I shouldn't have . . . have dumped all my . . ."

"That's all right," he assured her. "If you can't unload on me, who can you unload on?"

"We'll . . . manage," she said. "Somehow, we'll manage."

"I know."

"By the way . . . were you on the phone with somebody? I thought I heard you talk—"

"Just someone taking a poll. Nothing special."

"Oh, well . . . if we get somebody else with something like that, kick them over to me. You shouldn't have to be bothered with stuff like that."

"You're too good to me." Then he turned to her and said, "Betty . . . I want to be a good father. It's important to me. More important than you could believe."

She walked over to him, rested a small hand on a shoulder that dwarfed it. "Everything *will* be okay. As long as we stick together, we can manage somehow."

"Somehow," he echoed, and tried to smile.

And failed.

Chapter 8

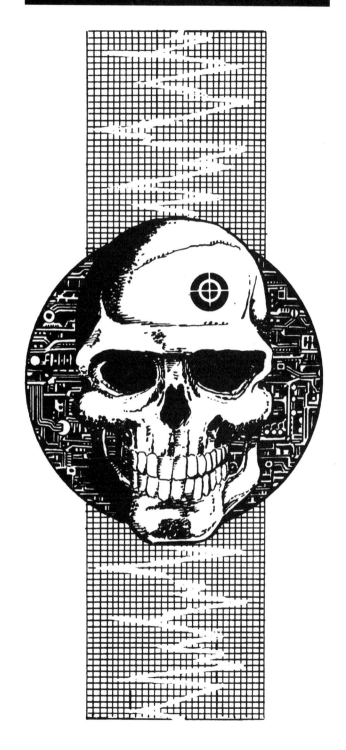

When Mr. Needleman saw the latest Martian to appear at the clinic, he didn't stare. He didn't gasp. He didn't shout for joy, or announce to anyone who would listen that he was not crazy; that he was right, the Martians had landed, and the entire world now had less than a snowball's chance in hell.

Instead he simply fainted dead away.

The Hulk and Doc Samson looked down at him with a mixture of bemusement and pity. "What's his problem?" asked the Hulk, chucking a thumb at the prostrate form.

"I don't know. Give me a moment," Samson said as he easily hoisted Needleman on his shoulder and walked off down the hallway to find a physician, an orderly, or someone else who could attend to him.

Bruce had arrived under his own steam, his powerful leg muscles covering miles of distance with every leap. He had kept a wary eye out every moment, certain that sooner or later one of the various individuals who had it in for him would attack. He told himself that it wasn't really paranoia if people really *were* out to get him. Somehow, though, that was cold comfort.

"Dr. Banner . . . ?"

He'd been lost in thought, so Bruce was slightly distracted

when he turned and looked at the man who had hailed him. From the description that Samson had provided, recognition was instant. "Dr. Trotter?"

"The same."

Bruce immediately felt himself warming to the man. There was a great deal of charm in the smile that was buried beneath the bushiness of the beard.

With his cane, Trotter gestured toward a room at the end. "Why don't we go and chat there?" He led the way, with the Hulk following only a few steps behind. He held open the door, and Bruce ducked a bit as he passed through the door frame.

Bruce turned to face him. "So. Tell me about this . . . miracle."

Trotter outlined it for him in brief strokes, all the time watching Bruce carefully to see what his reactions were. But Bruce's face was perfectly inscrutable. "So?" said Trotter when he was done. "What do you think?"

There was a rap at the door and Samson entered. He glanced from one to the other, and was pleased to see that there was no hint of tension in the room. When dealing with the Hulk, that was always desirable. "So where do we stand?"

"At a crossroads." Bruce's eyes narrowed. "Then again, I've been there before."

"Is there anything I've overlooked in my explanations?" asked Trotter.

Bruce draped his hands behind his back. "There's something you have to understand, Doctor. A number of times in my life, I've placed my trust in people. And more times than I can count . . . they've betrayed me in some way. Turned out to be using me for their own ends, some of them fairly nefarious."

"Now, that's hard to believe."

"It's true."

"Oh, I believe it's true," said Trotter. "What I find hard to believe is that you used the word 'nefarious' in a sentence. This, I never heard someone do before."

Bruce actually chuckled softly. "I'm sorry. Would you prefer if I spoke in monosyllables and forgot how to use personal pronouns?"

Trotter laughed in response, and Samson took this as a good sign. The two of them seemed to be developing some degree of trust, and that was going to be absolutely essential if there was any hope of making this work.

"What you tell me, Dr. Banner," Trotter said after a moment, "this is a sad thing. You know why this is a sad thing? I'll tell you why this is a sad thing. It's because I can really help you. My background's impeccable. Leonard here, he vouches for me. Here I come in, with all this . . . what's the word? Pedigree. All this pedigree, but I'm getting all the *tsuris* left over from everybody who did you dirt before. I can't make up for all those people, Bruce. All I can do is try and fix it so they don't bother you again."

Slowly Bruce nodded, and then he turned to Samson and said, "Leonard, could you and I talk in private for a moment?"

"This is not a problem," Trotter said. "I'll be right outside, with my ear shmushed against the door, if you need me." He waved cheerily and stepped outside.

Samson stared at Bruce, arms folded. "Still so anxious as you were before?"

"Anxious in several different meanings of the word."

"Did you consult with Betty?"

Bruce looked down at his feet. "Of course."

Samson made a sort of clucking noise. "You'd think you'd have gotten to be a more skilled liar than that."

"I didn't see a reason to tell her."

"How about that she's your wife?"

"How about," Bruce shot back, "that I didn't want to raise her hopes only to have them dashed again . . . or give her reason to be worried if it could be avoided. She's been through enough, Leonard."

"We all have, Bruce."

Banner lapsed into silence for a long moment. "If I do this . . . I can't shift back and forth between the way I look now and my—pardon the expression—puny form."

"That's the theory," Samson agreed. "Now maybe in time, you could. But . . ."

"But why would I want to? If the Hulk ceases to exist—if I'm just Bruce Banner, husband—that's all I want out of life, isn't it? All I need?"

"You've certainly given me that impression."

"How would the surgery be done?"

"Close in, laser scalpel. Your skin would heal almost instantly, of course, but even your body's incredible regenerative powers would be slow enough for us to insert the device. For anybody else, it would be minor surgery that would require, at most, a day or two's recuperation. For you, it would be like an ordinary person getting a mole removed."

"When can we do it?" Banner asked, his mind clearly made up.

Samson gestured expansively. "Anytime. I suspected you'd be fairly anxious to just go ahead with it. Dr. Trotter arranged for an accomplished surgeon, Dr. Schwartz, to do the surgery."

"He can be trusted, too? Remember, Leonard, I'm basically sitting perfectly still and allowing relative strangers to put lasers to my head."

"Don't worry. I've known Marty Schwartz for years. Besides, Bruce, the thing to remember is this: it's not as if Marty's, or Dr. Trotter's, motivations are unknown here. They've been very up-front about it. They want to be known as the men who cured the Hulk. Can you blame them?"

"No," said Bruce. "But they've got to promise to keep it under wraps for at least a year."

"A year?" asked Samson. "Why?"

"A year to give Betty and myself a chance to completely disappear and set up a new life somewhere. So that when the story finally does break, we'll be a nice, normal couple in a nice, normal world . . . so normal that it couldn't possibly occur to anyone who knows us that that nice Bruce and Betty whoever-they-are could possibly be associated with something as unsavory and frightening as the incredible Hulk."

Samson nodded slowly. "All right, Bruce. I'm sure that will be fine for all concerned."

Bruce clapped his hands briskly, barely remembering at the last moment and softening the blow, lest the impact of his hands devastate the room and perhaps the entire building. As it was, Samson felt his ears pop.

Bruce sat on the edge of the table, gripping it firmly. The small operating room was simple and functional, and everyone present was a doctor (although from a variety of disciplines).

Schwartz was still looking a little uncertain. "Are we sure about this? Strapping down a patient's hands prevents any sort of involuntary jumps or—"

There was a soft chuckle from Banner. "Somehow I doubt that any restraints would really be up to the job, Doctor. The slightest pull and I snap them. Don't worry. If I do 'jump,' I'll heal immediately. It won't be a problem."

"Well . . . I just . . ." Schwartz cleared his throat and glanced at Samson and Trotter, who were nearby. "I just . . . I wouldn't want to make you . . . y'know . . . angry. Because I'd heard that . . ."

"You wouldn't like me when I'm angry?" Bruce shook his head. "Ugly rumors, that's all. Actually, I'm a sweetheart. Slow to anger, quick to forgive. That's me."

Trotter was checking over the instruments, and then he walked around to Banner and held the device up in front of him. Bruce squinted. "Looks like a microchip."

"That's about right."

"I should just warn you, Doctor," said Bruce, his gaze flickering to Trotter. "If this should turn out to be . . . oh, I don't know . . . a bomb, say. Or a mind-control device. Or . . ."

Trotter sighed. "You know, Bruce . . . if you were around for the creation of penicillin, you would have been right in there saying, 'Bread mold? It's a trick. It has to be a trick. They're trying to poison us.' You still nervous, Dr. Banner? No one's twisting your arm . . . as if we could. No one's forcing you. You want to do it, do it. You don't want to, then leave. It's your decision."

"I've made it." He gripped the sides even more firmly, taking care that the sections of the table didn't snap off in his hands. "Let's do it."

There followed a long silence as the Hulk stared straight ahead. He heard the soft buzzing of the laser scalpel, and was dimly aware of a soft tug toward the back of his head. He felt flutters of nervousness once more, but he conjured the image of Betty to his mind. She was smiling at him, looking so sweet, so gentle.

And he pictured her holding a child. Their child, a small, healthy infant, in her arms. A bundle of life that they had created. Imagine that. Imagine that after so much destruction, so much havoc that he had wreaked . . . to have actually *created* something. What a notion. What a concept.

Was there a chance? Was there really a chance that—?

"Done."

Bruce turned and looked questioningly at Schwartz. "Are you sure? It seemed like almost no time at all . . . and I don't feel anything. But what should I . . ."

Then he felt it.

He gasped, sliding off the table, going down to one knee with such an impact that the room trembled. "Bruce!" said Samson.

Trotter raised a hand, waving Samson back. "It's all right."

"My . . . *my head!*" roared the Hulk, clasping it with both hands. "Buzzing . . . noise everywhere . . . some sort of . . . can't think, *can't think . . . you bastard, what did you . . . ?!*"

"Like this you don't talk to me!" Trotter said sharply, as if scolding a child. "This is to be expected. The bio-chip is tapping in to your neural pathways and reordering them. This I told you. It's bound to be disorienting. It should pass quickly . . . five, six seconds . . ."

The Hulk rolled onto his back, gasping.

"Thirty seconds, tops," Trotter amended, sounding just a touch uncertain.

"Doctor!" Samson said urgently, his intense gaze going from Trotter to Bruce and back again.

"It will be all right!"

Bruce rolled to his hands and knees. His fingers convulsed, tearing up pieces of the linoleum. He stared downward at his hands . . .

And suddenly started to see something.

The flesh was turning pale green, as if the color was melting away.

Then his hands began to shrink.

He felt his whole body starting to contract. There was intense burning as his skin shriveled, his muscles tightened, his bones contorted to accommodate the new shape. Pain, wracking pain was all through him, but he could handle that. He was used to that. What was new to him was the astonishment, the hope, the prayer that might finally be answered.

The pain pulled his hand into a fist and he slammed it on the floor with all his strength. Nothing happened. A few fragments of linoleum flew, but that was all.

He felt cold. Sensations of heat and cold meant little to him, but now there was a definite chill in him.

His breath came in ragged gasps. His clothes hung on him like potato sacks. His mouth felt completely dry and his vision was slightly blurred. His glasses fell out of his newly loose shirt pocket, the glasses that he still wore out of habit for reading even though he probably didn't need them. They clattered to the floor and he fumbled for them, picked them up, and placed them tremblingly on his face.

The world snapped into focus, and he was looking into Doc Samson's face. Doc had crouched down and was looking closely into his eyes. "Bruce?" he whispered.

"Leonard?" Even his voice sounded different. Not deep and raspy, that kind of rumbling speaking-from-a-wind-tunnel tonality that he'd possessed ever since the transformation. "Leonard? I'm . . . I'm cold."

"Good," said Leonard, grinning. He looked up at Trotter. "Do you think we could get Dr. Banner something to put on?"

"Absolutely," said Trotter, who wore a smug look of self-satisfaction. "You know, I think he wears my size now . . . which is fine, if he doesn't mind dressing like an old man."

Bruce staggered to his feet, his legs feeling uncertain beneath him. He felt fantastically light, as if tons of excess weight had miraculously been removed. He took a step and lurched so badly, misjudged so thoroughly, that he would have fallen if Samson hadn't caught him. He steadied himself and then started forward again.

He reached for a metal surgical tray and picked it up, staring into it.

The pale reflection of the man he'd once known looked back at him.

"Congratulations, Dr. Banner," said Trotter proudly. "Welcome back . . . to the land of the living."

Betty sat and stared at CNN, watching the same parade of news stories go by for the umpteenth time. Morbidly, she kept waiting for some mention of her husband to crop up on it.

Where in God's name had he gotten off to?

Apprehension had been building in her all day. It had been a very lightly attended daycare that day, because there was a flu going around and a lot of kids were simply home sick. With such sparse turnout, Betty had taken the rest of the day off to come back and be with her husband.

And he was gone.

Where had he gone off to? They'd agreed that simply wandering around wouldn't be a wise pastime for him, and yet he was nowhere to be found.

What if he didn't come back?

She felt as if she hadn't been treating him particularly well lately. She had an excuse, though, didn't she? With all the turmoil in both mind and body that she was experiencing—fear for the future egged on by her rampaging hormones—it was no wonder that she was short-tempered, apprehensive, crying all the time.

She had wanted a normal life, a normal husband. How fair was it to harangue Bruce simply because fate had made it nearly impossible for them to entertain such a hope?

But how fair was it, in turn, for her to have thrown away all—

There was a knock at the door.

Whenever there was a knock, it was always reason for concern.

What if it was the army? Or S.H.I.E.L.D.? Perhaps some demented villain come calling, stopping by for a spot of tea and fifteen rounds of mindless destruction.

On the other hand, what if it was merely someone trying to convert her religion?

That would be a stumper, all right. As she headed for the door, she put her palms out flat as if weighing two things. Religious nut. Demented villain. Which was more annoying, which one, which one?

Still uncertain of which would be tougher to handle, she peered through the peephole. Then she immediately gasped in recognition, turned the lock, and opened the door.

"Leonard!" she said. "Come in! What are . . . ?"

Samson remained where he was on the stoop. "Betty," he said gravely. "First, I should say congratulations on your pregnancy. I wish you well . . . I really do. But there's something else we have to discuss first."

She paled.

"There's no easy way to say this, so I'll just give it to you straight out: something's happened to Bruce," he said.

She gulped, resting a hand on the door frame. "What?"

"It's . . ." Samson seemed stuck for the words.

"Is he alive? Just tell me if he's alive."

"He's alive, but he's . . . well . . ." And Samson wasn't quite able to maintain the deadly serious demeanor anymore. A smile started to pull ever so slightly at the corners of his mouth.

Betty stared at him, completely lost.

"You'd better see for yourself," Samson finally said. He stepped aside.

Bruce had been standing directly behind him, but because of Samson's size and Banner's relative lack thereof, he'd been effectively invisible. He was wearing surgical greens, which might have looked rather odd to the casual passerby. Other than that, he looked utterly normal. He was wearing glasses, and his sandy-brown hair dangled boyishly in his face. His arms were gangly, and the pants hitched as tightly as possible considering how slim he was. His flesh tone was slightly pinkish, as if he'd been standing out in the sun for a little too long.

He looked Betty in the eyes, on a level gaze with her for the first time in over a year and a half, and echoed words that he'd spoken to her that day of the personality merging. Words that had been tinged with just an air of menace but now seemed amused and welcoming.

"Honey," he announced. "I'm home."

Betty tried to form words but couldn't manage any. She came forward on unsteady legs, reached out for him, and embraced him. He laughed and they staggered into the living room, still in each other's arms. Samson, grinning like an idiot, came in behind them and closed the door.

"My God," she whispered, "my arms go around you. Completely around. See?" She interlaced her fingers in the small of his back. "See there?"

"I see," he said, trying not to laugh. "Betty, careful! Don't squeeze me too hard! I'm kind of fragile these days. Wouldn't want me to break a rib."

"I won't! Don't worry, I'll be careful! I—how? How did this happen?"

"Miracle of modern technology," said Bruce.

"A miracle . . . yes, it's a miracle! And you!" and with mock irritation she slapped Samson on the chest. "You certainly took your sweet time dragging out the news! Great little prank there if I'd had a stroke while waiting for you to tell me whatever news you had!"

"I'm sorry, Betty. Couldn't resist."

She looked back to Bruce. "Is it . . . permanent? Are you going to change back?"

"We're not sure." He looked to Samson for confirmation, and Samson nodded. "We think not. We hope not. We'll have to wait and see but . . . things look good at the moment."

"No," she said, kissing him firmly. "Things look great. So . . . what happens now?"

"Now?" said Samson. "Now, Mr. and Mrs. Banner . . . with any luck at all, you live happily ever after."

PART TWO

DREAMS

Chapter 9

The nursery was perfect.

It had been done up in soft, gentle tones of gray. A mobile hung over the perfect little crib, and the carpet was soft white and gray shag. Tranquil lullaby music floated through the air.

Betty sat in a rocking chair, gently tilting back and forth, cradling the baby, who was tightly wrapped in a soft, gray blanket. She looked down at him lovingly and he gazed back up at her. He smiled. Her son, little Ross, had smiled at her. They always said that when babies smiled at this age, it was simply gas. But she didn't believe it. How did the omniscient, omnipresent "they" know anyway? Probably "they" consisted of soulless, heartless men with no romance in them whatsoever. She was a mother. She had carried the child around in her for nine months. She knew him, and he was a part of her. And that part of her that connected her to her son told her that this was absolutely, positively, no-two-ways a smile of genuine contentment and love.

His cheek was eminently tweakable. She reached down and tweaked it.

He opened his mouth, and the noise that came from it was nothing human.

It was a roar, deafening, so deafening that Betty clapped both hands to her head. In doing so, she lost her grip on the baby. Ross rolled off her lap, the blanket coming loose, and he fell to the floor.

She cried out his name, and it seemed to echo all around her. Ross, for his part, pulled himself to his feet, his little bowed legs supporting him without effort. He staggered over to the crib, got a firm grip on it . . . and started to lift it.

Betty was out of the chair, running toward him, reaching out desperately to try to intercept him. She screamed as loudly as she could. There was no noise from her.

Ross raised the crib over his head and hurled it at his mother. The crib crumbled, knocking her to the floor, wood flying everywhere. Pinned under the debris, Betty stretched out a hand, trying to pull her son back to her.

He was heading for the nursery door, which was closed. It didn't slow him for a moment. He plowed through it, knocking it free of its hinges. But then, as if changing his mind at the last minute, he didn't go out. Instead he turned, looked at his mother with eyes flecked with gray. She cried out to him, begging him to calm down, to come back to her.

He crouched for a moment, as if gathering strength, and then leaped skyward. He crashed through the ceiling. For just a moment Betty saw pale white sunlight, and then the ceiling caved in on her. She shrieked, the agonized cry of someone who had just lost that which she loved most in the world. . . .

"*Betty!*"

Her name was called, as if from God on high, and the voice of God sounded like Bruce. . . .

"*Betty!*" it came again. And this time she woke up in response to it.

From the darkness of a bedroom lit only in pale moonlight,

Bruce looked down at her. His hand was on her shoulder. "Betty, wake up! Honey—?"

"*Oh God, Bruce!*" she wailed, and grabbed for his arm. It was soft and not particularly well muscled, and she loved it all the more. No longer massive and green, but normal—gloriously, wonderfully normal. Despite the fact that once her husband had been a walking tank, she nevertheless felt *more* safe with him in his permanent human form.

He held her close, giving thanks once more for being able to do so without being concerned he might snap her spine. "Bad dream, huh?"

"Ohhhhh, Bruce," she wailed . . . and then was appalled to realize that he was laughing slightly. She pulled back from him. "What's so funny?" she asked, unable to mask her annoyance.

"I'm sorry, Betty . . . I swear . . . it's just, the way you said, 'Ohhhhh, Bruce,' well . . . you sounded just like Mary Tyler Moore."

"Very funny," she said humorlessly and thudded down to the mattress.

"I said I'm sorry," he said, lying down next to her and rubbing her shoulder. "What happened in the dream?"

"Nothing."

"Hulk baby, right?"

Her eyes went wide and she rolled over to look at him. "How did you know?"

"You think I haven't had those dreams?" he asked reasonably.

"I was . . . afraid to ask."

"There's nothing in this world that you have to be afraid to ask me. What, you were concerned I'd be upset? That you might put frightening thoughts in my head? Betty . . . there's nothing you can come up with, no matter how horrifying, that hasn't already occurred to me. Don't forget, I'm a walking worst-case scenario."

Slowly he moved his hand down and across her swollen belly. "But maybe . . . just maybe . . . we've got a little best-case scenario."

Suddenly she gasped, as did Bruce. "Did you feel that?" she whispered.

"He kicked. My God, he kicked. What . . . what does that feel like, from the inside out?"

"Like I've . . . like I've got something in me that I've got no control over."

"Does that frighten you?"

"I guess it should. Except . . . it doesn't. Isn't that funny? With all our history, you'd think that would be something that scares me more than anything else. But I kind of like it. Here," she took his hand, "he moved over here."

She took Bruce's hand and slid it across her belly a few inches. He kept his palm flat against her stomach for a long moment, almost willing the baby to move. And sure enough, the baby did, shoving back against Bruce's hand.

"Incredible," he whispered.

Bruce curled up against her in the old way called "spoons," since it was like spoons fitting snugly against each other in a silverware drawer.

"What time is it?" Betty whispered.

He craned his neck and looked at the glowing LED numbers of the digital clock: *5:37.*

"A little after five-thirty."

"You want to get up? I'm still tired."

"My first class isn't until eleven," Bruce said. "And we were up late. I'm feeling lazy."

"Okay." She paused, and then said softly, "I'm not scared, Bruce. Whatever happens, if we're together . . . we can handle it. I know it. I just know it."

He squeezed her belly slightly and was rewarded with another thud in response. He lay there next to her and remained that way, his breathing becoming gentle and regular, matching hers.

There was another kick against his hand, and another. He felt it more and more strongly.

He tried to awaken Betty. She groaned softly, started to lift her head . . .

A gray fist punched through her stomach.

Dark blood fountained, splattered against the wall, soaked the bed sheets, the mattress. Betty continued to scream as the baby ripped through her stomach. Betty's head lolled back, her sightless eyes aimed at the ceiling. Bruce fell backward off the bed, plummeting into a pool of blood. He couldn't feel the bedroom floor beneath his feet.

The baby straddled the corpse of his mother and raised his arms to the ceiling, howling in triumph. Then he turned his baleful gaze toward Bruce and bellowed, *"You're next, Daddy! I'll get you before you get me—!"*

Bruce awoke, gasping, his hand still on Betty's stomach. Fortunately his being startled awake had not at all jostled Betty, who didn't even stir. She was even snoring slightly, a joyfully mundane sound.

The baby moved beneath his palm.

Very slowly Bruce slid his hand off Betty's stomach and rested his hand at his side.

And he did not fall back to sleep again.

Chapter 10

I t had been a perfect spot for them.

The Bethlehem, Pennsylvania, campus of Templar University had a feel and style all its own. As opposed to the relatively impersonal, big-city atmosphere of the main campus in Philadelphia, the Bethlehem campus was smaller and sylvan, with tall trees instead of tall buildings, and bicyclists who didn't have to wear masks over their faces to screen out carbon monoxide. More relaxed, friendlier.

It was also one of the better-kept secrets. For a number of years, the Bethlehem campus had been a haven for some of the best and brightest in the scientific community. It was hard to place precisely when it had begun, but for the past ten years, the campus had slowly been grooming its own stable of inventive geniuses and innovative, independent thinkers. Major corporations had taken notice. Oh, sure, there had been rough spots, such as the time that several of the more aggressive computer students had discovered a mutual and rather intense dislike for country-western music. So they had broken into computers at Fort Benning and come within seconds of launching several Titan missiles with the intended target being the Grand Ole Opry in Nashville. They thought better of it at T minus fifteen seconds and aborted the mission. The investigation was thorough, yet the perpetrators were never found as the students (and even teachers) closed ranks, and the legend surrounding Templar's Bethlehem campus only grew.

It was a campus where the occasionally odd and curious thing was wont to happen.

However, the acquisition of a new teacher by the physics department—one Dr. Bruce Lee Kirby—barely garnered any attention at all. He'd come highly recommended by Dr. Leonard Samson, who had himself taught at Templar for several years.

Dr. Kirby (jokingly dubbed "Rip" by several students) was somewhat lean, with thick black glasses and red hair carved into an odd buzz cut, accentuating his slightly "dorky" air. But he was quite pleasant, with a full and hearty laugh, a quick sense of humor, infinite patience with his students, and a general air of being pleased just to be there.

The students quickly sensed that he knew his stuff. More than knew it . . . he was a quick thinker, and was capable of going off on fascinating tangents about all sorts of possibilities.

He spent long days at the campus. When he wasn't in his office, he could generally be found in the laboratory. His particular field of specialty seemed to be harnessing different forms of radiation.

His wife, whose name was Elizabeth, was extremely nice. They had a house near campus. He generally walked to the university from home, and oftentimes she accompanied him for the exercise. She was pregnant, nicely rounded at about six months along. They would always greet whatever students they passed, and always by name; no matter how casual the acquaintance, they never forgot a name. It was as if they were taking detailed note of everyone around them. This was naturally interpreted as being extremely friendly. Of course, it could also have been taken to mean that they were rather paranoid, but nobody thought along those lines. What, after all, did they have to be paranoid about?

Dr. Bruce Lee Kirby finished writing on the board and turned to face the class. It was a small class, around twenty students. The room was warmer than Bruce would have liked, and sweat was making his shirt stick to his chest.

He tapped the formulae with his knuckle and said, "So are we all clear on this? These are the very formulae that the scientists for the Manhattan Project used to develop the atomic bomb. I hope none of you has any plutonium on him, because otherwise we could all be in big trouble."

There were nods from throughout the room. Then one kid said, "Doctor, did the scientists on the project really understand what it was they were getting into?"

"In theory, yes," said Bruce. "Of course, there's a huge gulf between theory and actuality. Did they truly grasp the immensity of the power they were unleashing? After the results of the Trinity test in Alamogordo, Dr. Oppenheimer and the rest of the scientists in the Manhattan Project might very well say they did. After all, the Trinity test was a twenty-two-kiloton implosion-type fission bomb. The Hiroshima bomb, by contrast, was thirteen kilotons—gun-type, as opposed to implosion. Nagasaki's was the full twenty-two. But even so . . . I tend to think they didn't. The sheer destructive power of the A-bomb was beyond anything in the history of humanity. How do you quantify, intellectually, a device that could kill one hundred thousand people in a heartbeat, as it did in Hiroshima . . . forty thousand more in Nagasaki?"

"I thought Nagasaki had the bigger bomb," pointed out another student.

"Yes, but the terrain was hillier. That afforded some protection. And that doesn't begin to include the people who were injured or died from radiation later on . . . plus who can even begin to calculate the long-term birth defects, or even something as ephemeral as the destruction of our collective peace of mind? The bomb's out there, and has hung over us as a threat for half a century now.

"And mull this over: The damage that one of those first A-bombs caused was the equivalent of twelve thousand metric tons of dynamite." There was a soft whistle from several class members, and then Bruce added, "And today's thermonuclear weapons are eight to forty times as powerful as the bomb dropped on Hiroshima." The whistling immediately stopped.

"What kind of radiation does the bomb hit you with?" asked one student.

Bruce shifted slightly from one foot to the other, doing his best not to look uncomfortable. "Neutrons and . . . gamma radiation. However, the damage done by the radiation depends heavily on where you are in relation to the bomb. For instance, the gamma radiation at two-thirds of a mile from ground zero is only about a hundredth as strong as radiation at ground zero itself."

"But it can still do damage?" asked another.

"Oh, it's been known to."

One girl leaned forward and looked very serious and very troubled. "So . . . does that mean that Dr. Oppenheimer has potential to be one of the greatest mass murderers in history?"

"Murderer?" Bruce cleared his throat. "That's a rather harsh term to apply to a scientist, Bobbie."

"He invented it. It's not like it's accidental. When you invent a bomb, you figure it's going to be set off. People are going to die. If you build something with the intention of killing people, doesn't that make you a murderer?"

"It was wartime, Bobbie. It's a different situation."

"It's not wartime now," pointed out one guy. "And we get to worry now about small, crazy nations, or terrorists, or whoever, building bombs and blowing a few hundred thousand more people to ashes. Oppenheimer and the others, they should have looked ahead. They should have known what they were setting us up for."

"James, you're trying to second-guess history. The object was to end the war—"

And now another girl, clearly of Japanese ancestry, spoke up. "No. The object was to teach Japan a lesson. To scare them into surrendering, which they did, so there wouldn't be months more of land wars. If there had been more fighting, and more people had died . . . still, sooner or later, the war would have ended, and that would have been that. Instead, we get to carry around the threat of atomic death on our backs, just so in the 1940s they could cut corners and end things quickly. But they didn't end things, did they? It's dragged on for half a century, and now it's all our problem. Isn't that right, Dr. Kirby?"

Bruce let out a long sigh. "Believe me, kids . . . you're going to find out as you get older that the *right* thing isn't always the same as the *correct* thing. At the time, the atomic bomb seemed the way to go. It was the correct thing. Whether it was the right thing, well . . . I'll leave it for you people to decide . . ."

There was resolute shaking of heads.

". . . in a philosophy class," he finished. He glanced up at the clock and saw that the period was over. He dismissed them, then leaned against his lectern and only at that point discovered that he had crumbled the chalk into a fine white powder.

"Kids," he moaned softly.

"*Kids?*" Betty said incredulously.

She was lying flat on an examining table. Her shirt was pulled up to just under her bosom, her pants rolled down to below her stomach, and her belly—covered with clear jelly—was fully exposed. Her obstetrician, Dr. Joy Thomas, was running the flat probe of the sonogram over the general area of her womb.

"Kids?" Betty repeated. "What do you mean, 'The kids are doing well'? You mean it's . . ."

"Twins, I'm quite sure," said Thomas. "I thought I detected two heartbeats last month, but I didn't say anything at the time. Now I'm pretty positive. Look," and she angled the monitor around so that Betty could see it more clearly.

Betty didn't know what the hell she was looking at. To her it appeared as large blobs of shadow and nothing else.

Seeing Betty's confusion, Thomas took a pencil and indicated, "You see there's a leg . . . there's another . . . and a third, which means either it's twins or a three-legged baby. There's the spine . . . this is one of the heads, or maybe both . . . they're very close together, it's hard to tell."

"Two hearts?"

"Two strong hearts, beating away. Definitely twins. Congratulations."

"My God," murmured Betty, "Bruce isn't going to believe it."

"I hope he can handle it." Dr. Thomas smiled. "Oftentimes it's a tough thing for the husband to handle. Giving him news like this . . . it's kind of like dropping a bomb on him."

"Yes, well," said Betty sanguinely, "it won't be the first time that's happened to him."

When Bruce emerged from the classroom, there was a familiar figure waiting for him, leaning on his omnipresent cane.

"Amos!" said Bruce, pumping Trotter's hand enthusiastically.

Trotter was eyeing his hair. "This you think improves your looks?" he asked, skimming the top of the buzz cut with his palm.

Bruce laughed softly. "It's to keep Betty happy. She's a big believer in changing appearances when we go from place to place. That's what happens when you grow up watching *The Fugitive*. Hopefully, though, we'll be staying here awhile."

"This I can't blame you for. It's lovely. Can we talk for a bit?"

"By all means."

They walked out onto the campus at a leisurely stroll. "I'd like to get a firsthand report on how it's going, Bruce," said Trotter, stroking his beard.

"So far, so good."

"Any stirrings? Close shaves? Problems I should know about?"

"None."

"Any moments of great stress?"

Bruce thought about it a moment. "Well, there was that night it was raining, and we were coming back from a movie. Blew a tire. I stood there in the rain, jack in my hand, trying to pry loose the hubcap. Finally did that. Then I couldn't loosen the lugs . . . then one snapped off . . . then the car fell off the jack and the rain came down twice as hard. You wouldn't have recognized me. I was cursing, shouting . . ."

"And? What happened?"

"Triple A towed the car."

"I mean with you? Nothing turned green or swollen?"

"Nothing," Bruce said with a smile.

"So? This is good news."

"It is. It truly is." Bruce sat on a bench and Trotter sat next to him.

"And your wife? She's doing nicely, yes?"

"She's doing great. Baby's coming along. There's the normal worries. . . ."

"Such as?"

Bruce adjusted his glasses. "Oh, such as that the baby will be a monster. Or smash its way out of the womb. Blood everywhere.

Beast incarnate. That sort of thing. Nothing I'm sure you haven't heard before."

Trotter stared at him for a long moment. "And this you're calling normal worries?"

"Normal for us." He sighed heavily and turned to look at Trotter. "I'm more worried about me than the baby, frankly. And not just because I've got a half-ton alter ego in my past."

"What, then?"

"My . . ." He fidgeted a few moments more. Trotter waited patiently. "My father was extremely . . . abusive. Abusive in ways I've never even discussed with Leonard . . . that I'd rather not discuss with you, if that's okay." Trotter nodded slightly in acknowledgement, and Bruce continued, "The point is, abuse is passed down. Things that are done to us, we turn around and do to our children. One of the reasons I think my mind . . . splintered . . . in the first place was that I was afraid of being too emotional. I'd seen what unrestrained fury could do to a marriage, and to a man . . . and to the children. But now, through the efforts of Leonard and yourself, I'm a whole person. I'm the person I was, in many ways, afraid to become. And now I have a child on the way. Amos . . . what if . . ."

"What if you become like your father?" Trotter said, his voice muted. "Bruce, believe it or not . . . I understand exactly what you're going through. My father, likewise, was not the . . . kindest man in the world."

"I can't believe he was on par with mine," said Bruce.

"The point is, Bruce, it's not automatic. This 'pass-along' thing, yes, there's truth in that. But it's not like male-pattern baldness or eye-color—things we have no control over. The mind, Bruce," and he tapped Bruce squarely on the forehead, "the mind gives us the ability to triumph over conditioning, rather than being slaves to it. This you understand, right?"

"Right. But I still can't help being afraid."

"Fear is good," said Trotter amiably. "Fear of consequences keeps many people honest. Fear of being ostracized keeps many people sociable. Fear of dying keeps most people alive. We have a society built on fear. This may not be a pleasant thing to acknowledge, but, well . . . there it is."

"There it is," agreed Bruce, although he wasn't one hundred percent sure just what it was he was agreeing to.

"So where are you off to?"

"To the lab. I've got a little project I'm working on. Are you interested in seeing it?"

"Bruce, my boy, I consider you one of the greatest, grandest experiments I've ever embarked on. Believe me, anything that you're involved with, I'm interested in seeing."

They headed off toward the lab.

Bruce looked up from the applesauce chicken (Betty's specialty) and said across the dinner table, "You'll never guess who I saw today."

"Lou Ferrigno?" Betty replied after a moment's thought.

"No."

"Chris Farley?"

"Look, do you want to hear or not?"

"Okay, okay," she said. "Who?"

"Dr. Trotter. The man who—"

"I know who he is. Why didn't you bring him home for dinner? I would've loved to meet him."

"I suggested it, but he had other plans. At some point, I'm sure, we'll get together."

Betty picked up her dish and headed into the kitchen as Bruce continued, "We ran kind of late. I was showing him things in the research lab, and before we knew it—"

"What kind of things? You working on a new project?"

"Just started, yes. Kind of new. Also kind of old."

"Meaning what? What are you working on?"

"A gamma bomb. So . . . any apple cobbler left for dessert?"

He heard dishes crash. He raised his eyebrows questioningly. "Betty? You okay? What happened?"

Betty walked slowly back into the living room, looking ashen. Her hands, from which the dishes had slipped, hung loosely at her side. "You're not serious."

"Of course I'm serious. I love your apple cobbler."

"*Not the damned cobbler!*" She couldn't believe it. "Bruce, are you nuts?! A *gamma bomb?*" She rapped on the top of his head. "Hello? Anyone home in there?"

"Ow! Stop it!" He flinched. "I'm not invulnerable anymore, you know."

"Good. That way we've got a shot at something getting through! You're not seriously thinking of re-creating the gamma bomb! That's what started all this!"

"Betty, calm down. . . ."

"*Calm down!* Bruce, you think I don't see this coming?"

"See what coming?"

She circled the living room, gesturing wildly, almost knocking knicknacks off the shelves. "There you'll be, in the lab, late one night. Something'll go out of control, or there'll be sabotage, or something else because there's *always* something else. I'll be looking out the window, wondering, 'Gee, when's Bruce coming home?' And then all of a sudden, blam, there'll be a mushroom cloud in the sky, and a burst of green light, and next thing you know, hang on, kiddies, he's back again! It's irresponsible!" She grabbed a pen and pad of paper and started to scribble something as she said, "No, it's worse than irresponsible! It's predictable!"

He sighed deeply. "Betty, you're being ridiculous. Nothing like that is going to happen."

She'd stopped writing before Bruce began speaking. When he finished, she ripped off the paper from the pad and tossed it at Bruce. He stared at what she'd written: *Nothing like that is going to happen.* He looked up at her and she'd just finished writing something else. "Betty . . . it will be different this time."

She tore off the sheet and flipped it to him. He read, *It'll be different this time.*

"Like I said. Predictable," said Betty, dropping the pad and pencil onto the desk.

He held up the pieces of paper and looked at her dourly. "Very funny, Betty."

"Look very closely, Bruce. You'll see I'm not laughing."

"Listen, will you just sit down for a moment? You're getting yourself all worked up. It's not good for you, and it's certainly not good for the baby." Gently but forcefully he guided her over to a chair, and she allowed him to seat her. "Now just . . . just listen, okay?"

"If you keep telling me to listen, I'm going to stop listening."

"All right. Just li—uhm. Just look. I've just been very . . . troubled lately."

"Oh, well, that makes sense," she said sarcastically. "When I'm feeling troubled, I get my hair done. When you're feeling troubled, you create a nuclear explosive device. This is a testosterone thing, isn't it?"

"Are you going to let me get through this or not?"

"I'm not sure. I haven't made up my mind yet."

"I've just . . . been thinking a lot lately. Thinking about dead children."

She stared at him, confused. "Well, that's certainly the kind of thing you want to say to a six-months-pregnant woman."

"And that I would bear some responsibility for them."

She started to speak again, but then stopped, and then started again. "Uhm, Bruce, I'm okay, I'll let you get through this . . . if nothing else just to find out where you're going with this."

"I appreciate that," he said, not sounding the least bit sarcastic. "Betty, I created bombs. The gamma bomb. A weapon of devastating power. Then, while I went on with my life, the government turned around and manufactured them, stockpiled them. Media attention was drawn to it, and the government wound up disassembling them. But that doesn't change the fact that I helped contribute to the nuclear paranoia that currently grips our society."

"Okay, but . . ." Betty interrupted, "it's like you said. The bombs have been dismantled. They can't hurt anyone anymore. So what's the problem?"

"The problem is that I put so much time and energy into a weapon that could cause massive destruction. And what's happened since then? Weapons designed to 'stop war' becoming more powerful, more devastating. And what did they develop as well? Enhanced radiation weapons—"

"What kind?"

"Neutron bombs. Isn't that just marvelous?" he said in annoyance. "Bombs that kill people, but leave property intact. That's completely botched priorities. And I want to do something about it. Put the priorities back in place."

She wanted to say something bright, such as "How?" but she kept her mouth shut, figuring that Bruce would explain.

"What I want to do is develop a weapon that does what a weapon should do. Stop the enemy without killing the enemy. The opposite of a neutron bomb."

Understanding dawned in her face—understanding and perhaps even a small bit of support. Buoyed by her hint of a positive reaction, Bruce continued with greater enthusiasm. "Would you mind if I put it in layman's terms?"

"I would be thrilled if you did."

"All right. What the new gamma bomb would do is break down materials of significant density, while not harming—for instance—humans. The gamma bomb, if it works out properly, would be capable of destroying a tank while leaving the tank operators completely unscathed . . . or, at most, second-degree burns. Guns would likewise be rendered inoperable. The result would be bare-handed soldiers, which could still lead to fighting if you've got soldiers who are that single-minded. Still, war would be pretty much unfightable. None of the standard tools of the trade, as it were, would be available."

"And this is what you've started working on in the lab?"

He nodded eagerly. "What do you think?"

"I think, if you can pull it off," she said slowly, "you might have some potential here."

"That's very gracious of you."

"Bruce," she stroked his hand gently, "I'm not some sort of ogress, you know. I'm capable of listening. I can even wind up agreeing with you sometimes . . . although I'm not going to pretend that your working with a gamma *anything* doesn't make me very nervous."

"I'm being very, very careful. And when the bomb's in final form, even if it went off—which it won't, but even if it did—the whole purpose of the design is *not* to affect people. That includes people already exposed to gamma radiation."

"I hope so. Because I can see that, no matter what I say, you're going to do this thing anyway. Just don't screw up."

"I won't," and he patted her on the shoulder. "So . . . how about I get dessert? You stay put, take it easy. Relax."

"Easy for you to say." She propped up her feet as Bruce strode into the kitchen. She heard him taking dishes down from within.

"And how was your day, dear?" he said heartily. "Had your doctor's appointment today?"

"Yup, yup. Saw her. She, uhm . . ." Well, there was no reason to hold it off any longer. ". . . she said we're having twins."

She heard dishes crash. *Good*, was all she could think. *What goes around . . .*

". . . come around, Doctor. You're going to have to come around sooner or later."

In Major Talbot's office, Leonard Samson sat in a chair and regarded Talbot with undisguised boredom. "I've heard this song before, Major."

Talbot leaned against his desk and said, "No, you've heard the tune, Dr. Samson. Let's try completely new lyrics. How does 'treason' sound to you?"

Samson tried to stifle an urge to laugh, and was not completely successful. "It sounds to me like you're reaching. Even desperate. May I ask, just out of curiosity, just what I've been doing that is contrary to the interests or national security of the United States?"

"Simple." Talbot looked entirely too smug. "The Hulk is a cause for national concern. If you have information that is indicative of his whereabouts and you're holding it back, then you are operating against the best interests of your country."

"Despite doctor-patient relationship."

"That's correct."

"Despite the fact that, aside from that time in Chicago when he claimed he was set up, we've seen nothing of the Hulk for nearly a year."

"That's correct as well."

Doc made a soft popping noise with his mouth. "You know what I think, Major?"

"No, Doctor. I'm all ears. Precisely what do you think?"

"I think budget time has reared its ugly head, and that you suddenly have to justify the Hulkbusters on some sort of Congressional level. I think they're ready to trim back, even eliminate the money that's been lavished on this project which is designed specifically for the continued harassment of one individual. I think," and he leaned forward and smiled pleasantly, "that you are running scared."

Talbot pulled himself up stiffly. "You are entitled to your opinion, Doctor . . ."

"Am I? Thanks ever so. Nice to know there's still a few freedoms left around here."

". . . but I'm warning you that withholding information might be antithetical to your continued freedom. Do I make myself clear?"

"Loud and clear, Major," said Samson. "I'd like to thank you for insisting I come out here and waste my time. Tell you what, though. I'll send you a bill. And despite the fact that it's for the military, I won't even inflate the price beyond any sort of reasonable level. In any event, I strongly advise that you pay it. I'd hate to have to come back . . . and I regret to tell you that I don't take giant armored robots in trade." He walked out whistling, entirely too happy, and closed the door behind him.

Talbot threw a pencil that ricocheted off the door. Then the phone rang. Immediately he picked it up and snapped, "Talbot! Whattaya want!"

Then he was dead silent for a moment before snapping to attention. "Yes, General," he said. "I'm sorry. No, sir, that's not how I usually answer the phone." Pause. "Yes, sir, I know the Hulkbusters project has generated a lot of negative . . ." Pause. "Yes, sir, I know he hasn't been seen, and out of sight is out of mind. But may I point out that . . ." Pause. By this point he was grinding another pencil under his palm. "Yes, I know you've been in there fighting for the appropriations, sir. I know there's other considerations. But I still feel . . ."

Long pause. A very long pause, in which Talbot's face got darker, more threatening, as if a cloud had passed over him.

"Yes, sir. Thank you, sir," said Talbot. "I know you did your best, sir." Slowly he replaced the phone on the cradle.

And then he ripped it out of the wall.

Chapter 11

Betty had never been much for "get-togethers."

It was certainly not her first time at such a gathering. After all, as the daughter of General "Thunderbolt" Ross, she'd been pressed into service as hostess any number of times when her father was entertaining hotshots, officers, and important dignitaries. But it wasn't something she looked forward to.

But this wasn't just any get-together. This was her baby shower.

The baby wasn't due for another two months, but Marcia Worell, wife of Dean Worell, was going to be leaving for a six-week European tour and Marcia just simply *had* to be there for the shower because she never, just never, missed a baby shower for any wife of a faculty member. And since the sun at Templar's Bethlehem campus had a disturbing tendency to rise and fall on Marcia Worell, it was decided to just go ahead and have the bash early.

The women were gathered in Betty's living room. Betty felt uncomfortable with the display of gift-giving and attention. Truthfully, the main thing that concerned her was suddenly finding herself thrust into a spotlight. Spotlights are hot and uncomfortable places to be, particularly when one wants to remain discreet. But she had figured that if she simply went along with it, then it would be over and done with, and she could get back to her nice, normal, low-profile life. If, however, she had made a fuss over it, or tried to resist, that would have been regarded as curious—even bizarre— behavior. She would have been Elizabeth Kirby, that odd woman who didn't want to have a baby shower. A trivial thing to be remembered for, of course, but since Betty's goal was not to be remembered for anything, it seemed advisable to avoid it if at all possible.

Surrounded by boxes, Betty opened up the third layette in a row and tried to be as thrilled as she possibly could be. All the women clucked and cooed, oohed, and aahed. Betty surveyed them and thought, *Lord, just give me a machine gun and a sympathetic jury. That's all I ask . . .*

"Here!" said Marcia. She was holding up a wire coat hanger, festooned with ribbons. "Here you are, Liz!"

Betty took it and stared at it. "Uh . . . thank you . . . uh . . . may I ask what the purpose of this is . . . ?"

"The *purpose*?" Marcia laughed and the women followed suit. "Those are the ribbons from the presents you've opened so far. You're supposed to tie them on to a hanger. I thought you might want to put on the rest."

She looked at the cheery faces of the women. "This is, like . . . a tradition or something?"

There was a chorus of, "Yes! Of course!"

Clearing her throat, she said, "But, I mean . . . giving a coat hanger to a pregnant woman? Isn't that . . . I dunno . . . a little strange? I mean, when you think of coat hangers and pregnancy, you think of . . . well . . . you know . . ."

The women looked at each other, and then Marcia laughed. Quickly the others did, too. Marcia affectionately slapped Betty's knee. "Liz, you are such a kidder!"

"Aren't I, though?" asked Betty, who absolutely detested being called Liz. Bruce had made the (apparently) fatal mistake of introducing Betty with the more formal "Elizabeth." Marcia, in that immediate and aggravatingly friendly way some people have, promptly started addressing Betty with the "familiar" form of "Liz." Betty had corrected her a couple of times, to no avail. So she had given up and instead simply tried to keep her distance from Marcia, with varying degrees of success. And she figured that she should count her blessings. At least she wasn't being called "Lizzy."

Betty rose from the couch and said, "Who's for coffee?"

There were several raised hands. Marcia started to get to her feet and say, "Don't trouble yourself, Liz. I'll make the coffee—"

"No!" said Betty, already up and heading for the kitchen. She certainly didn't need Marcia poking around or getting into things. Not that there was anything particularly incriminating in the kitchen; it wasn't as if there was a gamma bomb ticking down in the cupboard. Nevertheless, Betty had developed a serious aversion to anyone sticking their noses into things unasked.

She entered the kitchen and started making the coffee. From the living room, laughing voices floated in to her.

It grated on her, and she had no idea why.

No, that wasn't true. She did have an idea why. It was because this was what normal life was all about. Baby showers, and a nice house, and having other wives over. Friends, or at least acquaintances, making a fuss over you. Whipping up coffee. All these were elements of everyday, routine life. Everything she'd wanted. And she wasn't at all sure how to react to it.

She figured that perhaps it was like women who lost a great deal of weight because they wanted to feel good about their appearance. But they still felt unattractive and insecure, because they were unable to think of themselves as slim. They still felt fat.

Perhaps that was what Betty was going through. She'd spent so much of her life being trapped in bizarre and outrageous circumstances, that she'd completely lost the ability to feel normal. On the outside, for all appearances, she was a normal, everyday, pregnant wife of a teacher. On the inside, she was still the beleaguered soul mate of the rampaging Hulk; someone who had undergone a transformation or two herself. Normal on the outside, and a paranoid part-time freak on the inside.

"Better get used to it, *Liz*," she murmured to herself. "Maybe, finally, it's a nice normal life for you, just like you always wanted."

Suddenly she felt an odd sort of warmth, and wetness.

She looked down.

Something dark and liquid was trickling down the inside of her leg, spotting on the floor in a small pool.

Then the pain came . . . .

God, no . . . too early . . . and blood . . . there shouldn't be bl . . . she thought, and then she collapsed.

Templar University Hospital was a teaching hospital, and also considered to be one of the finest in the state.

For Bruce, it was one of those situations where all the pedigree in the world, all the reasons *not* to be concerned, were completely irrelevant. He was concerned, he was frightened, and he had a splitting headache.

He stood in the corridor at the hospital, pacing, feeling like a father in some old-time situation comedy. He'd rushed straight over from the school the second he'd been informed. He'd been in the lab, putting the finishing touches on the gamma-particle projector. It was a small, gun-shaped device that was the only piece of actual hardware he intended to produce. The rest of the bomb was going to be charts, diagrams, detailed theories. All of which, when the time was right, he was going to make sure to keep his name divorced from. He felt strongly about the rightness of the project, but he felt equally strongly about keeping even the fabricated moniker of Bruce Lee Kirby out of any sort of limelight.

All of that, however, was secondary to his primary concern at the moment for Betty.

Dr. Joy Thomas emerged through large swinging doors and Bruce immediately went over to her. He didn't even have to pose a question.

"The babies are definitely coming early, Bruce," she said without preamble.

"Is she going to be all right?"

"We're doing everything we can—"

"*Is she going to be all right?*"

She took him by the shoulders, knowing that right now he didn't need to hear some careful, neutral, make-no-commitment answer. Particularly in times of emergency, people didn't want their medical practitioners to be cautious. They wanted them to be God.

"I'm not going to let her die, Bruce," said Thomas firmly.

"And the babies . . . ?"

"If I can save them, I will. You just have to trust me."

"I want to be with her."

"We're bringing her into the OR very shortly, soon as she's stabilized. You can't do anything to help her. Just stay here and pray, all right?"

He looked unsteady, pale. Well, there was certainly reason enough for that. She aimed him toward a couch, sat him down in it, and then hurried off to be with her patient.

She had not meant the instruction about praying literally. Nevertheless, Bruce sat there for a moment. Then he intertwined his fingers and spoke very, very softly.

"Dear God," he whispered. "I'm a scientist. A rational man. Always looking for the scientific answer. But when my life fell apart, I found that I was more inclined—rather than less—to want to believe in you. I suppose because the only comfort I could take in everything I was put through was that it was for some sort of . . . of purpose. Because if it was all just random, cruel tricks of fate—if my life was really that pointless—I doubt I would have lived through it. I would have—I don't know—blown my brains out or something. And in recent years, I was certain that my marriage to Betty *was* the reason I'd been put through it all. That I'd been tested, and somehow I'd lived up to it or passed it or whatever it was I was supposed to do . . . and I'd been given Betty as a reward. I know that's a selfish and egocentric point of view to have, but . . . well, that's how it seemed to me. And I just . . ." He choked a moment, and continued, "Please. Don't . . . don't take her away from me. Not after all this. Not after everything we've been through. It's not fair. I know, I know . . . life isn't fair. But please . . . make it something better than what it is. For me, at least. And for her. And them . . . whoever and whichever they turn out to be. Give us some happiness . . . please . . ."

Betty lifted her head groggily from the pillow. "Bruce . . ." she said uncertainly.

"It's me, Betty," said Dr. Thomas, taking Betty's hand. She checked the fetal monitor. She didn't like what she was seeing.

"Bruce . . . where's Bruce . . . ?"

"He's outside."

"Are the babies out yet?" Bruce and Betty had intended to try to do the birth without aid of anesthesia, feeling that it would be best for the children. But that plan had flown out the window.

"Not yet. Soon, Betty, very soon. We're going to do a C-section to get the babies out. Do you understand?"

"Yes . . . C-section, yes . . ." And suddenly, with surprising strength, she gripped the doctor's wrist firmly. Her voice dropped to a hoarse whisper. "The babies . . . save them. . . ."

"We will," promised Thomas, unsure of whether she was lying or not.

"If it's me or them . . . save them. . . ."

"It won't come to that," Thomas assured her. She eased Betty's head back onto the pillow, and a low sigh emerged from Betty's lips.

Moments later, they were wheeling her into the OR.

It was not too long after that that it all went straight to hell.

Time passed.

And more time.

Bruce began to sense that there was a problem, but no one would tell him anything. He kept going to the nurses. They kept shrugging or saying that the doctor would be with him shortly.

In the meantime, the hallways seemed to have become filled with more intense activity. Doctors ran past, barely affording him a glance. He heard people being paged, one after the other, and they were all being summoned to the same area. Considering that, as luck would have it, there were no other women in labor, Bruce was fairly certain that it all related to Betty.

And he couldn't get an answer.

The heavyset nurse, although she was trying to look sympathetic, also let her impatience show. "Dr. Kirby, someone will be along shortly, I assure you."

"You've been saying that for," he glanced at his watch, "nearly three hours now. I'm entitled to some sort of update!"

"Dr. Kirby, you're shouting."

"I'm not shouting!" he shouted, and then reined himself in, trying to compose himself.

The nurse's lips were thin and pressed together. "I don't have to put up with that sort of attitude, Doctor."

"I'm sorry. It's just that I'm concerned about—"

"We're concerned as well, Doctor. Everyone is concerned. This is a very concerned hospital. Now, you're just going to have to take your seat and let us do our jobs. All right?" The last sentence was nominally a question, but it came across far more as an order.

He felt his hand trembling, his head pounding. He went into the men's room to splash cold water on his face and help calm down. He stared into the mirror, gazed at the soft, "human" face that looked back at him.

If it were the old days, he'd be able to walk right in. No one could stop him. He'd be able to stride up to the doctor and command attention. No nurse would dare give him lip. He would simply glare down at her from the insulation of his seven feet of height, his half-ton of muscle. *Let's see them bark orders then. Let's see any of them show how tough they are if—*

His fist was already slamming against the mirror before he even realized that it was in motion. The wall mirror shattered. It didn't fall apart, but instead radiated outward in a webbed pattern from where he'd struck it. His reflection was shattered into what seemed a million fragments.

His hand was cut, although not badly, and convulsed into a fist. He stared at it as if it weren't even connected to him.

Blood was trickling from the cut in the side of his hand. The blood was dark green.

He blinked, grabbed a paper towel, and wrapped it around the injured hand. He looked at the blood that was absorbed by the towel, and was astonished to see that it was the normal, dark red one associates with such things. Slowly he peeled away the paper towel and saw a similar color on the side of his hand. No hint of green at all.

Not wanting to think about it any further, he started the water running and held his hand under the cold stream. It soothed the dull throb, and he watched with a grim satisfaction as the unmistakably red blood swirled away down the drain. He cleaned it off and applied pressure until he was convinced that the bleeding had completely stopped. Then he shook the hand, trying to ease the tingling he felt, and walked back out into the waiting room.

A tall, familiar figure was waiting for him.

"Hello, Bruce."

"Leonard! Thank you, thank you for coming." He went to shake Samson's hand and immediately winced under Samson's firm grip. Samson noticed the twinge of pain on Bruce's face. "You okay, Bruce?"

"Yes."

"I mean . . . *really* okay?" Samson stressed the word sufficiently that the subtext was clear.

"Yes," Bruce repeated, with equal significance.

"Okay, then." He rubbed his eyes, looking very tired all of a sudden. "So . . . I appreciate your calling me."

"I . . . this will sound weak of me, Leonard. I didn't feel as if I could handle the waiting alone. Isn't that ridiculous?"

"No. No, it's not ridiculous at all. I'm glad that I was able to be of help."

"If you really want to be of help, you'll find out what's going on. No one's telling me anything."

"I'll see what I can do."

He headed toward the nurses' station, Bruce trailing behind him. "Now watch out for her," Bruce cautioned as they approached. "You'll get zero cooperation out of—"

"Hello, Daphne," Samson greeted her.

The heavyset nurse looked up at him, and her face promptly transformed into radiant pleasure. "Leonard! It's great to see you!"

Bruce glanced in confusion from one to the other. "You know each other?"

"No, Bruce, we're just both incredibly lucky guessers with names." He smiled briefly to indicate that it was nothing more than a gentle gibe, and then turned back to the nurse. "Daph, we got one frantic husband here."

"I'll say." She glanced at Banner. "Frantic enough to be two frantic husbands."

"Truer words were never spoken," muttered Bruce.

"Can we get a sit-down? An update? Something?"

That's when they heard the scream, followed by a second. And the second was Betty's.

Betty lay on the operating table, her view of the rest of her body blocked off by a partition. There was a great deal of bustle in the OR, terms being tossed around she didn't understand. She heard steady beepings from monitoring machines, several sets of heart-beats. Hers, which was slower, and two more that were moving far more rapidly.

She hummed softly to herself, not quite knowing why. She wondered if they knew she was awake, or could hear her hum-ming. They certainly didn't act like it. Dr. Thomas was there, but she didn't seem to be doing the bulk of the work. Instead she was acting more like an assistant to another doctor, an older man with dark, baggy eyes.

Music was playing softly through speakers. Something classical. Mozart, she thought.

There were many other people there, swarming around. Betty tried to figure out what purpose each of them served. An anesthe-siologist, and another assistant . . . and a nurse, she looked so young, with dark blue eyes, trying to do her job as efficiently as she could. But it was obvious even to Betty that the nurse was new at her job.

Then Betty felt movement, or imagined she did, from the area of her stomach. Fingers were reaching in, pulling, pushing, sepa-rating folds of skin, and she heard a sound like a sort of moist suck-ing . . .

And the nurse lost it.

She wasn't doing anything except holding a tray of instruments, but they slipped from her numb fingers. Her eyes widened in horror, and then she screamed. A scream of undiluted terror that drowned out Mozart, drowned out the sounds of metal rolling on the floor.

Betty didn't know what had happened, didn't know what the nurse was reacting to. She was so detached from what was going on around her that at first she drew no connection to herself as the cause of the nurse's unprofessional panic.

And then, somehow, it suddenly penetrated. The realization flashed into her mind, a sunburst of understanding. She was the source. . . . No. Not her. The babies. Something had gone wrong, hideously wrong, a nightmare given life and form. From the pureness of her womb had sprung forth something unimaginably awful. . . .

The first true awareness that the surgeons had that Betty was conscious was when her own screams joined those of the nurse.

"Betty!" howled Bruce, and before Samson could make any sort of move, Bruce burst through the swinging doors in the direction from which the screams had come. An instant later, Samson was right after him.

Bruce barreled down the hallway, dodging gurneys and people in wheelchairs. From behind Bruce floated the nurse's shouts of "*Stop him!*"

Two orderlies responded. One tackled Bruce around the knees, the other around the chest. Between the two of them they could easily have broken him in half. In fact, one of them could likely have done the job.

Bruce writhed on the floor, trying to shove them off himself. He cursed at them, felt a pounding in the base of his skull, tried to push them away . . . and then suddenly they were off him.

Doc Samson had come in behind them and had lifted them off as if they weighed nothing. They struggled at first, and then they saw who and what was holding them and they stopped and stared.

In the meantime, Bruce clambered to his feet and kept going. The entire altercation had consumed barely seconds, and Betty's scream was still ringing in his ears.

"Bruce, wait!" Samson called, tossing the orderlies aside as if he'd forgotten about them entirely.

It was too late.

Bruce located the OR and burst in.

Usually the unexpected and unannounced arrival of a frantic husband—equipped with not so much as a protective mask—would garner the immediate attention of everyone in the OR. Not this time. The place was such a hive of consternation that it took long seconds for anyone even to realize that an intruder had shown up.

Bruce heard crying—the crying of twin voices—and sobbing, and hysteria, and off in a corner a nurse was propped against the wall, mask down and giving dry heaves. One doctor was sharply rapping out orders.

"*Betty!*" Bruce shouted, which finally prompted everyone to notice him.

There was dead silence, his arrival just the latest surprising moment in an afternoon that had caused reactions in operating room personnel ranging from shock to outright hysteria.

He heard Betty's choked sob, barely above a whisper. "Get out . . . you did this to me, you bastard, get out."

And there was the crying.

His gaze shifted to the incubators. Two were in position.

One was empty.

But he heard two voices. He looked to the other incubator in confusion. It was at that point that the doctor tried to regain command of the situation and ordered Bruce to leave.

Bruce didn't hear him. Blood was pounding to his ears, drowning out the doctor, Betty, the cries of the children . . . all of it.

He saw their faces, their twin mouths twisted in identical high-pitched wails. But he couldn't see either face completely clearly, because they were too close in to each other. Both of them in the one incubator, for good reason.

They were indeed twins—twin boys—but there would be no confusing one with the other.

For one was pale, milky white . . . and the other was a ghastly charcoal gray.

And they were joined at the head. Siamese twins, the left temple of the gray one's skull connected to the right temple of the pale one.

Bruce's head swam and a voice said, *Oh God, wake up now, please, it's time to wake up. . . .*

And he heard a laughter from somewhere deep within his head. A deep, foreboding laugh, and at first he thought it was the ghost of his father creeping around in his mind, rejoicing in the misery that his son was about to face.

But then he decided that it was more insidious than that.

He decided that the mocking voice was, in fact, the voice of God. Laughing at His handiwork. Chortling at the answer given to Bruce's prayer.

Here, before Bruce's horrified eyes, was living proof that God was completely insane.

It was the last thought that went through Bruce's fractured mind before he passed out. He never even felt the strong arms of Leonard Samson catching him.

His mind was lost to the laughter of a deity gone mad.

Chapter 12

Word spread quickly, and the hospital in Bethlehem, Pennsylvania, was under siege in no time.

General facts (but not details, such as the names of those involved) had gotten out almost immediately. Hospital officials, when contacted, confirmed the fact of the grotesque birth, although not specifics.

This was more than enough to set the crush of media attention into movement. The legitimate press and the tabloids were neck and neck for the story. Bare hours after the birth, the hospital was mobbed with camera crews, print reporters, wire-service newspeople. They were all over the place, running the hapless hospital security, which was woefully unprepared for a situation of this magnitude, ragged. Reporters in every corridor, in stairways, elevators, at nurses' stations, under nurses' stations, in supply closets. Seeking firsthand accounts, pictures, information and more information. Why? Because if there was any sort of personal hideous tragedy inflicted on a member of society, it was a guarantee that totally unconnected strangers everywhere had a right to stick their noses into it and become a part of it.

Everyone in the world had their own tragedies and traumas. And all this played into one of the great truisms that helped make the United States the country that it is today, the truism being that misery loves company.

Hospital authorities took several immediate steps, partly at the urging of Doc Samson. First, they contacted a private security service and hired forty more guards to try to keep a lid on the press. It was about half the number they really needed, but as much as the budget would allow.

Second, complete and utter confidentiality of the identities of both parents and children was instituted. Strict orders were issued to every staff member, from the chief of surgery to the guy who'd been scrubbing toilets for three weeks. The parents were Mr. and Mrs. Doe, the children Baby Doe White and Baby Doe Gray. The records were taken by the top hospital staff and secured. It was made clear that if the names were leaked, then the source of the leak would be located and terminated. And if the leak proved impossible to pinpoint, then entire departments would be given the heave-ho.

It was quickly apparent that the threat was not a bluff, and even tabloid reporters offering sizable bounties for pictures of the "freak babies" didn't have any luck.

The entire maternity ward was blocked off. Emergency measures were put into effect as other obstetricians associated with the hospital contacted all their patients who were due anytime within the next several weeks. Temporary affiliations were granted at other hospitals so that doctors who usually worked with Templar University would be allowed to operate out of alternate facilities. Current patients in the obstetrics ward were checked out a day early or, in one extreme case, simply moved to another hospital.

It was certainly a good deal of disruption and confusion. But it was decided that all of it was preferable to subjecting the newcomer to the bunker that the obstetrics ward of Templar University Hospital had become.

Into the bunker now strode a new arrival.

He was tall and slender, and moved with such casual grace that one would have thought he was a dancer rather than a doctor of medicine. Indeed, he seemed to walk as if his contact with the surface of the earth was tenuous at best.

His hair was black and cut very short, and a band of silver hair hugged either side of his head and converged to a point on the back of his skull. His face was triangular, and sported a mustache that reached to the lower part of his jaw. His eyes were dark and seemed to look beyond whatever was in his direct sightline. Anyone whom he walked past invariably did a double take and was seized with the oddest feeling of *déjà vu*.

He had glided into the hospital's main reception area and spoke in a carefully modulated, deep timbre of a voice with utter authority. "Obstetrics, please," he had said. There was no trace of a question in his tone.

"There's a situation up there, sir," said the rather harried receptionist. "Unless you're on official business . . ."

"All my business is official," he said.

Something in his voice prompted her to look up at him. He didn't smile, although she had the impression that he did.

A man suddenly staggered up. "Excuse me," he muttered, shoving past the tall man. He leaned forward and grunted at the receptionist, "My name is Sanders . . . and I . . . I need to see some-one immediately. . . . I'm in tremendous pain . . . I don't know what's wrong with me."

The tall man rested a hand on the would-be patient's shoulder and said firmly, "I know what is wrong with you."

Sanders looked up at him slowly. "You do?"

"Yes. You are a reporter. Your name is not Sanders. It is McGee. You are on deadline, and are attempting to do whatever you can to get near the subjects of your intended story."

McGee straightened up. "What are you, some kind of mind reader?"

"When necessary. However," and he held up something that McGee immediately recognized as his wallet.

He snatched it from the tall man's hand in irritation. "You know, pickpocketing is illegal."

"Indeed. You can inform the police, if you wish. However," and his gaze riveted on McGee's, "your problem is that you genuinely *are* in pain."

McGee blinked. "I am?" He rubbed his stomach in confusion.

"Yes. You see, you have several large kidney stones. And you are going to be preoccupied for the next few hours endeavoring to pass them."

The reporter grunted. "Oh God . . . you're right. I feel them."

"Yes, well . . . I *am* a doctor."

McGee staggered away, groaning. The tall man turned back and looked at the receptionist.

"You *must* be a doctor," affirmed the receptionist. "The way you were able to tell what was wrong with him . . . ?"

"Years of discipline. Now, the way up to obstetrics?"

She pointed. "Follow the green line along the floor to the second bank of elevators. Third floor up. Here," and she handed him a pass. "You couldn't get past security without this."

"Oh, I doubt that. But I will be more than happy to do things by the numbers."

"That's very kind of you," she said gratefully. The tall man strode away, and it was only a few minutes later that she realized she had forgotten to find out precisely what the nature of his "official" business was. By that time, however, he was long gone.

They had given Bruce the room next to Betty's in order to simplify life. They hadn't checked him in. Leonard had simply dictated that he have somewhere to cool off and be alone, to try to cope with what had happened.

For long hours he had remained there, staring up at the ceiling. Now he finally rose from the bed. He stood there for a moment, summoning his nerve, and then he emerged into the hallway and stepped into the adjoining room.

Betty lay there on her side. She was looking right at him, and yet—as he moved and her gaze didn't shift—he realized that she was staring off into space.

"Betty?" he said softly.

No response.

"Betty, I . . . know you must hate me right now. I can't blame you. If I were you, I would hate me too."

Still no response.

He moved toward her and sat on the edge of her bed. He took her hand. It felt like a dishrag.

He tried to think of what to say, and nothing came immediately to mind.

And then Betty said very softly, "I want you . . ."

"Yes?" He was eager to hear. "You do?"

"I want you . . . to kill me."

"You . . ." He couldn't find his voice for a moment. "You . . . you don't mean that."

"Yes," she said very distantly, "yes . . . I do."

"You're . . . you're just depressed. I mean, even after a *normal* delivery, there's depression. It's hormonal."

"Hormonal." She laughed without any amusement. When she spoke it was with a distant singsong in her voice. "Hormonal. Bruce, it's not hormonal. What it is is a sham. A joke. I've been dying by degrees over the past years. Little pieces of me, eaten away. Like the Sondheim song . . . every day a little death. People don't die all at once. They die a little at a time. Things happen that

175

rob you of your will to live, bit by bit. In the body, in the soul. And when you reach your limit, whatever that is, then you die. That's pretty simple, right?"

"Betty . . ."

"So I don't want to wait around. I'm telling you now, if this isn't enough to kill me immediately . . . then I don't want to wait around to see what else happens."

"*Stop it!*" he told her, sounding more angry than he would have liked. He calmed himself and continued, "Betty, honey, this isn't like you. You're . . . you're the strongest person I know."

"No. No, Hulk is strongest one there is," she said and laughed again in that dead voice. "Hulk make baby. Hulk make two babies. Hulk kill wife. Hulk kill happiness. Hulk . . ."

Bruce got up and started to walk away. At the door he was stopped by her voice as she said, "Bruce? I don't hate you."

He placed a hand against the door frame. "Thank you."

"I hate myself for falling in love with you."

He couldn't look at her. It didn't matter, though; she'd stopped looking at him as well. Then he walked out into the hallway, leaving her behind.

Doc Samson stood at the observation window outside the nursery, looking at the two children in the incubator. Inside, Doctor Thomas was checking their charts, monitoring their life signs. She glanced out at Samson, who she knew was watching her, and shook her head grimly.

There was a tap on Samson's shoulder. He braced himself, prepared to throw another reporter out on his ass. Instead he found himself staring into the eyes of a tall man with black and silver hair.

"Dr. Strange!" said Samson in relief. He shook Strange's hand firmly. "Stephen, thank you for coming on such short notice."

"Not a problem," said Strange. "I just wish to be sure that I'm not putting any local noses out of joint."

"Believe me, you're not. This is a superb hospital, Stephen, with great facilities and top-notch staff. But this," and he gestured toward the twins, "this is something that's way out of their league."

"I suspect it's an entirely different league altogether," said Strange. "Siamese twins who aren't identical. Gray . . . that was Bruce's original color when he became the Hulk."

"That's right. And he reverted to gray for a time." He sighed in amazement as he observed the twins. "Gray- and white-skinned, joined at the head. The two aspects of Bruce in microcosm," said Samson grimly. "Baby as metaphor. It's insane."

"It's an insane universe," Strange told him. "I've had the opportunity to converse with it from time to time on that very subject." He squinted, studied the babies some more. "Still, I don't understand how it's possible. Conjoined twins, like any set of identical twins, have identical genetic makeup. So how can one look normal and one look abnormal?"

"You don't understand, Stephen. They *do* have the same genetic makeup . . . a genetic makeup that resembles nothing seen before, thanks to the gamma bomb accident that permanently altered their father's genes. Bruce is a shapeshifter; he always has been, ever since the accident. The shapes are reflections of his personalities and his inner turmoil. The twins inherited that trait from him."

"But that doesn't explain why one is normal and one isn't."

"Yes, it does. They're two different people, Stephen." He placed his hand against the glass. "For all the work we do with the human mind—for all that societal influences, environment, and family life affect the way people turn out—nobody is born a complete *tabula rasa*. We all have *some* aspects of our personalities intact when we're born. Look at any nursery. One baby might always be crying, fidgety, cranky . . . and another is calm, laid back. One bellows to be fed, the other just whimpers a little. And the two young Banners were born with certain preencoded personality traits reflected in their physical makeup."

"Could their forms change, then?"

Samson shrugged. "I have no idea. Best guess? No. When you've got a condition that is so deeply rooted at both the cellular and psychological levels, you'd have to change the person completely. Make him something completely apart from what he was born as. Behavior modification that brings him around 180 degrees. Not impossible. But not likely."

"Stephen."

Strange turned in response to the new summons and saw an odd-looking, redhaired man facing him. He frowned slightly. "Bruce?"

"I'm afraid so."

Strange studied him for a moment. "I believe you can very likely sue whoever cut your hair that way."

"I'll take that under advisement, Stephen. Leonard, I see you took my advice about bringing Stephen in on this." He shook Strange's hand firmly. "I can't think of anyone better."

"Now hold on, Bruce. Don't put too much faith in me. There's only so much I can do. And before I do any of it, I have to speak to whoever's in charge."

"Then let's get to it, shall we?"

They did not *all* get to it, however. Dr. Strange got to it, in deep conference with Dr. Thomas and the attending surgeon, Dr. Sorrento. Bruce, in the meantime, sat in his room with Doc Samson, one leg propped up on a chair. "I spoke to Betty," Bruce said after some time.

"Didn't go well, did it?"

He looked at Samson bleakly. "She wants to die, Leonard. I've taken a beautiful, vital woman . . . and I've broken her will to live."

"Bruce . . . you didn't ask for this."

Bruce looked sadly at Samson. "I was selfish, Leonard. I wanted to prove that I could be a good father."

"That's so important to you?"

He nodded, and then tapped his forehead. "He's still up there, you know. Brian Banner, my beloved late father. Rattling around inside my head, spooking me. Still with his claws in my peace of mind. And I thought . . . I thought that if I ever had the opportunity to be a father, then maybe I could do a good job of it. Be kind, be loving. Establish a connection with my child that was strong and supportive. Teach him to walk proudly instead of tentatively. To triumph over his environment instead of falling victim to it. Give him a sense of himself, teach him all the lessons so that he could be a good person. If I'd managed to do all that, then maybe . . ."

"Maybe you could shut your father up once and for all?"

Bruce nodded. "Exactly. So you see? Out of my selfish needs, Betty gave birth to . . . to her greatest nightmares. And I've inflicted those nightmares on the one creature on this planet I'd rather die than hurt."

"It will work out, Bruce. I'm sure of it."

Bruce gave him a look that spoke volumes. And what it said, in essence, was, *Let's not kid a kidder, shall we?*

That was when Dr. Strange stuck his head out of the consulting room. "Bruce," he said, and there was an unmistakable grimness in his voice. "We have to talk, immediately."

Bruce stood, as did Samson.

Strange moved over to them and said, "Listen carefully. We're going to have to separate the twins."

Bruce looked in confusion to Samson and then back to Strange.

"Well, yes, I assumed that was a given. At some point down the line, once they've had a chance to become stronger and—"

"No, you don't understand. Their vital signs are not stabilizing as we'd hoped. If we do not separate them immediately, we're likely to lose them both. As it is, they're very, very weak. Thank God that their brains are fully and separately developed. If those were merged, I don't think we'd have a chance. As it is, the pale one may not make it, no matter what we do. The gray one is a little stronger, but not by much. Plus there are . . . other considerations."

"Such as?"

Strange cleared his throat slightly. "I'd think it's obvious. Bruce, the gray child . . . we have no idea what it's capable of. What if it . . . mutates further? What if it develops supernormal strength? He could kill his twin with a thrust of his fist. What if he tried to push the other away, and in so doing, ripped apart—"

"I get the idea!" said Bruce, trying to block all those hideous possibilities from his mind's eye.

"The operation is their only chance," said Strange, "and I just wish that we had some way of improving the odds."

Bruce seemed to look off into the distance, and he said softly, "Maybe we do, Stephen. Maybe we do."

Chapter 13

Betty lay on the bed, staring at nothing. Then she closed her eyes and sent off a prayer that maybe, just maybe, she might have a cerebral hemmorhage or something and just die peacefully in her sleep.

And then a gruff, angry voice said, "What the blazes do you think you're doing, young lady?"

Her eyes snapped open.

Her father was standing there, as big and barrel-chested as she remembered him. The medals on his uniform glistened. He had his hat tucked smartly under his arm, and he was standing at attention.

For someone who she had thought was dead, he seemed to be in excellent health.

"Daddy . . . ?" she whispered.

"Get up, young lady. When Thunderbolt Ross enters a room, everybody had better know enough to snap to. Do you know enough?"

"I . . ."

"*Do you?*"

She sat up, smoothing the lap of her hospital gown. "I'm sorry, Daddy."

He lanced her with his steady, unrelenting gaze, and then

started to pace. His head swiveled like a tank turret. "Now, then . . . you want to tell me what the ding-dong blue blazes you think you're doing here? Lying around, feeling sorry for yourself?"

"I'm . . . not well, Daddy. I just had surgery. . . ."

"*Faw!*" snorted General Thunderbolt Ross. "So you had a little surgery done on you! So what?"

"Daddy, they cut me open! Have a crumb of sympathy, okay?"

"Sympathy!? When we hit the beach at Normandy, you think we got any sympathy? Blasted right we didn't!" he continued before Betty could even open her mouth. "You think we didn't get sliced open? Sniper fire opened up my right thigh! I had enough blood pouring out of me to float the *Nimitz*! Did I lie down and say I needed a rest? Did I complain? Blasted right I didn't! Know what I did do? I stormed the hill and took out a whole nest of those Nazi swine! That's what I did!"

"Daddy . . ."

"And there were people worse off than me! Much worse! I remember Corporal Ellison. He wound up taking so many holes in him, when the wind blew just right he sounded like a harmonica. But he kept on going. Lost his hands to a grenade. Didn't stop him. Tore apart a battalion with his teeth."

"Aw, Daddy, come on . . ."

"And then there was Slaughterhouse Straczynski. Right leg got blown clean off. He picked it up, hopped back into battle, and used it to club an entire Panzer division to death."

"Daddy, for crying out loud, don't you think you're exaggerating just a *little*? Huh?"

He stared at her, looking offended, and then "harrumphed" slightly. "If that's what you want to believe, then go ahead. I was there, young lady, and you weren't. But maybe you think you know better. After all, you had the best education available. You're a bright girl. Not as bright as you think . . ."

"What do you mean by that?" she said suspiciously.

He snorted disdainfully. "You think I didn't know about your infatuation with Banner? That the main reason for it was because I disapproved? You resented me, Betty, admit it."

"I did *not!*"

Ross actually chuckled deep in his wrinkled throat. He produced a cigar and lit it up, taking a deep, confident drag. "You did exactly *because* of the education I gave you. Because I sent you away to school, and that made you mad as hornets. So when Banner came along, you saw that I couldn't stand the spineless milksop. You showered your attention on him in order to get my goat. No, no, don't bother denying it again," he ordered, waving off her objections. "Because let's face it: It worked. Your getting involved with him really stuck it to me. Burned my biscuits something fierce, young lady."

"I'm sorry." She looked down. "It was childish. But . . ."

"But what?"

"Well . . . maybe that's part of what made me interested in Bruce at first. But as I got to know him, I was . . . I was genuinely attracted to him. I mean, he was so sweet and kind and . . ."

"And everything I wasn't?" he said softly.

She looked back up at him, her eyes moist. "I didn't say that."

"You didn't have to." He paused. "I suppose it's better that it worked out that way. You married him, after all. You can't have any sort of long-term relationship that's got spite as its foundation."

"I know. I know."

"And now you don't like how things are going, eh?"

"Well," she gestured helplessly, "I can't exactly say everything's wonderful, can I?"

"*Fah!* Was everything wonderful when we stormed the beach at Norman—"

She moaned and dropped down, her face in her pillow. She

stayed that way for what seemed forever. Then she felt strong fingers stroking her hair. She started to sob.

"When you were a little girl . . . at night, when you were sleeping," he said in a voice more gentle than she could ever remember him using, "sometimes I'd come in and just stroke your hair. You had beautiful hair. Still do."

"I wasn't always sleeping," she whispered. "Sometimes I'd wake up from it. And it . . . it felt so nice, that I wouldn't move at all. Not do anything, because I was afraid that you'd stop if you knew I was awake."

"I might have."

"And you'd sing sometimes. You'd sing 'Me and My Shadow.' Do you remember?"

"Of course."

"I . . ." She could barely get the words out. "I thought you didn't love me. Because Mommy died and left you stuck with me. Because I wasn't a boy. I thought . . ."

"Hogwash," he said brusquely. "Boys are overrated. Give me a loving daughter any day of the week."

"I . . . tried to be . . . I think I screwed it up. . . ."

"Everyone screws up. It's a human thing to do. You should never be ashamed when you screw up. However," he added forcefully, "if you don't *fix* the screwup, then you've got no business showing your face in public. So here you are: You've rejected the man who is still your husband, milksop or not. You've rejected your children . . . and I take some responsibility for that, because you're doing to them what I think you believed I did to you. But I didn't, Betty. I never did."

His voice grew dark. "But what you've also done, Elizabeth, is something for which I have no tolerance at all. Not a scintilla. What you've done, Elizabeth, is reject life. Reject that miraculous spark that your mother and I gave you."

She hung her head. "I'm sorry, sir."

"The idea! Crying that you want to die. That you want to just end it all. What kind of weak-kneed garbage is that? It's embarrassing! To me! To your mother! To the United States of America! To the entire civilized world, if you ask me!"

"I *said* I'm sorry," she repeated, and this time there was clear irritation in her voice.

"You can save your sorries! This whole blamed country is going right down the tubes! People saying they're sorry for this, or sorry for that, or sorry for some other blamed thing! Except it doesn't mean anything! People apologizing right and left, but no one assumes responsibility! There's no consequences taken! You know what 'I'm sorry' means?" He snapped his fingers. "That! Nothing! Easy to say, easy to toss out. But it doesn't amount to a hill o' beans, young lady!"

"Well, *fine,* then!" Betty said angrily. She swung her legs down and off the bed, yanking the IV with the saline solution out of her wrist. "I'll show you!"

"Don't show me, blast it! Show yourself!"

She grabbed a robe that was hanging nearby, draped it over herself, and stalked toward the door. But before she got there, her father's voice barked sharply, "Betty!" She stopped and turned to face him.

He was standing at full attention, his hand snapped up and to the brim of the hat that he now wore proudly on his head.

Betty brought her arm up, just as she had seen so many men do through so many years. They stood there for a long moment, salutes held perfectly still.

"Go get 'em, honey. Storm the hill. Make me proud," he said, and snapped his hand down.

She did likewise and said with full confidence, "I will, sir."

She went to the door of the room, threw it open, and found

that she was standing on a beach. Overhead the sky was dark, and there was the unmistakable sound of mortar fire, coming closer, coming toward her.

An explosion at her feet blew her backward. She felt herself lifted high in the air, a broken marionette, and she thudded into her bed . . .

Fully awake.

She trembled for a long moment, stabilizing her senses, refamiliarizing herself with her surroundings.

Her father wasn't there, of course. He was long gone. Nor was there fighting right outside her door. But there were, she realized, a husband and children who needed her. And she wasn't going to do them a damned bit of good lying where she was.

She got up, took her robe, slipped her feet into the hospital slippers that had been provided, and headed for the door. But when she reached it, she paused suddenly, a little nervous to see what might be out there. She thought she was awake. Then again, everything made sense while she was dreaming, so for all she knew, she was still knee-deep in weirdness.

Slowly, tentatively, she opened the door a crack and peered through.

It was a hospital corridor.

"Can't be too careful these days," she murmured.

etting out of the hospital had been much easier than Bruce thought it would be.

None of the reporters knew what the father of the "freak" children looked like. As he was heading out, he took care to identify himself to hospital security so that he would not encounter problems getting back in. He made it to his car and sped to the main campus. It was a pleasant day and, under ordinary circumstances, he would have walked it. But this day he needed to save as much time as he could.

It was still fairly early. Bruce had lost track of time; the events of the past days had caused the passage of hours to collapse into each other.

Classes were drawing to a close, with final examinations approaching rapidly. Bruce had so looked forward to this time. He was eager to see just how much the students had absorbed, how good a teacher he had been.

He had been working so hard to create rather than to destroy. Create an exciting academic environment. Create a challenge for the students, and stimulate their thoughts.

Create a child.

Now he had no time to oversee his students, and his dream of bringing life into the world seemed to be tottering on the brink of extinction.

His pace took him quickly across the campus toward the laboratory at the research center. From a distance, heading down another path, he spotted Dean Chase and Professor Felder, steeped in some sort of intense discussion. He waved to them. They glanced up and then appeared to pick up their pace and head off in another direction. Slightly odd behavior, but Bruce was sufficiently preoccupied with his own concerns that he gave it no further thought.

Moments later he reached the lab. He fumbled with his keys, his hands trembling with stress, before he finally managed to open the door.

The lab seemed cold this morning. Like a morgue.

The gamma gun wasn't a "gun" in the traditional sense that one envisioned such things. It was a cylinder, with tapered edges, about three feet long and ten inches in diameter. The triggering and regulating mechanisms were situated in the middle of the cylinder, consisting of a small array of numerical sequencing pads and microcircuitry. It was called a "gun" because it injected and focused the gamma particles as the source for the larger weapon that Bruce hoped to complete someday.

His first instinct was to take the gamma gun and just go, just get out of there, get back to the hospital as fast as he could. But he'd been running a test on it the other day, and had not been satisfied with the wave-pattern buildups. It had been uneven, too difficult to control. He was sure it wouldn't take much adjustment. Indeed, he would have attended to it the other day, but he hadn't wanted to be late getting home. Lord, what a trivial reason that seemed now. But he couldn't have known. Besides, back then—a lifetime ago, it seemed—he had thought he had all the time in the world.

He started working quickly, forcing his hands to stop shaking. Panic wasn't going to help him, nor was tension. He made himself proceed in an efficient, scientific manner.

Long minutes passed as he charted the wave flow, made notations, made adjustments. Slowly, hope began to build in him. It would only be a few more minutes, and then he'd be ready to—

The door, which he had closed behind him, opened.

His view of the door was blocked by some equipment. He stepped away from the gamma gun, moved around the equipment . . .

And froze.

His entire attention was squarely on the gun barrel pointed at him from less than five feet away. For anyone with a smidgen of marksmanship ability, it was point-blank range. And the man who had the gun on him appeared to have more than just a smidgen.

He was wearing an army uniform. Beneath the brim of his hat, his eyes glinted with steel.

"Dr. Banner," he said. "It's hard to recognize you with your dazzling new 'do. I'm Major William Talbot."

"Of course," said Bruce, forcing his voice to remain even. "It's hard to recognize you without your giant robots."

"Ah yes," said Talbot sadly. "Well, you see, that's part of the problem. No, don't move," he warned, his voice suddenly sharper as Bruce took half a step to his right. Bruce stopped where he was and Talbot went back to sounding casual. "You see, Project Hulkbuster was cut from the military budget. Armor mothballed, staff dispersed. I've been reassigned. Tragic what a state the leaders of our country have brought us to."

"Listen to me—" Bruce began urgently.

"Just a warning," Talbot said. "You start to make the slightest move towards changing—a hint of green—and you're dead."

"I don't change. Not anymore. I've beaten it. It's over."

Talbot seemed genuinely interested. "Is that a fact?"

"Yes."

"Well, that's interesting. And it jibes with what I've found out. You see, I was en route to my lovely reassignment—running a damned recruitment board—when word hit the national media about the rather odd birth that had taken place in these parts. To most people it meant simply 'freak,' but for someone like me, it cried out as a lead. I got down here within hours after the birth. Did some checking around, poking and prodding. Army identification opens up a lot of doors. Found out the proud father is a teacher here and started showing around this. . . ."

From the inside of his jacket he pulled an 8 × 10 glossy of Bruce. "At first folks didn't recognize you, what with your having whacked off all your hair, as I said. But then they did. I told a couple of key school personnel just exactly who you were, and what your story is. They seemed less than enthused. I hate to be the bearer of bad tidings, Doctor, but . . . I strongly suspect you haven't got a hope in hell of getting tenure. Or even making it through the semester, for that matter. I'd been over to your house and was getting impatient, so I came back here . . . and happened to run into a couple of extremely frightened faculty members who told me they'd seen you heading in this direction. Wasn't that superb timing?"

Bruce's mouth had gone completely dry. The barrel of the gun had not wavered so much as a millimeter. "Major, listen to me. There are lives at stake. . . ."

"Oh yes, indeed. Yours, for starters."

"There's something here in the lab that can save my children—"

"Save the monsters?" He seemed amused. "What a concept."

"They're not monsters! They're innocent babies who deserve at least a chance of survival! Look, Major," he tried to sound reasonable, "you want me, not them. I'm the one who you blame for all the trouble that your uncle ran into. I'm the one who was the Hulk. If you want to take me in, fine. You got me fair and square. Take me in. Just give me the time to save my children's lives. They're Betty's children, too. Your uncle was married to her. He loved her. Don't you think he'd want to save her children if it was at all possible?"

It seemed that the gun was wavering just slightly.

"We live in an unjust world, Major. I never asked for anything that happened to me. I'm a victim, as much as your uncle was. As much as those children are. Let me at least have a chance to end the cycle of victimization. Anything you want to do with me afterwards, fine. My word of honor, I'll go with you."

"Word of honor, eh?"

"Yes."

Talbot appeared to give the matter some thought. Then he said, "You know, Doctor, a friend of yours recommended a musical play to me. *Les Misérables.* What with the budget cut, I found extra time on my hands. I went to see it. He was right. Fabulous show. I was so taken by it, I read the book. And this situation between us, right here . . . it reminds me so much of the moment when the fugitive Jean Valjean confronts Inspector Javert in the sewers of Paris. Valjean says much the same things as you are. Begs for mercy, promises to return. Javert lets him go . . . and then is so completely unable to cope with a world of grays, rather than issues of stark black and white, that he kills himself. And I've been pondering that for a while. That whole notion. Examining one's life and priorities, and realizing when mistakes have been made. Realizing that you've persecuted a fundamentally good and moral man and, in so doing, become far worse of a person than the one whom you'd been tormenting. And you know what I've decided?"

"What?"

Talbot squeezed the trigger. The bullet smashed into Bruce's chest, ricocheting off his third rib and rearranging the contents of his left lung. Bruce didn't even feel the pain; that would come later. Instead all he felt was the impact that knocked him off his feet, slamming him to the ground. The world seemed to tilt at a forty-five-degree angle.

And Talbot shouted, "I've decided that *Javert was a freaking moron!*"

Talbot approached and fired again. Miraculously, Bruce actually found the strength to roll mostly out of the way. Rather than lodging in his heart, the bullet instead tore through his left biceps. Talbot didn't seem terribly concerned.

"So what if you don't change into the Hulk anymore?" asked Talbot as calmly as if chatting about the scores at Wimbledon. "Doesn't mean that you won't again. And it doesn't mean that you should be exonerated for past sins. Considering how shabbily my priorities have been treated by official channels, however, you'll pardon me if I don't trust them to do the right thing."

Bruce, trying to lift his head, coughed out blood, and also a word. "*Murderer . . .* "

"That's only in peacetime," said Talbot, standing right at Bruce's feet. "In time of war, you're called a soldier. Well, Dr. Banner, as far as I'm concerned, our country's been at war with you from the moment you smashed your first tank. I don't care if our leaders haven't declared it. I don't care if Congress won't fund it. It's a war just the same. But now," and he cocked the trigger, "now the war ends."

They were using the largest operating theater in the hospital. It seemed as if every available staff member was in there.

From overhead in the observation room, Doc Samson looked down upon the scene.

The twins were unconscious, tubes sticking out of almost every visible part of them. Dr. Sorrento was drawing a line down the section of the skull platelets where they were joined.

Dr. Strange, in mask and gloves, was in a last-minute conference with Dr. Thomas. He glanced up in Leonard's direction . . . and then his eyes widened in surprise. He made a small motion with his head to Leonard's right.

Leonard Samson looked to his right and was astounded to see that Betty had entered the small observation room. "Betty, you shouldn't be up and around! You just had surgery."

"I'm not going to lie around. We took far worse at Normandy."

He stared at her, his head tilted slightly in question. "I beg your pardon?"

"I'm all right, Leonard. Really. I'm fine."

"Are you sure you want to watch this?"

She nodded her head slowly. Now all of the OR personnel were glancing up at her. Strange was looking up questioningly. Samson gave a little shrug.

"Is there a way to talk to them?" asked Betty.

"There's a PA here," he said, tapping a small panel. "They use it during operations when students are observing, for questions. But an operation of this complexity . . . well, they don't generally encourage a lot of distracting chitchat."

"But they haven't really started yet."

He hesitated, then flicked the switch. Betty leaned forward. "Excuse me . . . can you hear me?"

There were nods. They were all looking up at her now.

"I just . . . I wanted to tell you . . ." Her voice sounded as if it were going to choke.

"Betty," he whispered, "they know. They know you're count-ing on them—"

"No, that's not it," she said firmly. She coughed and then said, "I just wanted to tell you . . . that the one on the right . . . his name is Ross. And the . . . the gray one . . . his name is Brett. Ross is . . . it's my maiden name, but it's more to remember my dad. And Brett is a combination of 'Bruce' and 'Betty.' I just wanted you to . . . to know who you were operating on."

Dr. Strange nodded in understanding. Betty clicked off and then leaned back on her heels.

"Betty, I really think you should leave," said Leonard. "In fact, considering your mental state, I may have to insist . . ."

She turned to him and her gaze drilled through to the base of his skull. "I don't care if you were struck by gamma rays and turned into a muscle man, or bitten by a gamma-irradiated chicken and can lay gamma-irradiated eggs. If you try and take me out of here, I'm going to knock you on your gamma-irradiated ass. Do we understand each other?"

He stared at her, and—despite the gravity of the situation—had to fight not to let the corners of his mouth turn up. "That's not exactly conduct becoming to a woman who almost became a nun."

"Yes, well," and Betty turned to look back down into the OR, "I've known some pretty tough nuns in my life."

They watched in silence, and then Betty said softly, "So . . . where's Bruce?"

"I don't know," said Samson. "I was reluctant to tell you. I don't know where he got off to." He paused. "I . . . I hope you don't think he abandoned you, or doesn't love you, or doesn't want to be here."

"I'm . . . trying not to think anything," said Betty in an even voice. "I'm hoping . . . and dreaming . . . and fearing. That's all. That's all anybody's life boils down to: hopes, dreams, and fears. And I hope, and dream, that the children will live to experience it and . . . fear they won't. Everything else doesn't matter. If Bruce can be here, and wants to be here, then he will."

Bruce lay in a pool of his blood, gasping for air that wasn't coming.

Talbot stood over him, weapon aimed squarely between Bruce's eyes. "The pain must be pretty bad," said Talbot. "Don't worry. It won't last for much longer."

And indeed, the pain was tremendous. Overwhelming . . . for someone with normal thresholds of pain.

But Robert Bruce Banner, for years, had learned to live with pain. Learned to live with the agony of his body twisting and distorting, muscles rippling and stretching, bones distending—agony that was unimaginable because there was nothing like it in the natural world. It was like giving birth from every pore of your body. It was enough anguish to drive anyone subjected to it on any sort of a regular basis completely insane.

And Bruce Banner, to save his sanity, had learned to cope with it. Learned to block off portions of his mind, to disengage his pain receptors, to send away the sensations of suffering into a far, remote corner of his mind and lock them away. He had not had to do it with regularity for quite some time, but it was not a technique that one forgets.

Bruce had not forgotten it now. Pain that would have immobilized another man visited Banner, and he didn't answer the knock. Instead he shunted it off, refused to acknowledge it, and called upon the adrenaline and reserves of desperation that might be his only salvation. He did not admit to himself that the wound was fatal. He did not allow for the possibility that he was going to fail, and that his children could die. And he would be damned if the last sight he saw was the smug face of Major William Talbot.

And just as Talbot started to squeeze the trigger, Banner slammed his feet up into Talbot's crotch. It wasn't as forceful a move as Bruce would have liked, for his strength was ebbing fast. But it was enough, for it caught Talbot completely off guard. Talbot gasped, his arm jerking. The gun fired high and blew a clock off the wall. As Talbot staggered, Bruce hooked the back of Talbot's knees and pulled forward.

Talbot's knees buckled and he went down. The gun clattered to the floor.

Immediately Bruce was atop him, scrambling over him. Blood was fountaining from his wounds, covering both of them, as Bruce struggled to grab the gun. He got his hand on it, but his fingers were covered with blood and he couldn't get a firm grip.

With a roar of fury that vied with anything ever issued from the Hulk's throat, Talbot lunged at the weapon. For a moment they were both grabbing it, struggling for position, cursing and shoving on the floor . . .

And then Talbot got the edge. His hand clamped around the barrel and he pried it out of Banner's fading grasp. And before Bruce could make another move, Talbot swung the gun around in triumph and brought the butt of it crashing against the base of Bruce's skull.

Pain exploded inside his head, stars blasting from behind his eyes . . .

And there was something else.

A cracking . . . a distant sensation of something cracking beneath the surface of the skin.

Talbot let out a triumphant laugh and hit Bruce again in exactly the same place, in exactly the same way.

And a very faint, very subtle buzzing noise—which Bruce hadn't even been really aware was there in the first place—ceased.

Bruce screeched as thoughts, emotions, unchanneled sensations roared through his brain with freight-train speed.

Talbot was unaware of the source of Banner's agony. He was completely obsessed with paying Bruce back for the physical discomfort that Bruce had inflicted on him. The crazed soldier grabbed Banner's throat, cutting off his air, working his fingers up to the underside of Bruce's chin.

"You gave it . . . a good try, Banner," grunted Talbot. "But it wasn't . . . good enough by half . . ." and he squeezed harder and harder . . .

And suddenly realized he wasn't making any progress.

Banner's throat had abruptly become tougher, harder. He could feel the neck muscles hardening. It was like trying to strangle a spool of phone cable.

And Talbot understood, with horror, what was happening. He'd gotten overconfident, too caught up in his personal vendetta.

He'd blown it.

No! Not yet! he thought frantically, and he tried to bring the gun to bear and fire while there was still time.

But Bruce's hand clamped onto the business end of the gun. A hand that was already abnormally large, tinted with green. Banner was snarling, pain slamming through him, but this time instead of pushing it away, he channeled it, focused all his anger and fury on the would-be assassin astride him.

Banner's hand convulsed, closed tight, and shattered the gun . . . and Talbot's hand as well. Talbot felt the bones breaking beneath the viselike grip of Bruce Banner, and he shrieked.

Bruce Banner laughed. It was a very ugly sound, a liquid sound for there was still blood in his lungs, but it was mattering less and less because his body was healing itself. It was getting larger, more powerful. Over the past months he'd actually started to get a tan, so his skin was a darker brown than usual, but that didn't matter, because the green it was turning into was as emerald as ever.

And Talbot ran.

Or tried to.

He didn't get very far, because Bruce grabbed him by the scruff of the neck and just shook him. Shook him like a cat worrying a mouse. Talbot's brain slammed around inside his cranium so hard and so violently that he thought he could hear it slosh. Then, suddenly, the ceiling seemed to be approaching him very quickly.

He slammed into it face first. Fortunately for him it was only acoustical tiles. If it had been something more sturdy, he would have wound up with his eyes literally in the back of his head. As it was, the tiles cracked and tumbled to the floor.

"Please . . . don't . . ."

He was swung down, his feet still dangling some distance above the floor. He found himself face-to-face with the infuriated visage of the incredible Hulk. There was a smattering of green blood on his chest in silent acknowledgment of the wound he'd sustained in his more vulnerable form. Otherwise he was whole—and pissed.

"Please . . ." whispered Talbot.

"Ooooh," the Hulk cooed mockingly. "The 'P' word. You're asking for mercy, is that it?"

"Look, you've . . . you've got to understand."

"Funny . . . that's just what I said to you in Chicago, for all the good it did me. Tell me, Major. Tell me what I have to understand."

"I was doing . . . my job . . . as a soldier."

"You tried to kill me!" roared the Hulk with such force that it blew back Talbot's hair. "You *shot* me! And now you want me to ignore that! And let you go, so you can . . . what? Dog my every step?

Maybe you'll go after Betty next time, huh? Threaten to kill her, too? You're a loose cannon, Talbot—and a loose end—and I'm going to *tie you off!*"

One massive hand gripped Talbot's head, the other Talbot's legs, and—shaking with rage—the Hulk started to bend the terrified soldier backwards.

Talbot screamed once more . . . and then literally disgraced his uniform.

The Hulk paused, as he saw the humiliation and anguish in Talbot's face. "Oh, Lord," he muttered, and dropped Talbot to the floor. Talbot lay there trembling, unable to make a coherent utterance other than a few inarticulate noises.

Contemptuously the Hulk turned his back to him and picked up the gamma gun. Then he spoke to Talbot without looking at him. "You know . . . there was a time when the term 'good soldier' was an oxymoron to me. But I understand now. General Ross, or your uncle . . . if it had been one of them, they'd have spit in my face and told me to do my worst. If you weren't able to live up to that example, well then, someone should." And now he did turn to glance at Talbot, his face filled with scorn. "Go ahead, Talbot. Do your worst . . . if you can think of doing worse to me than you've already done to yourself."

Without another word he walked out of the lab, leaving a whimpering Major Bill Talbot behind.

And as the Hulk left, he stepped over the fallen clock. It had stopped at the time it was broken: 10:47

At 10:46 A.M., the twins were separated.

And at 10:48 A.M., Ross Banner's tiny heart stopped beating.

Chapter 15

He was bathed in a gentle light that played from an amulet at Dr. Strange's neck.

Betty stood by the other side of the incubator, with Leonard Samson near by. She looked down at the child, a finger gently stroking a paper-thin arm. There was only one other person in the room, a priest, giving the child the last rites. He finished and Betty said softly with him, "Amen." The priest looked nervously at the amulet that Strange wore. For one insane moment he thought that there was some sort of . . . of eye peering out from within the amulet. That the eye was even the source of the light. But he decided that dwelling on it excessively was probably not the best idea. And so he crossed himself before hurriedly departing.

"I'm sorry, Betty," Strange said. "I tried. We all did."

"And there was nothing all your . . . magic . . . could do for him?" Betty couldn't even bring herself to look into Strange's eyes.

"I'm afraid that medicine falls into the realm of the natural, not the supernatural. We separated your sons, Betty, but Ross went into cardiac arrest, and we simply weren't able to revive him. All I could do was . . . what I've done. 'Catch him' just at the moment of death, while he still possesses that ephemeral quality we call life."

"How long can you keep him like that?"

"Not for long. And even if it were indefinitely, it's not practical. It doesn't make any sense." As tenderly as he could, he said, "He's . . . gone, Betty. I've closed the door on his foot, as it were. But he won't come back through . . . he can't. All he can do is depart. Nothing can stop that. I kept him here so that he could have last rites, as you requested. But at this point . . ." He shrugged helplessly.

"Not . . . not yet," said Betty. "Just . . . give me a minute or two, okay?"

Leonard turned away, unable to watch, unable to keep his composure.

Betty reached into the incubator and removed Ross. He didn't stir. His chest didn't move. The only hint of life to him was the warmth from his body. Strange expanded the light from his amulet to encompass both Betty and her child as she moved slowly, heavily, toward a chair. She sat, and wished it rocked. But it didn't, so she settled for rocking her body back and forth very gently, pushing off the balls of her feet.

And in a voice as delicate as spun glass, Betty began to sing, "Me . . . and my . . . shaaadow. . .walking down the avenue . . ."

Strange kept the light steady.

Samson left the room, feeling that Betty didn't need to hear him break down.

It wouldn't have mattered if he'd stayed, though, because Betty was in a world of her own. There was nothing except her and her child, and the light that enveloped them. She continued to sing, her voice strong and steady, cracking only once as she tried to keep a handle on the emotions churning within her.

She went through the entire song twice. She even pretended that her father was joining in. And then his voice, if it was ever there, faded, and she sang solo, ". . . all alone and . . . feeling . . .

blue . . ." Then her voice trailed off. She said nothing for some time.

"Betty . . ." Strange said gently.

"Okay. Okay, I'm . . ." She lowered her lips to her child's face and kissed him once. "I'm . . . we're . . . ready."

The light faded as Betty held the child to her bosom, and she gasped and looked up at Strange, tears she could no longer hold back streaming down her face. "I felt him," she whispered. "I felt him leave, right through me. Oh, God . . ."

Stephen Strange went to her side, knelt down, and held the two of them. And there they remained for some time, mourning the short, tragic life of Ross Banner.

Doc Samson strode down the hallway purposefully. He was a psychiatrist. He knew precisely what misplaced aggression was, and all the reasons for it—and ultimately, the futility of it.

At that particular moment, he simply didn't care.

He strode into the main waiting area, and as before, it was mobbed with reporters. And just as he knew they would, they started to descend on him, hyenas around the lion.

For a moment the image of the biblical Samson, slaying the Philistines with the jawbone of an ass, came to mind. He didn't have a jawbone to use, but at the moment, the journalists were little more than Philistines, and he was more than ready to kick ass.

He grabbed at whatever got near. The first thing he snared was a couple of microphones. He pulverized them in an instant, crunching the metal between steely fingers. Before the reporters could even fully grasp what was happening, he grabbed the nearest television camera and yanked it away from the cameraman.

"*Hey!*" screamed the cameraman.

Samson was beyond caring. Gripping the camera firmly with

both hands, he slammed his palms together, crushing the camera in between. He snatched another, this time snapping straps that were holding it onto the cameraman's shoulder.

By now the reporters were suddenly realizing just what serious trouble they were in. They fell back as Samson raised the camera over his head and hurled it to the floor with sufficient force to demolish the camera. He noticed some parts remained intact. He ground them under his feet.

"What the *hell* do you think you're doing?!" the reporters shouted in various tones of indignation.

"Get out!" Samson told them.

"The people have a right to full—"

He sounded barely human, barely articulate. *"Get out!"* he howled in a cry of unadulterated rage. He grabbed some reporters at random and shoved them back with fearful force.

They tried bluster, they tried collective nerve, and none of it was able to stand up to the sheer fury of the green-haired colossus called Doc Samson.

"I've had it with you people! You vultures! You bottom feeders! Get out of here! Leave these people in peace! Have some respect! Have some *decency*, for God's sake!"

He shoved, he pushed, he manhandled, and he made it very clear that their presence would be tolerated no longer. A number of them darted into the elevators, others grabbed the stairs. The print reporters were scribbling as fast as they could even as they ran for their lives. The TV people left their shattered equipment behind, shouting dire threats of lawyers and lawsuits.

Samson didn't care. As far as he was concerned, no jury would convict.

He stood there for a long moment in the newly vacated waiting area, chest heaving, heart pounding.

A reporter with a notepad stuck his head back in through the stairwell door. "Excuse me . . . is it Sampson with a 'p,' or Samson without—"

"*Nyaarrrgghhhhh!*" was Doc's only reply.

The reporter slammed the door on his way out.

Samson turned away, growling, and saw Daphne staring at him, wide-eyed. "*What?*" he demanded impatiently.

She quickly turned her eyes back to her work.

Suddenly the door to the stairwell started to swing open again. This time Doc didn't hesitate. He yanked open the door and bellowed, "What do I have to do to get *through* to you?!"

The Hulk stared back at him. He had some sort of cylindrical device tucked under his arm. "For starters," he said, "you can try changing your tone of voice."

Doc gasped in amazement, which quickly changed to sorrow. "Bruce, you're . . . different again. What happened?"

"It's a long story, Leonard," said the Hulk tiredly.

"Where did you go? What's that thing?"

"This," and Bruce held up the cylinder, "fires concentrated gamma particles. I figure maybe it can help the boys. If their genetic structure is similar to mine, then their bodies will practically be sponges for the gamma rays. Perhaps they've even got a healing factor like mine. The gamma rays will augment it, maybe even jump-start it. We can . . ."

He stopped. He saw the way Samson was looking at him, saw it in his face, saw that there was something there that Samson didn't want to tell him.

In a voice like death, Bruce said, "Just tell me if they're both gone."

Samson shook his head.

He pictured Talbot delaying him and was suddenly sorry he hadn't ground the major's head into a fine powder. "Which one, then?"

"We lost Ross. I'm . . . sorry, Bruce."

Banner stared at him blankly. "Who the hell is Ross?"

"Oh, that's right. Ross is—was—the pale one. The, uhm . . . gray one is Brett. They're working on him, trying to stabilize him. Still touch and go."

"Who gave them those names? Ross and Brett?"

"Betty did."

"She's up and around, then?" Bruce said in wonderment. "That woman's resiliency is . . ."

"Bruce," he rested a hand on the Hulk's forearm. "She needs you now."

Banner hesitated. "I . . . don't know how I'm supposed to feel here, Leonard. I mean . . . I've just lost a son. But I . . . don't feel anything. It's as if I don't know how to handle it."

"You probably don't," Samson said reasonably.

"I didn't even know him . . . didn't have a chance. How do you mourn someone you don't even know? Can you? Just because they have their origins in your cell structure . . . ?"

"Bruce, trust me, these aren't questions you have to worry about. You haven't fully assimilated things yet. There'll come a point when you do, and it'll all catch up with you at once. And then you'll react however you react. For now . . . we just keep moving."

"Keep moving," Bruce echoed. "Like sharks, right? Move or die."

"Exactly."

"In that case . . . let's move."

"You can't be serious."

In a small room off the OR, Drs. Sorrento and Thomas—still both in surgical garb—gaped at the device that Bruce was holding. Strange and Samson looked on, Strange scowling and his arms folded.

Betty was seated near by. She was in a wheelchair, at Thomas's insistence. She didn't seem particularly lively, sitting there listlessly as the discussion seemed to drag on. Bruce had tried to speak to her, but she barely seemed to acknowledge his existence. It was as if, with the passing of Ross, the soul had gone out of Betty as well.

"I mean, you can't be serious," Thomas repeated. "You want me to turn an unlicensed device on a two-month-early premature birth? Expose him to gamma radiation which, to be blunt, Doctor, hasn't exactly made your life a bed of roses."

"I'm aware of that, Doctor. I'm also aware, from what you're telling me, that Brett's chances are not good."

"To be blunt, that's true," admitted Sorrento. "But even so, Dr. Banner . . ."

"There's no 'but' here, Doctor. This can help him."

"We don't know that."

"We can surmise," said Dr. Strange. "And we know that the child stands little chance without it. He's barely alive as it is. We've both seen the charts. Organs underdeveloped, immune systems failing . . ."

"I won't authorize it," Sorrento said flatly.

"Fine. I won't ask," replied the Hulk.

Sorrento couldn't believe what he was hearing. "I'm not going to let you just go waltzing in there and shower that child with gamma rays."

"It won't be a shower. More like a light sprinkle."

"This isn't funny, Dr. Banner!"

Bruce took a step forward, towering a foot and a half over Sorrento. "What's funny," he said with no trace of humor, "is that you're under the impression that you can stop me."

"I . . ." Sorrento smoothed down his shirt. "I will if I have to."

"What are you going to do? Hit me with your medical diploma? Strangle me with your stethoscope?"

"Dr. Samson," Thomas said urgently, "stop him!"

"Great idea," Samson said, the voice of reason. "I should point out to you, however, that if I try to stop him, he will probably resist. Having been in a couple of these tussles in my life, I can tell you that the damage to surrounding real estate is going to be considerable. The threat to life and limb of anyone within, oh, say, a two-block radius, is going to be substantial. And even then I can't guarantee that I *can* stop him. Oh, I've knocked him out before . . ."

"Lucky punch," said the Hulk sourly.

"But there's no guarantees. We're talking wrecked hospital ward . . . maybe even wrecked hospital, Dr. Sorrento. Do any of us want that?"

"By the way, I saw a real nice Porsche in the restricted parking lot. Bet that gets trashed early on," the Hulk said sanguinely.

The blood drained from Sorrento's face. Desperately, he turned to the sorcerer and said, "Dr. Strange, you see the problem . . ."

"Indeed," agreed Strange readily. Then he turned to Betty. "What do you think?"

"What do I think?" she said. Her hand was to her breast, as if she was trying to feel the place of warmth that the baby had occupied for so brief a time.

"Should we take this chance?"

"I don't know," she whispered. "I . . . you're asking me to decide between two impossible choices. Let another baby die, or perhaps doom him to . . . what? We don't know. Bruce, we don't know enough . . ."

"We know as much as we're going to." He paused. "Betty, I . . . I know you look at him and see a freak. But he's our child. . . ."

She looked up at him, her eyes red from crying but fierce as a storm. "Don't you think I *know* that?" she demanded hoarsely. "Do you think I'd reject him because of what he looks like?"

"I don't know," said Bruce. "With everything that's going on, I don't know what's going through your mind anymore."

"Bruce, maybe this isn't the best time," Samson began.

"No, Leonard, it's all right," Betty said waving him off. Slowly she rose from her wheelchair, walked gingerly to Bruce, and looked up at him. "Go ahead," she told him. "Say it."

He was unable to keep the hurt and anger, so long buried, out of his eyes. "You rejected me because of what I looked like. When Leonard performed the merge, you stayed away. It took you a long time to accept me. You might reject Brett now and regret it months later, but he won't be around anymore, like I was. . . ."

"You're wrong, Bruce," she said flatly. "I kept you at a distance, yes. But it wasn't as if you were simply the man I married in a new package. Your personality changed as well. You weren't the man I fell in love with—not at first, at any rate. And I admit, your . . . body . . . intimidated me. I'm not an Amazon, Bruce. I think I should be forgiven that. But none of that—*none* of that—has anything to do with this. Don't try to punish me because of whatever resentment you may still have."

"You cursed me out because of what I did to you. I didn't want any of that to weigh in decisions about the baby."

"I was in hysterics, Bruce," she said tiredly. "We don't always say what we mean, even under the best of circumstances. Hell, if the Hulk really smashed everyone he said he'd smash, the entire continent would be a wasteland of pulped bodies. What I'm saying, Bruce, is . . . he's my child. Maybe . . . I dunno . . . maybe you're right. Maybe his appearance might have . . . might have put me off. Made me afraid to love him. But, Bruce, I held Ross in my arms as he died. I don't want to have to go through that again. God, that sounds self-centered, doesn't it?"

"No," he said with great tenderness.

She rested her head against his chest and said, "Bruce, I don't care if his skin is gray or aquamarine . . . if he's got three heads . . . if he's got wings and a tail. He's my child, as much as he is yours. I don't want to have another baby die a meaningless death—to live a pointless life. There has to be some greater reason for this to have happened than simple cruelty."

Suddenly one of the residents burst in. Without preamble, he said, "Baby Banner. Blood pressure dropping, cardiac arrhythmia . . ."

"Let's go," said Sorrento to Strange and Thomas. Without saying anything more they went quickly into the OR, leaving the issue unresolved.

After a moment of silence, Betty stepped back and said, "Bruce, whatever decision you make, I'll support."

"Thank you, Betty," he said gratefully.

And in a flat voice, she added, "If you botch it up, I will kill you." It was clear from her tone that there was no hyperbole in the choice of words.

Chapter 16

A fairly old car pulled up to the hospital parking garage. The attendant stepped out of the booth and pointed to a sign that read, SORRY: FULL.

The car didn't move.

The attendant walked over to the driver's side and rapped on the window. It rolled down and the smiling face of an elderly bearded man peered through.

"Sorry, sir," said the attendant. "Things have been kind of crazy around here. We're parked solid."

"That's all right," said the old man, and he stepped out of the car. He patted the attendant on the shoulder and then started to walk away.

"Sir! You can't just leave it here!"

"I don't need it anymore. Keep it."

"Sir," and he grabbed the old man by the arm, "I have to insist . . ."

The old man pivoted and slugged the attendant. He dropped like a stone.

"No. *I* have to insist," replied the old man. He brushed his hands off and headed toward the hospital main entrance.

* * *

"No pulse!" called out one of the surgeons. "No rhythm!" And the steady, unchanging tone from the monitoring devices sounded through the OR.

"Start him on eppy!" snapped Sorrento.

"We're losing him," Strange said neutrally, looking down at the tiny patient who weighed no more than a couple of pounds. "His body's shutting down."

"What would you have me do, *Doctor*?" Sorrento demanded.

"I think it's about to be taken out of your hands," said Strange.

The OR doors burst open. The Hulk strode in, the gamma gun under his arm.

"Get him out of here!" snapped Sorrento to the other doctors in the room.

They stared at the Hulk. He stared back.

"Sir," one said to Sorrento, "with all due respect, you've gotta be kidding."

"This is wrong!" Dr. Thomas spoke up. "It's unethical and immoral!"

"I'll have your license, Strange!" Sorrento told him. "*You* could stop him!"

"Step aside, Doctor," Strange told him.

Sorrento started to object when suddenly his legs began moving of their own accord. Without intending to do so, he made way for the Hulk.

"Clear them out, Stephen! Hurry!" snapped Banner as the gamma gun whined to life. "I'm going to narrow focus as much as I can, but if there's free-floating gamma particles here, I don't want anyone else to catch any!"

"You heard the man," said Strange. "Everyone out."

Most left of their own accord. Strange only had to "push" a couple. Meantime, Bruce saw that a pale light had enveloped Brett, a pale light that seemed to be originating from Strange.

"He's in stasis, Bruce," said Strange, "but that can only perpetuate his condition, not cure it."

"Understood," said Bruce. "I presume you can protect yourself from the radiation."

Strange wasn't entirely able to keep the disdain out of his voice. "Oh, please . . . that goes without saying."

"All right . . ." He tossed a look up toward the observation booth. Betty and Samson were there, Betty with her eyes closed, rocking slowly, hands clasped.

She was praying.

Fat lotta good that's done so far, thought the Hulk cynically, even as he aimed the gamma gun. "All right, Stephen, here we go. Shut down the light and watch the monitors."

The pale, unearthly light faded, and Brett Banner proceeded to die.

Betty opened her eyes to slits and watched.

Bruce punched in a last adjustment and fired the gun.

Reflexively, Betty plugged her ears. Part of her was braced for the possibility of suddenly finding herself at ground zero if the thing blew up. She wondered if she would have time to be aware of it before she became a blackened piece of toast.

But there was no bright flash, no deafening explosion. Instead there was a loud humming and a faint sort of ticking noise as the gamma gun activated and fired.

A low-level bombardment of rads filled Brett Banner's body. Bruce was operating largely on guesswork, having calculated the degree of "hit" that he'd taken in the gamma explosion that had given the Hulk form. After that, he'd tried to calculate some sort of appropriate percentage to use on Brett, taking into account the far greater proximity, the child's relative lack of mass, and whatever other variables he could allow for. Bottom line, though, was that this was a best-guess scenario. He could practically feel Betty's gaze drilling into the nape of his neck, and didn't want to deal with the possibility that his best might not be good enough.

"Talk to me, Stephen."

"Still nothing," said Strange calmly. He had taken paddles and was rubbing them together to generate an electrical field.

Banner upped the intensity by a tenth of a percent.

Strange applied the paddles to the baby's chest and triggered them. A shock blasted through the infant's body, lifting him slightly off the table.

Watching from above, Betty gasped. Leonard Samson, who a year before had been watching Betty herself in similar dire straits, took her hand in his. "Steady," he said.

"Still nothing. Going again," said Strange, and he triggered a second shock.

The line on the heart monitor jumped and started to beep in a rapid series of bounces.

"We've got rhythm," Strange told him.

"We've got music," Banner replied, trying to take the edge off his growing concern. He wasn't sure what he should be looking for, how long he should be doing what he was doing. What if Sorrento was right? Hell, there was no "what if." Sorrento *was* right. The Hulk had taken his son's life into his own huge green hands, and there was every likelihood that he'd . . .

"Bruce," said Strange, and for the first time there was a touch of uncertainty in his voice. "Bruce, he's growing."

Strange was right.

Brett's mass was increasing. Before their eyes, the unconscious child's body was becoming larger, more substantial. The soft shape of his head firmed up, his arms became fleshier, the ribbon of veins that had been visible vanished. A thin fuzz of gray hair started to develop on his head.

"Shut it down, Bruce."

"But . . ."

"*Shut it down!*" ordered Strange.

Banner immediately complied. He hadn't been certain what precisely he'd been looking for to indicate that the experiment was a success, but this certainly seemed to be it. "What are his vitals?"

"Steady and strong," Strange said, checking all the monitoring devices in rapid succession.

The baby continued to grow. More hair was coming in, and there was greater and greater definition of his musculature.

Up in the observation room, Betty whispered, "Oh my God," visions of a giant rampaging baby deliriously dancing through her mind.

"Bruce." Strange sounded a bit apprehensive.

"I know, I know! I shut the gamma gun down, though! This is . . . this is I don't know what . . ."

"Can you drain some of the residual radiation off him?"

"Absolutely. Give me about two months to reconfigure the gun, we'll be all set," said the Hulk sarcastically.

Strange was about to reply when, suddenly, Brett's size and shape stabilized. His skin was still gray, and he was considerably larger than he had been moments ago. But other than his hue, there was nothing especially abnormal looking about him. Strange quickly weighed and measured him, and found that he was a hefty (but not freakish) ten pounds, two ounces, and twenty-three inches long.

"Heart rate normal. Breathing normal. BP normal." Strange nodded approvingly. "Congratulations, Dr. Banner. You appear to be a father."

Bruce gasped, unsure whether to laugh or cry, and ultimately making a noise that was a combination of both. He turned and looked up at Betty—but she wasn't there. Nor was Samson.

Then the door to the OR opened and Betty walked in. She was wearing surgical garb, a mask over her face. Samson was dressed likewise.

Bruce took her by the shoulders. "He's going to be fine, Betty."

"I know. I saw. I . . ." She wiped tears from her eyes and embraced him. When she did, she sighed. "Ohhh, hell . . . I'd gotten used to being able to put my arms completely around you."

"That's okay. We'll make do." He kissed her on the top of her head and then gestured toward the newborn table that Brett was lying on, sleeping. "Care to see your son?"

She moved toward him. His skin was still gray, although a much lighter shade than it had been previously. She wondered what that meant, if anything. "Well," she said after a moment, "at least he won't have to worry about suntans, huh?"

"Or about having a mother who loves him?"

"No," she agreed. "No . . . that won't have to be a concern of his at all." Through gloved hands she stroked his sleeping face. "I've got to admit, when he was growing there, for a moment . . ."

"I know, I know. I thought we were trapped in a Disney movie."

"I hate to say anything that will shatter the mood of ragged cheer," said Samson, "but, you know, we commandeered an operating room, pretty much threw out the personnel, took it upon ourselves to implement an unorthodox—let's face it, unprecedented—medical procedure on a preemie. People, we're not operating in a vacuum here. There's going to be hell to pay."

"Hell can bill me," replied the Hulk.

The old man from the parking garage walked past two security guards. They tried to stop him, first with gentle commands and then with reluctant force.

One guard wound up with two busted ribs and a concussion. The other ended up in traction for three months.

The old man headed upstairs, laughing softly to himself.

Samson and Strange were in Sorrento's office, trying to smooth things over. Their efforts were well-intentioned but didn't seem to be going anywhere, because the hospital personnel were hopping mad.

The chief of staff, Dr. Eisenberg, said furiously, "We have bent over backwards for you people! Cleared out the place, hired guards, withstood a media circus . . ."

"I know," said Samson, trying to be placating. "And don't think we don't appreciate it."

"Appreciate it?! I don't think you're even aware of it! And what do you do in return? Bully our people! Act like we're hired help! What kind of crap is this?" He stabbed a finger at them. "I know the deal with you people, you supertypes. Some people call you 'Marvels.' Well, maybe you've started believing your own press! Maybe you think you can go where you want, whenever you want, and do whatever the hell you want. Well, I'm here to tell you that it's not so! Not in the real world and not in this hospital!"

Except for one nurse, there were no hospital personnel on duty in the nursery. Then again, there was only one child there, and he seemed in fairly safe hands. The nurse kept a safe distance, still a little disconcerted by the child's unique skin tone.

Betty was sitting in a large rocking chair, holding a bottle to Brett's mouth. There were only a couple of ounces of formula in it, and it had taken a bit of effort to get him started. But once he had begun, he did so with some enthusiasm.

"Smile, honey."

She looked up and blinked against the flash of a bulb. Bruce lowered a Polaroid camera that a nurse had lent him.

"Oh, God, Bruce, I look terrible," she protested. "You're cruel and heartless, and I hate you forever."

With a soft whine of the camera's motor, the picture slid out the front. He examined it. "Hmm. You're right. You're all faded and streaky." He held it up.

"Wait until it finishes developing, O scientific genius."

"If you insist." He slid it into his pocket and watched her feed him. "We were talking about breast-feeding, as I recall."

"Well," said Betty after a moment. "I, uhm . . . I know we were talking about it. I was even looking forward to it. But I figured maybe we should wait a little just to make sure that . . . well . . . you know."

"I know what? Betty, what's the probl—" And then he realized. "Oooohh . . . you're worried about the strength factor."

"Right. We don't know how much of his daddy's power he inherited. And if his little jaws are . . . *ahem* . . . well . . . I'm just a little reluctant to put any delicate portions of my anatomy within biting distance until I'm a little more comfortable with the situation."

"Well, that's fine, honey. I mean, let's be philosophical. If God had meant women to nurse, he'd have given them glass breasts and rubber nipples, right?"

She chuckled, which shook up Brett. There was the slightest hint of confusion in his eyes, as if he were concerned that the world was rumbling around him.

"Bruce . . ." And she looked up at him lovingly. "Anything I said that might have hurt your feelings . . . I'm sorry. I just want you to know that . . ."

"I know, and I'm sorry, too, because what you said was right. I did 'do this to you.' "

"We'll deal with it, Bruce, just like I've said before. As long as we're together . . . we can handle it."

"Now, that's such a sweet thing," came an elderly voice.

Bruce turned to see a familiar person standing in the door. "Dr. Trotter!"

The nurse gestured briskly. "Sir, you can't be in here. Parents only. Please, go around and look through the glass."

Trotter didn't move. He just stood there, leaning on his cane. He was staring, enraptured, at Brett.

But Betty, in turn, was gaping at Trotter. She stared at him, scrutinizing his face, studying his eyes, the shape of his nose . . .

"Betty, this is Dr. Trotter. He . . . well, he cured me, at least for a time. We had a little problem, Doctor."

"Yes, so I see. This can be dealt with. Anything can be dealt with. Tell me . . . may I hold the baby?"

"Sir, I *really* have to insist," the nurse said more firmly.

"Oh, nurse, would it really hurt all that much?" asked Bruce. "We'd get him a gown, a mask . . . just be for a moment . . ."

"Keep him away," whispered Betty. "Keep him away from me . . . from Brett . . ."

"What?" Bruce was puzzled. "Betty, what's . . . ?"

"Bruce, don't you see? How can you not see?"

"See what?" He looked from Betty to Trotter and back again. "Betty, what's wrong?"

"Your wife, she doesn't like me, Doctor," said Trotter, sounding both disappointed and mildly amused.

"Betty, I don't understand what—"

And in a horrified, frightened whisper she said, "It's you. He's you."

"What?"

"He looks just like you . . . the way you used to look, except much, much older. Your voice, your mannerisms . . ."

"Betty, are you *insane?* This is Dr. Amos Trotter. . . ."

The nurse took Trotter firmly by the arm and said, "Sir, you're upsetting the patients! Don't make me have to—"

Trotter never even glanced at her. He swept her aside, sending her clattering over empty cribs. She struck her head on the ground and lay silent.

Bruce's jaw dropped in astonishment. "What's going *on* around here?! Dr. Trotter—!"

"Actually," said the old man, "I'm afraid I've got some bad news." And now his voice no longer had the pleasant, slightly Yiddish tremor to it. It sounded hale and vital and tinged with menace. "I'm afraid you've never actually met Dr. Trotter. The doctor is, I fear, dead. I killed him some months ago, when I first arrived, and took his place. We bore a passing resemblance to each other, and with my hair and beard, well . . . it's not difficult to pass yourself off as a recluse whom no one has seen for quite some time."

The Hulk stepped in between Trotter and Betty, casting a glance at the nurse to make sure she was okay. She moaned softly, which was going to have to be good enough for now. He looked back to "Trotter." "*Who are you?*"

"He's you!" Betty said, clutching Brett to her tightly. "I'm telling you, Bruce, he's you, *he's you!*"

The Hulk took a step forward, staring in disbelief. "But . . . but that can't . . . not unless . . ."

And Trotter began to change form.

His shoulders broadened, his legs became larger, more muscled, and then impossibly muscled. His clothes ripped, his face began to darken, his skin turning green. But not the emerald green of the Hulk; rather, more of a dull olive. His head got wider, his brow distending, pockmarks appearing on his forehead and all over his skin. As his clothes tore away, they revealed that under them he wore tight blue pants, a blue tunic, and scalloped metal wristbands.

He grunted from the stress of the change, but made no sound other than that. And within seconds, Bruce Banner was gawking at the last individual he ever wanted to see again. A face that had haunted his dreams from the moment that he'd first confronted it.

The face of his future self. The incarnation of Lord Acton's stated truism, "Power tends to corrupt, and absolute power corrupts absolutely." The Maestro of a time yet to come, of a people ruled by fear and a world devastated by war. A time where only strength mattered—and since he was the strongest one there was, then he mattered above all.

He sneered at the Hulk, yellow teeth drawn back in a contemptuous smile.

"Give me the child," said the Maestro. "Or die. It makes no difference to me."

Chapter 17

"Look, Doctor," said Stephen Strange, rubbing the bridge of his nose tiredly and trying to come up with some way of resolving things. "The bottom line is that one of the children lived. That has to count for something."

"The bottom line, Doctor, is that your people did whatever they felt like, regardless of chain of command or—"

"Look, we're going in circles here," Samson pointed out. "Fighting doesn't accomplish anyth—"

That was when the walls and floor shook with such violence that both Strange and Samson were thrown from their seats.

The Maestro circled warily, the Hulk standing his ground. "Betty, get out," Bruce said.

"No, Betty, stay," purred the Maestro. "It's been ages."

Betty, for her part, couldn't get out. Getting to the door meant getting past the Maestro, and he was too quick, too surefooted to allow that to happen.

"What are you doing here, Maestro? How did you survive?"

For the first time a flicker of astonishment moved across the Maestro's face. "Now, how did you know who I am? I mean, that Betty would have the intuition to see me for what I was . . . that concerned me enough to stay clear. But how do you know the name that I've taken? How do you know I'm called 'Maestro'? We've never met before."

The Hulk, in surprise, started to reply, but then he clamped his mouth shut. However minimal it was, he had some degree of upper hand against his future self. Saying anything would only serve to provide the Maestro information, and that Bruce could see no reason for doing.

"Oh, all right, don't tell me. Just give me the child . . . Brett, did you say his name was? I like the sound of that."

"You can't have him."

"Oh, come now, Bruce! I am the father, after all . . . as much as you. Don't I get visitation rights?" He paused. "No?" he prompted, sounding disappointed. "Oh . . . very well, then."

And with no further warning, he launched himself at the Hulk.

Betty screamed as the Maestro slammed into Bruce, driving him back through a wall. The entire floor shuddered from the impact.

The Hulk warded off the first punch, but the second roundhouse from the Maestro tagged him squarely in the jaw. He went down, tried to get up, but the Maestro's assault was quick, vicious, and merciless. Blow after blow landed on the Hulk's head and upper shoulders. He tried to ward it off, but the Maestro was wasting no time.

He lashed out as best he could, but the Maestro caught his arm, whipped it around, and twisted brutally.

There was an audible snap, and the Hulk howled, twisting in pain from the dislocated shoulder. A nauseating thought was that he'd gotten off lucky; the last time, the Maestro had broken his neck.

The Maestro didn't hesitate. He grabbed Banner up in his powerful hands, twisted quickly, and hurled the Hulk through the nearest window. Glass shattered as the Hulk crashed through and plummeted to the ground three stories below. The fall wasn't designed to kill him. No fall could do that. It was just to get him out of the way for a moment.

Betty, meantime, was out the door, dashing for a corridor. And suddenly the wall in front of her exploded as the Maestro appeared in front of her, cutting her off.

She tried to run the other way but didn't get more than a step before the Maestro snagged her arm, spun her around.

"*No! Noooo!*" Betty howled. "*Brett, no!*"

He snatched the child out of her arms. "I'll do right by him, Betty," snarled the hideous travesty that had once been Bruce Banner. "Believe me, he's better off with me than you."

"Give him back! *Give him back!*" Betty clawed at the Maestro's hair. He shoved her away, strands of his gray mane snagged in her fingers. She fell to the floor, sobbing, crying Brett's name.

The Maestro had the cane shoved through his belt. Now he pulled it out, gripping the gleaming diamond-shaped object that was atop it. In his other arm he cradled Brett, who was whimpering in confusion.

"I could kill you," he rumbled. "But I'd rather let you live, knowing you'll never see him again. A mild payback, bitch, for your betrayal."

"*I never betrayed you! Never—!*"

He said darkly, "Don't worry. You will."

Then he heard commotion from either direction. From the left, the Hulk was smashing his way back in. From the right he heard other voices—voices he hadn't heard in decades but were still immediately recognizable.

The talisman on his cane glowed, a rainbow of colors coalescing around him. Brett began to wail more loudly, frightened by the noise of the air and the shouting of his mother.

From around the corner came Doc Samson and Dr. Strange. Exploding through the far wall came Dr. Bruce Banner.

Too late.

The Maestro's form began to dissolve, breaking down into an assortment of colors. He laughed as he vanished, saying, "Well, well! A regular doctor's convention! A pity we can't stay!"

"*Stop him!*" Betty called out.

Like the Cheshire Cat, the only thing left of the Maestro was his demented smile. And a second later, with a roaring of air and a final, brief cry of an infant, he was gone.

For a moment, no one moved.

"Impossible," breathed Strange. "It's in my sanctum . . . how could . . ."

Still disbelieving what had just happened, Betty passed her hand through the air. "Bring him back," she whispered, and then louder, agonized, "*Bring him back!*"

"What happened?" demanded Samson. "What the hell happened here?!"

In quick, short strokes, Bruce outlined exactly that. Samson's eyes grew wide as the Hulk told them the identity of Brett's kidnapper. Bruce had told him months ago of his monstrous future counterpart, and the traumatic events surrounding their previous encounter.

"All right . . . nobody panic," began Dr. Strange.

Betty looked ready to slug him. "Don't tell me not to panic! Some bizarre version of Bruce just kidnapped my baby! I'll panic if I want to! I'm going after him! Wherever he went, I'll—"

"No," said the Hulk firmly. "I'll go after him. I know him. I can handle him. We just need to figure out how and where—"

"The how I can tell you," said Strange, frowning. He was making arcane gestures in the air, and something popped into the air in front of him. It was a glittering jewel.

"That was his!" said Bruce in confusion. "It was on top of his cane. Where—?"

"From my sanctum sanctorum," Strange told them. "It's called the Timeond. It's a mystic talisman. I acquired it from a rather odd silver-haired gentleman in a trenchcoat. . . . It's too involved, I'll tell you later. It opens portals through dimensions." He looked at the Hulk significantly. "It was the source I drew upon to send you to the Crossroads."

That brought the Hulk up short. The time of the Crossroads was a very confusing period in his life. Given over entirely to savage, undiluted berserker rage, the Hulk had literally become too dangerous to remain on Earth. So Dr. Strange had sent him to an interdimensional axis point called the Crossroads. From there, the mindless Hulk had gone from one world to another, seeking a place that he could consider home. He never found one, and eventually circumstances arose that ended up delivering him back to Earth.

"How did the Maestro get his hands on it?" asked the Hulk.

"I don't know," Strange admitted in frustration. "I thought somehow he had absconded with it from my sanctum. But I just recalled it from there; it was untouched."

"Can we use it to go after him?"

"We can open up the portal, yes, but trying to determine from which direction he came is more problematic. . . ."

His voice trailed off as he stared at Betty's hands. With catlike speed he reached over and grabbed her by the wrist, turning her hand over. He saw the gray white strands entangled in her fingers.

"His hair?" he asked.

"Y . . . yes," said Betty, confused. "I . . . tried to stop him. . . . I know it was idiotic, but . . ."

"Not only was it not idiotic, but it may also have given us our one shot." He took several strands from her, held them in one hand. Then he put the Timeond into the other and brought them together. His hands flared in a burst of light that hurt anyone who was looking directly at it. "A simple spell should enable us to track him now, back to whatever dimensional point he originated from."

"All right . . . I'm ready," said the Hulk. "Send me after him."

"Us," Samson said firmly.

"No, Leonard," the Hulk said with equal conviction. "Stephen has to stay here to keep the portal open, and I need you to stay here as well. We don't know what's waiting on the other side. You're the only one besides me who knows about the Maestro. If I don't make it back—if he's left some sort of booby trap behind, or if things don't pan out—I'm going to need somebody to be able to come in after me. And besides, if for some reason the Maestro comes back, I want you here to protect Betty."

Samson didn't look particularly thrilled. "All right, Bruce. Twenty-four hours, but no more. Then I'm going in, too."

"With any luck, it won't come to that. Stephen, fire it up."

Strange nodded, continuing the incantation he had already begun. The amulet at his neck, the eye of Agamotto, opened, and light radiated forth. Samson, Bruce, and Betty shielded their eyes as the air in front of them rippled, colors splitting apart and shimmering.

Bruce stood in front of it, squinting, as the air became a dazzling, multicolored whirlpool. With a high-pitched whine that seemed to shimmer with power, the beam from the Eye of Agamotto stabbed through, vanishing into midair.

"Follow the light!" shouted Strange above the roar of the air. "The beam will guide you to him! Take you down the right road! And be careful! The Crossroads is a temporal nexus! Time doesn't pass there the same way it does here, and strange things can happen! Do not lower your guard for a moment!"

"How does he get back?" cried Betty.

"Through his original point of entry! So remember where you come through, Bruce!"

"I will! I'll come back with Brett, and with the Maestro's Time-ond!"

"Just get Brett and leave!" Betty urged him. "Forget about the Maestro!"

He gave her a desperate look. "I can't! You know that! If we leave things as they are, he could come back at any time, try and take Brett again for whatever the reason he took him in the first place!"

"All right, all right! Just . . ." She couldn't find the words. As the colors danced in front of them, the roar of the air growing ever louder, she held him as tightly as she could. He leaned down and she kissed him, her mouth wet with tears.

"Bring him back," she whispered into his ear. "Don't let it all have been for nothing."

"Piece of cake," he told her.

He turned to Samson, who put a firm hand on his shoulder. "Twenty-four hours, Bruce!"

"Be back in less than one, Leonard! Stephen . . . keep a light burning for me in the dimensional window!"

Then he turned to the portal, this time not shielding his eyes or looking away at all. He took a deep breath.

I don't know why this has happened. I don't know why most of the things in my life happen. Maybe none of us does. But I know this: I won't let it all be for nothing. God, if you're listening . . . just this once . . . either work with me, or ignore me. Just don't make it any harder than it is, okay?

And with that silent, if somewhat sardonic, prayer, Robert Bruce Banner leaped into the nexus, and vanished from time and space.

PART THREE

FEARS

In the highest tower of the green castle, which looked down upon the darkened city called Dystopia, the one-eyed, wizened man who was known simply as the Minister gazed upon the city with unease.

He paced his room, his long red robes sweeping along the floor. His face came to an almost perfect triangular point. The pale skin was leathery, and his right eye was gone. He'd lost it years before when the Maestro had demanded it as a show of loyalty. It had since been replaced by a glowing red mechanical lens that was—the Minister hated to admit—infinitely more efficient. He had developed it over the years, improved on its abilities. Things that he had learned in his studies, in his delving into all manner of laws both natural and unnatural, had honed his skills until he could perceive things beyond normal human vision.

Even things he did not want to see.

He turned his attention to the skies.

His right eye sensor saw things that no one—not even the Maestro—could see. Ripples in the sky, shades of colors beyond the range of normal vision. Shadings and twistings that had no business being there, and were an ill omen. A very ill omen.

Now—now with the Great Conquest about to be embarked upon—it seemed that somehow, impossible as it might be, the forces of nature were aware. Temporal ripplings crackled through the skies, imperceptible to anyone else but the Minister.

He did not like how this was shaping up. No. No, he did not like it at all. . . .

Chapter 18

The savage Hulk sat at the Crossroads, stewing.

Above him, hands pointed in different directions, indicating alternate roads that he could pursue. At the moment, however, he didn't feel like going down any of them.

Much of his understanding was clouded. He didn't fully comprehend how he had come to this particular situation. There were brief, tantalizing memories dancing at the fringes of his mind. But nothing that he could really hang on to, or analyze. Indeed, he had only recently started recapturing any degree of what could laughingly be referred to as "intellect." But it was only a minuscule portion, not good for much except firing his fury or stoking the flames of his anger.

He had seen places he did not comprehend. And there were voices whispering to him, bizarre little aspects of his mind that advised him or spoke to him about things that mattered little to him . . . or else things that he didn't want to dwell on.

So there he sat, his back leaning against the Crossroads signpost. Beyond the roads that stretched in all directions, there was nothing. Just emptiness, a vast and endless void that seemed to moan at him. Wind whistled past constantly; he was never sure of where it came from, or where it was going. It was simply there.

Just like him.

Then he heard something . . . saw something . . .

A beam of light arcing just above him. It wavered for a moment and then bent off and went down one particular direction.

But the Hulk didn't care about that direction particularly. What interested him, instead, was the origin. For something about the light stirred one of those fragments of memory that he'd been unable to fully grasp.

He had seen it before—something very much like it—and his fractured brain began to associate it with someone . . . a man . . . a man in a red cape . . .

"Magician," he growled, a dim and distant hate beginning to bubble within him. Yes. Yes, that was it. The magician . . . the one who had condemned him to this nonplace. That light had the feel, the stink, of the magician.

Possibilities lurched into his tortured mind, presented themselves. Gates of logic swung on rusty hinges.

The light might mean the magician . . . and the magician might mean freedom . . . and revenge . . .

"Smash them," he rumbled as he lumbered to his feet and headed in the direction that the light had come from. "Smash them all."

Memories of the place tugged at Bruce Banner's mind.

He viewed the Crossroads as if he were looking through gauze. His recollections of it were filtered through the fogged prism of his time as the mindless, berserk Hulk. He couldn't recall details so much as sensations. How things had made him feel rather than what had actually happened to him.

The time in the Crossroads had been one of the loneliest, bleakest periods of his existence. In a way, he was glad he didn't remember much of it.

Above him glistened the light from the eye of Agamotto. Ironic, he mused, that it had been the power of Dr. Strange that had consigned him to this place. And now he was allied with the mage, counting on Strange's power to see him through. Amazing what a jump of a few hundred points in IQ could bring about.

The road he trod was fairly narrow and, oddly enough, a pale pink. There were other roads as well, a variety of colors, winding above and below him, fading off in different directions. Winds shifted and seemed to take form, shimmering in different aspects before vanishing once more.

Far below him, where nothingness lay, the winds seemed to be the strongest. He didn't particularly like the looks of that, and he had a feeling that falling off the road would be an extremely bad idea. So he watched his step.

He followed the trail of light, and then he felt the road shaking slightly beneath his feet in time to his steps. Was the pathway through the dimensions that rickety?

He stopped walking.

The road, however, continued to shake in a slow, steady rhythm. As if something very massive, very heavy, was coming his way.

Then he heard a growl, building into a roar, and squinted into the distance. Something was coming up on him fast, a green juggernaut that had spotted him and was picking up steam with every step.

"Aw no . . . it can't be," he said.

It was the savage Hulk—Banner himself, from the time when he was a mindless brute, trapped in the Crossroads.

It didn't seem at all possible, except that Strange's cautions about temporal flux suddenly came back to him. The warning that time didn't necessarily pass normally there.

"You," growled the Hulk, "you are here . . . to destroy Hulk . . . but Hulk will smash you . . ."

Banner took a cautious step backward. There was simply no comparison between the robot approximation from Chicago and this formidable creature which stood before him. The savage Hulk radiated undiluted power.

And Banner was at a serious disadvantage, for his earlier incarnation had an unlimited capacity for strength-generating anger. Banner, however, had a built-in flaw: if he became too angry, too out of control, he would very likely revert to his helpless human form. In a pitched battle against a frenzied, monstrous opponent, a normal Bruce Banner—as angry as his mind might be—would last no time at all.

"Hulk," he said as firmly and forcefully as he could. "Stop. Stop where you are."

His monstrous counterpart stopped in his tracks. He growled, his head tilting slightly, as he studied Banner.

"I don't want to fight," he said. "I'm not here to hurt you. I'm just . . . passing through."

"You are . . . magician's friend?" rumbled the Hulk.

Banner let out a slight sigh of relief. He was going to be able to communicate with his doppelgänger. Perhaps there would be a minimum of problem with this after all. "Yes, I'm the magician's fr—"

"*Hulk hates magician! Hulk will smash magician's friend!*" And with that, the Hulk of the past charged his future incarnation.

Banner tried to leap over the Hulk's head, but the Hulk was moving too quickly. He slammed into Banner, tackling him around the waist. The two of them went down in an emerald tangle of arms and legs.

"Get off me, you green oaf!"

The Hulk roared in his face in response. Banner never realized until just that moment that the Hulk's breath was nothing to write home about. He wondered why no one had ever mentioned that to him. Then again, who'd have the nerve?

A second later a massive green fist drove down toward Banner's head. He yanked clear at the last second, drove a leg up, and flipped the Hulk over his head. The Hulk landed heavily but was on his feet in a second, moving with a speed belied by his bulk.

The Hulk swung a roundhouse that Banner dropped below. Banner lashed out with a leg, knocking the Hulk's feet out from under him and sending him heavily to the roadway once more. Banner leaped forward, landed atop him, driving his knees into the Hulk's chest. There was a grunt from the Hulk, and then Banner swung his palms together on either side of the Hulk's head, boxing his ears. The Hulk roared, disoriented, his head ringing.

Banner turned and ran as fast as he could. His legs pistoned, driving him forward, as he followed the trail of the light.

The road was shaking violently under him, but he couldn't be sure if the impacts were coming from his own feet or the Hulk's in pursuit. Banner risked a quick glance over his shoulder.

No sign of the Hulk.

Just for a moment he allowed himself an inward sigh of relief. Maybe whatever temporal currents were surging through the nexus had swept the Hulk away into some alternate—

The Hulk crashed into him from overhead, both massive feet driving into the small of Banner's back.

The wind was knocked completely out of him as he was slammed to the road. He hit with tremendous force, and for one horrific moment he thought he saw a crack ribboning out in front of him.

Above him the light continued to gleam . . . but began to fade just slightly. Colors from all around began to swirl around it, as if the temporal energies were beginning to assail it.

And then a fierce kick in the head spun his senses, and Bruce Banner rolled off the edge of the road. The only thing that kept him from plummeting into the abyss was the desperate grip of his fingers. His legs pinwheeled in space, trying for purchase, finding none.

The Hulk crouched over him, bellowing, "Now! Now Hulk will smash you!"

"You green goofball!" Banner shouted back at him. "Don't you understand anything? I'm you! *You!* I'm the Hulk, too!"

For a long moment, the Hulk paused, glowering down at the hanging Banner. Banner could actually see the Hulk's pea brain digesting the information, trying to understand it and cope with it.

"Green skin . . . is Hulk too?" he asked finally.

"That's right, yes!"

"Not anymore," grunted the Hulk, and he kicked Banner loose.

The instant Banner lost physical contact with the pathway, it was as if he had been sucked into a whirlpool.

The temporal energy whipped around him, spinning him. He felt reality shifting around him, completely disorienting him. He was yanked away, tumbling helplessly, away from the road. The winds howled around him. . . .

He struck something.

He hit it sideways, with his gut, and almost slid off it. But he managed to grab it and hold on, scrambling and hauling himself up.

It was a fragment of road, free-floating through the ether. A road had shattered somewhere, and this one piece of debris had, by luck, floated directly into the Hulk's path.

Finally, a break. Not much of one, but a break.

It was pale pink, just like the one that Banner had been on before. And it was . . .

Drifting downward. The winds were holding it aloft momentarily, but it was the most temporary of supports. Within minutes, perhaps even seconds, the pink platform that was his salvation could lose its bracing and fall off into the nothingness below.

Banner craned his neck and looked upward, saw the distant gleam of the light beam.

He had exactly one chance.

He crouched, preparing his leg muscles for what was possibly the single most important leap of his life. Nothingness yawned beneath him. Temporal insanity reigned around him.

Betty, he thought, and then leaped.

He arced higher and higher, approaching the road. He almost overshot it, but reached out and snagged it with one foot.

The road twisted.

It almost sent him tumbling off back into the temporal ether.

From behind him, the Hulk charged, uncaring about the road beneath his feet . . . uncaring about anything except getting his hands on his foe.

"No! Stop!" shouted Banner, knowing what would happen a second before it did. Because suddenly he understood just what it was he had landed on earlier. It had been a fragment of the very road that he was standing upon now. A fragment that had come from the road when it shattered—except that it hadn't yet . . .

But it did now.

Unable to take the stresses of both the temporal fluxes and the sheer pounding of the green gladiators, the area between the two Hulks splintered and fell apart, leaving them with a huge gap between them. Massive blasts of wind-that-was-not-wind ripped up through the chasm.

Uncaring of the strength of the gusts, the Hulk tried to vault the gap. He made it about halfway before the wind caught him. He roared in protest as he was carted away, driven higher, ever higher. There were networks of roads above, and that's where he seemed to be headed.

The road in front of Bruce Banner started to crumble as well.

Bruce ran, ran for his life, for Brett's life, his arms pumping. The cracks spread out in front of him and he covered the distance as fast as he could. He had no idea how far he was supposed to go, or where his destination was. A minute, a year—he had no clue at all.

Then, suddenly, he saw it.

The road simply seemed to end a short distance in front of him. The air was shimmering, calling to him . . .

And then the road ahead of him cracked.

It split completely in half, snaking out in two different directions, each with its own closure point. The light path had shimmered out of existence. He was on his own.

"*Oh, hell!*" shouted Dr. Banner.

There were cracks everywhere now, throughout both roads, in both directions. Whatever had been set in motion could not be stopped now. Within seconds the entire road would be gone, and he had absolutely no time to decide which way to go, no guidance, nothing except gut instinct.

From somewhere in the distance, he heard the roar of his uncontrolled alter ego. Something deep within him wanted to respond in kind, but he shoved it away. He dove through the exitway to the right, once again breathing a quick prayer.

And once again, his prayer was answered by a deity obsessed with perverse humor.

Chapter 19

The Minister stepped out on his balcony, blinking against the sunlight of the new day.

There was no trace in the sky of the temporal surges he had detected the day before. Nevertheless, he could not shake the feeling of discomfiture.

The feeling that something new had been added into the mix. Something deadly. Something that could take the Great Conquest and turn it into a complete balls-up.

He could tell the Maestro about it, of course. But the Maestro had never been one for unsubstantiated intuitions. Anything that the Minister had to tell him had best be backed up by solid facts that could be examined clinically in the cold light of day. Unfortunately, the Minister had nothing like that.

He just had an uncomfortable feeling in his gut.

Below him, the main marketplace of Dystopia was coming to life. Dealers, traders, and marketeers of all types were hauling out their wares, imploring passersby and newcomers to come closer, give a look, make an offer; any offer would be entertained, discussed, worked out between friends. It was a fairly colorful agglomeration of tents, storefronts, and thrown-together stands. During its busiest times, the crowds were shoulder to shoulder (although naturally they managed to melt apart and make room if the Minister happened to walk among them).

His attention shifted in the direction of the Wastelands and he frowned. It was over there, he realized, that the heaviest concentration of . . . what*ever* it had been . . . seemed to coalesce.

But it was gone now. Gone, and the sun beamed down unrelentingly upon the Wastelands.

He didn't like it.

Not at all.

Old Boz had felt old since he was young.

His hair had thinned while he was still in his late teens, and whatever remained had gone gray by his late twenties. He had begun siring children when he was sixteen. Over a period of ten years, he fathered seven. During that time, two of them died. His wife had died giving birth to the last one, and over the next few years he had buried another three. By the time he was thirty-four, he looked fifty-four, and walked with his shoulders permanently stooped. There was a world-weariness about him. A sense that nothing new could faze him, no matter how hideous, for his life was nothing but a series of calamities.

The Wasteland was scorching hot, as usual. Boz had thought there would be a storm the night before. Certainly there was something in the air. But it had never quite broken completely. Now it was early morning, and Boz was preparing for another day of hard, backbreaking work. This day, he anticipated, would be much like those in the past, and a very close approximation of those in the future. Eventually those future days would not include him, and he wondered—not for the first time—if the Survivalist Encampment would be able to survive his passing.

They came to him for everything. For help with the crops, for personal matters. Everything. And he had no one to turn to. No one.

He checked the thin moisture recycling tube that led into his left nostril. It was firmly in place. The loose-fitting, simple day garment was draped over a chair. He slid his arms through the sleeve, felt the creaking in his joints.

Then there was a pounding at his door. He turned and saw one of the younger ones, a kid name Mazz. Mazz was barely thirteen. He looked twenty, and was already graying. The Wastelands did that to you: shortened your life. Some might call that a hardship. In some ways, it was the greatest blessing this world had to offer.

"Hail, Mazz," Boz said. "How does it go?"

Mazz skipped the entire traditional greeting. Instead he was chucking a thumb over his shoulder and saying urgently, "Boz, you've got to see this. You won't believe it."

There was very little Boz wouldn't believe. But he followed Mazz out.

They moved quickly across the fields. Boz glanced at them as they went past. The crops seemed to be coming in nicely, for once. That was a pleasing change of pace.

Far, far in the distance, the fortress of the Maestro loomed. It was a reminder of everything he was, and everything they were not. In many ways, Boz feared the notion of their becoming too successful. As long as they remained struggling farmers, eking out a living, then the Maestro would leave them relatively alone . . .

. . . relatively . . .

He winced, thinking of that day long ago, and pushed the memory away.

But if they became too successful—if they thrived, grew, developed much beyond what they were just now—then the Maestro would come in and take over. Would commandeer their resources, as he had other encampments, other endeavors. When the Maestro set his sights on you and decided that it was time to yield to his authority, then that was pretty much that.

Mazz was running ahead and Boz did everything he could to keep up. Ahead of them were the cliffsides, one of the few sources of shade in the Wasteland. And then Boz thought he saw something odd projecting from one of the rocky formations, about six feet above the ground. And it was clear that the projection was the source of Mazz's consternation, because the young man was standing under it and pointing urgently. Boz drew close—and blinked in surprise.

A green creature who bore a striking resemblance to the Maestro was hanging halfway out of the rock. His head, arms, and upper torso were visible. The rest of him was, somehow, *inside* the rock formation, as if he had grown out of it overnight. His eyes were closed, his jaw hanging slightly open. It was hard to tell if he was breathing or not.

"Oh, bugger," sighed Boz. "Not another one."

"Yeah, but I never seen one come here before. Whattaya think, Boz?" demanded Mazz.

Boz scratched his head. "I . . . don't know what to think. It's . . ."

The creature's eyes suddenly snapped open. He looked around in confusion. "Where am I?" he demanded.

Boz and Mazz drew back, too petrified to say anything.

It was at that moment that the creature seemed to notice his own condition. With a grunt of annoyance, he braced both hands against the cliffside and started to push off against it. The rock broke beneath him as he pulled out his waist and then kicked free completely. He skidded the six feet to the ground, and then staggered to his feet, dusting the rock powder off himself.

"Well, it should be easy enough remembering where I came through, right?" he said. They nodded but did not comprehend. Then his eyes narrowed as he stared at Boz. "Wait . . . I know you. Boz, right? Leader of the Wasteland Survivalists?"

Boz bobbed his head, still utterly perplexed. "How . . . how do you know me?"

"I was here. I was with the Maestro . . . the day he made off with your daughter. With Char."

Mazz, who was standing several feet back, looked with alarm at Boz. It was an unspoken rule in the Camp that no one ever mentioned Char. There was too much pain associated with her memory, and no one wanted to inflict that upon Boz.

Boz, admirably restrained, simply nodded. "I . . . remember that day. Remember it all too well. But I do not . . . do not remember you."

"I was right there, alongside the Maestro."

"He says he doesn't remember," Mazz said in a tone that was a little too sharp for comfort, considering who and what they were addressing. Boz shot him a silent look to remind him of that.

"Are you sure?"

And at that point, even Boz could no longer restrain himself. "Are you sent here to torment me? Is this some . . . some perverse jest on the part of the Maestro?"

The green newcomer looked confused. "I . . . don't underst—"

"Char is gone! Gone, those twenty long years ago when the Maestro took her! I never saw her again! My beautiful little girl, probably long dead from the 'attentions' of the Maestro! I don't know what you are, or who you are, but don't talk of her! I . . ." His eyes reddened, but he didn't seem to have enough moisture in his body to generate tears. More softly, he said, "I beg you . . . don't talk of her."

But much of what Boz had said, the green behemoth didn't seem to have heard. He was still working on a new piece of information.

"Twenty . . . *years*?" he said.

There was a long pause, where all three of them stood and

looked at each other, each trying to assess the other's reactions and comprehend their respective situations.

"I think . . . we should talk," said the Hulk.

Survivalists walked nervously past Boz's hut. Every so often someone would try to peer in before losing the nerve and quickly continuing on his or her way.

Inside the hut, the Hulk waved off the offer of water. It was generous, for that was a very precious commodity out here on the Wastelands. He was, in fact, parched, but couldn't bring himself to take anything that these poor people had.

Besides, he was too busy trying to cope with what he'd learned. Namely, that he had not arrived in the same time that he had first visited that era. That he was, instead, at a point twenty years after that, placing him roughly 110 years into the future from his point of origin.

"What about the Outlaws?" asked the Hulk. "What's happened to them? Where are they?"

Boz frowned, recalling. "I know of whom you're speaking. I always predicted they'd be nothing but trouble. It was around that same time, twenty years or so ago. Not much to tell, really. The Maestro's forces, led by the Maestro himself, finally managed to track them down in their underground lair. They killed them all, I think."

Bruce couldn't find his voice for a moment. "All?" he whispered.

"So I understand."

Bruce rose from the chair and stood at the doorway, staring out at the fields, watching the Survivalists toiling.

"Did you know them?" asked Boz.

How to explain?

Explain that twenty years ago, he had come into a world that he barely recognized. A world that had been ravaged by two more wars, including an atomic one. Wars that had wiped out every super-powered being on the face of the earth—except one. Robert Bruce Banner, for whom free-floating radiation was not a threat, but a treat.

But it had been a Robert Bruce Banner who was not the man he used to be. He had been driven to the edge of insanity by years of hurt, betrayal, and loss. And the radiation had changed him, mutated him still further . . . and had, apparently, driven him over that very edge upon which he had teetered for so long. While survivors of the wars had cowered in underground bunkers, he had been topside, fashioning Dystopia upon the ruins of what had once been—Banner believed—New York. He had built a power base for himself, ruling from on high like some demented Wizard of Oz. He had called himself the Maestro, and he had done whatever he wanted, wherever he wanted.

The leader of the underground dwellers had been the Hulk's onetime partner, Rick Jones, aged beyond belief. The field leader had been Rick's granddaughter, a flame-haired hellion named Janis. Their discovery of Dr. Doom's time machine had set everything into motion: They'd used the machine to go back in time and recruit Robert Bruce Banner in the battle against his future self.

The future in which the Maestro ruled had not necessarily been Bruce's own; in fact, the very action of bringing him forward had been enough to render it an alternate timeline, since the Maestro had no recollection of the confrontation in his own past. The battle had been devastating nonetheless, fought on a variety of levels, from the physical to the psychological. First the Maestro had crippled him, and then he had turned around and tried to recruit him as an ally.

Their final combat had been the worst. Smashing through Rick's trophy room, filled with artifacts from the bygone days of the great heroes, Rick had died, and Banner himself very nearly had as well. But he had tricked the Maestro, won through cunning where sheer physical strength had been insufficient. He had tricked the Maestro into stepping onto the platform for Doom's time machine, and sent him screaming back through time—back to the very instant of the original gamma-bomb explosion that had created the Hulk in the first place.

He'd placed the Maestro squarely at ground zero, too much force for even the Maestro to withstand. Even as, miles away, gamma rays had irradiated Bruce Banner and begun his long, tortured odyssey as the Hulk . . . at that same moment, the journey had ended as the Maestro was reduced to ashes.

So how in hell had the Maestro wound up in the maternity ward of the hospital? Why was he surprised that Banner knew who he was?

There was only one answer—a hideously simple one, really.

The Maestro whom he had originally faced had been part of an alternate timeline.

But where there was one timeline, there was potentially another. And another. Each with small variations, each coexisting on an interdimensional plane.

And this Maestro—this new one—was from another of those realities. This reality, to which the Hulk had now come. A reality in which his reign had continued unabated, the Outlaws' resistance ultimately futile.

"They must not have found the time machine," he whispered. "That was the key point—the difference in the realities. They never found Dr. Doom's time machine, never brought me forward—and the Maestro eventually caught up with them and slaughtered them all. He won. In this reality, the bastard won."

"I don't understand," said Boz.

There was no point in trying to explain it. He could barely fathom it himself. "*All* of them died? All the Outlaws? Are you sure?"

"That's what I hear. That's what we were told. Hard to say for sure."

And then the ground started to shake beneath him.

"What's that?" he asked.

"The riders. The Maestro's riders." Boz listened for a moment. "Not coming this way, by the sound of them. Running roughly parallel, I'd say. At first I thought you were one of them, although we couldn't glom at all how you'd gotten stuck in rock like that."

"It's kind of compli—" Then the full measure of what Boz had just said registered. "You thought I was . . . one of them? They . . . they look like me? How many of them . . . ?"

"Are there? Dunno. If you head up to the ridge you can catch a glimpse of 'em for yourself."

Moments later the Hulk lay atop the ridge, on his belly. Boz, who was next to him, had lent him a pair of binoculars, tinted against the glare of the sun.

There were about twenty or so riders, astride those huge outlandish mutated dogs that were the Maestro's mount of choice. They thundered across the plains, creating the vibrations that the Hulk had felt.

He couldn't believe what he was seeing.

They were him. They were all him.

Oh, they weren't identical by any means. Some were hairy, some smooth. Some were smaller, some larger, some with more pronounced brows, some smoother. One was very wrinkled. Another had veins that were oddly distended. Some had short hair in bowl cuts, others had long and flowing. One had a beard. One was bald. One even had skin that was rocky and fragmented, evocative of the Thing.

It was insane. It was completely and utterly insane.

"The riders of the darkness," Bruce whispered, as if concerned that they could hear him even though they were far off.

"What?" asked Boz.

"It's a poem," said Banner. "By Lawrence Durrell.

"So the riders of the darkness pass
On their circuit; the luminous island
Of the self trembles and waits,
Waits for us all, my friends
Where the sea's big brush recolors
The dying lives, and the unborn smiles."

"That's a poem?" asked Boz.

"Yes."

"It doesn't rhyme, and I don't understand it."

"Well, it's kind of like life that way. No rhyme or reason." He peered through the binoculars again. They were riding in the direction of the castle. "How long have they been around?"

"They've been building up in number slowly over the past two decades—ever since the fall of the Outlaws, in fact. Slow but steady. First one, then another, then more and more . . . there's maybe fifty or sixty of them by this point. All answerable to the Maestro— or the Maestro's son."

His voice barely a whisper, the Hulk said, "Son?"

"Oh yes. No one's ever known who the mother was. Probably one of the Maestro's chumlies."

"Was he . . . born . . . before or after the first of the riders started showing up?"

"Before. Shortly before."

"Green also?"

"No, oddly enough. Gray. Gray as slate."

And the unborn smiles. And although the Hulk already knew the answer, he said, "And . . . what's his name?"

Chapter 20

Brett."

Brett stopped walking the moment he heard the growling voice of his father. He turned and smiled at him. "Good morning, Father."

The Maestro put an affectionate arm around him. Brett was as powerfully built as one would expect. His face was slim and handsome, and had only one disconcerting feature: He had Betty's eyes. The Maestro found it annoying to have her eyes gazing at him from across the span of more than a century. But he had learned to live with it.

After all, it was the only "soft" thing about Brett. He had grown over the past twenty years into a powerful specimen. His chest was rather broad, his arms cabled with muscles. His waist was surprisingly narrow, but his legs were long and deceptively lean. He couldn't jump as high nor as far as his father, but he was a fleeter runner by half. The combination of the Maestro hurtling through the air and Brett charging at high speed on the ground was more than enough to intimidate any opponent. All in all, the disgusting presence of Betty Banner's genes in him didn't seem to have totally befouled his genetic makeup.

Two Hulks walked past in either direction, offering greetings to the Maestro. He acknowledged each of them in turn and then said briskly to Brett, "Have you had breakfast yet?"

"No, sir."

"Then join me." He clapped him on the back. "I want to talk about final details for the Great Conquest."

"It sounds very exciting."

"It is, Son. It is." The Maestro sighed. "In a way, I'm doing it for you."

"Me?" asked Brett. "Why?"

"I'll tell you at breakfast. Oh . . . check on the Minister, will you? I haven't seen him out and about yet, and I'd asked him to get back to me by this morning with that update on our breeding facilities. I don't need him lying about."

"Yes, Father."

"Good lad," said the Maestro, as Brett headed off down a corridor. He tried to imagine what his life would be like without his son. In many ways, he felt, Brett had kept him sane. Had kept him focused, clear in purpose, and ambitious. One can never grow complacent with a growing offspring around.

Why, he might not even have aspired to become the greatest conqueror in the history of the world if it hadn't been for Brett.

Yes, indeed. He had a lot to be thankful for.

The Minister heard a knock at his door. "Yes?"

"Minister? My father wishes to see you."

"My pardons," said the Minister, looking for reports that he had been in the middle of preparing. "I have been . . . indisposed. If you could, Brett, please tell him that I will be down momentarily."

There was a pause from the other side of the door as Brett obviously considered whether or not to make an issue of it. But then he said, "Very well. I will tell him so."

The Minister quickly finished with a few last-minute details. Then he glanced once more out the window . . .

And frowned.

Far in the distance, something was hurtling through the air. It had originated from the general area of the Wastelands. The Minister's right eye construct zoomed in on the object.

No, not an object. It was one of the Maestro's . . . cronies. He was garbed in the ragged clothing sported by Wastelanders. He was soaring quickly, angling down toward the city of Dystopia itself.

Now, that was mildly curious. The assorted Hulks who had been coming to join the Maestro one by one certainly had freedom to go wherever and do whatever they pleased. But why the Wastelands? That was such a godforsaken area.

Ah, well. The Hulks moved in mysterious ways. . . .

When Bruce Banner had been preparing to leave the encampment of the Survivalists, Boz had been helping him adjust the hood of his borrowed garments.

"You know," Boz had said, "up until the moment you saw the—what did you call them? the riders of the darkness—up until that moment, I had been concerned that you might be like them. One of them spying on us for some reason. But in your face, I scanned an expression of such loathing—such fear—I knew then that was not the case. You're not like them at all."

"The loathing you saw, Boz, was for what they were. The fear was the concern that I might someday become like that."

"That will not happen," Boz had told him. He had paused and then said, "Why are you here? Why have you come to us?"

The Hulk had studied him for a moment. "To do whatever I have to do. More than that, you don't need to know."

"I will make one request of you . . . in exchange for the clothes, although I know them to be meager. Please . . . if you find my daughter, Char, and she wishes to be freed of the Maestro . . ."

"Then free her?"

Boz had looked surprised. "Is that possible? That . . . had not occurred to me."

"Well, then what were you going to ask me to do?"

As if it should have been obvious, Boz had said, "I was going to ask you to . . . to end her misery."

"You mean . . ." The Hulk had been appalled. "You mean kill her?"

Boz had turned away. His back to the Hulk, he simply nodded quickly.

"It won't come to that. Trust me." And with that the Hulk had leaped heavenward, toward Dystopia.

Now, as he glided through the sky, having been propelled by his mighty leg muscles, the Hulk surveyed the lay of the land below him. He needed a relatively deserted area to go to ground, and he spotted one at the outskirts of town. No one below seemed to notice him in passing. Either that or, with all those alternate versions of himself on the scene, the residents of Dystopia had become—there was no better word for it—jaded.

He landed, crouching, like a thief. He glanced around, satisfied that he had not been observed, and then he headed into town.

It was still relatively early in the day, but already the streets of Dystopia were alive with industry. The shadows were long, cast by the skyscrapers—most of them crumbling and unsafe, which didn't stop squatters from having taken up residence in many of them.

Hundreds of shopkeepers and traders were already open for business. Much business was done on the barter system, although old and popular standbys such as gold or precious gems were still popular, as was the so-called "oldest profession."

Bruce Banner moved through the streets, his rather conspicu-
ous green-skinned form hidden beneath the loosely fitting clothes
given him by the Survivalists, the hood pulled down and low. His
sheer size was not inconsiderable, but these were mutated times.
There were others on the street who were just as large, some even
conspicuously deformed.

A woman sidled over to him, rubbed against him. She wasn't
wearing much to speak of. "Scanning for a good squeeze?" she
purred.

He paused, mentally translating some of the patois that the
street people used. Much of it seemed left over from the computer
age. "Scanning" instead of "looking," for example. He tried to
remember some of the cadences and rhythms that Janis and her
cohorts had spoken in.

"Scanning to be in the know," he said.

"In the know of what?" she asked, running her hands along his
muscled arms and making a little noise of pleased discovery.

"Outlaws."

The woman recoiled from him, taking a step back. She practically spit a reply. "Outlaws? You scammin'?"

"No."

"I ain't in the know of no outlaws. No one is anymore. That
was a long time ago." She started to move away, but he gripped
her firmly by the arm and pulled her back.

"Get in the know," he said, his voice low and threatening. "Get
in the know, and then come back and slide me what you find out."

Her attitude was defiant, but also mildly curious. "What's in it
for me?" she demanded.

He had nothing, unfortunately, to give her. No goods to barter,
no gold or precious gems. Sex? Not only wasn't he comfortable
with the notion, but it was what she dealt in already. She probably
didn't need overstock.

One other option occurred to him. He didn't much like it. But he was trying to move quickly, accomplish as much as possible. Dystopia was a brutal world, and unfortunately he was going to have to tap in to that brutality if he was going to achieve his goals.

"Here's what's in it for you," and he applied just a touch of pressure to her arm. "I let you live."

"You threatenin' me?" She tried to pull away. "Lemme go! Hey! This guy won't lemme go!"

No one got near. Instead, they hurried past.

He drew her face very close to him, allowed her to gaze deeply into his eyes. She saw the green tint of his skin and she froze, petrified.

In a voice thick with menace, he dropped any of the comforting, familiar slang and snarled, "Right now, and until I tell you otherwise, you have one job and one job only: find out about any of the old Outlaws. Talk to whomever you need and get me the information. You won't say who you need it for, or why you need it. You will simply get it. Or I will kill you. If you try to leave the city, I will kill you. You are now my personal property. If you do not like your new status in life . . ." He let the end of the sentence dangle, waiting for her to complete it.

She could barely get the words out. "You'll . . . you'll kill me."

"Do you doubt me?"

"N-no. . . ."

And he realized bleakly that the reason she had no doubt of it was that the pure evil that made the Maestro what he was was alive and well within him.

He released her and turned away, his loose clothes swirling around him.

He had no intention of killing her, of course. Or even harming her in the slightest.

By the same token, he had no intention of making her his sole foot soldier.

By midmorning, he had made the same "offer" to a number of other indigents in Dystopia. Find out what he wanted to know.

Or else.

The vast table was scattered with the remains of breakfast. The Maestro was having his teeth picked clean by one of the many scantily clad girls who lived in the fortress. At the other end of the table was the Minister, going over various affairs of state. In between the two was Brett, chin propped on one hand, watching the back-and-forth. He seemed to find it all equally fascinating, no matter how humdrum it might be.

"I hesitate to bring this up once more, Maestro," the Minister said with that carefully deferential tone of his. "But your . . . associates . . . are starting to strain our resources to the utmost."

"I don't see the problem here, Minister," replied the Maestro. "They've been very resourceful scavenging, now, haven't they?"

"Yes, that's true," admitted the Minister. "But they've depleted all means of sustenance within a three-hundred-mile radius. They've made a number of raids that were unauthorized and—"

"Unauthorized?" There was tremendous danger in the Maestro's voice. "Minister, if my Hulkbusters wish to do something to maintain their upkeep, then the mere desire is sufficient authorization. Is that clear?"

"I was merely trying to point out th—"

"*Is that clear?*"

Brett was impressed to see that the Minister did not look the least bit intimidated. Nor, however, was he insane enough to reply with anything less than an utterly neutral tone, "Yes, Maestro. Quite clear."

The Maestro leaned back in his chair, nodding approvingly.

And then Brett spoke up. "In any event, much of this concern will shortly be moot. I doubt very much that my father failed to take this situation into account."

At this, the Maestro grinned a wide, yellow smile. "True enough. After all, it was my initiative to assemble the Hulkbusters. And I am very aware that for every action there will be an equal and opposite reaction. I would not have introduced the Hulkbusters into our little sphere if I weren't prepared to deal with the consequences of their being here. This relates to what I was telling you before, Brett." He leaned forward, his large fingers interlaced. "Once, in a time long past, it was a glorious age of combat. Even the wars that devastated this world were nuclear examples of those defining times. Power pitted against power, heroes against villains. Destruction, havoc, spoliation . . . God in heaven, it was glorious. It made me what I am today; had the fires of war not forged me, I would be less for it. And I do not want to take the chance of you being less than your potential would permit, Brett."

"That's very kind of you, Father. And that's why . . . ?"

"Yes!" declared the Maestro, thumping his hand on the table, just lightly enough not to break it. "That is the reason for the Hulkbusters. That is the reason for the Great Conquest. The son of the Maestro deserves nothing less than an epic adventure. Centuries ago, the defining battles of the humans were the Crusades. And since we are far more than humans, then we must have our own Crusades. Something epic beyond all imagining, audacious beyond comprehension. You understand, don't you, Son?"

Brett stared at him for a long moment.

The Maestro's brow darkened slightly. "You understand, don't you?" he repeated.

"Of course, Father," Brett smiled. "I'm sorry. I was just . . . imagining it. It's incredible."

"Naturally. If it's my undertaking, then nothing less than incredible will do. Minister!" he said briskly. "We are finished here."

The Minister still had more items to cover, but wisely divined that now was not the time. He rose, about to leave the great banquet hall, and then paused and asked curiously, "Maestro, did you dispatch one of the Hulkbusters to the Survivalist camp in the Wastelands?"

The Maestro frowned, trying to recall. "I don't believe so. Why?"

"I saw one returning, that is all."

"Hunh," the Maestro said, and then he shrugged. "I doubt it's important. Ask around, see who was out there and why. The Survivalists are hardly in a position to be a threat, but I'd like to know what's going on. Knowledge, after all, is strength. And I try to be the strongest one there is . . . in all things."

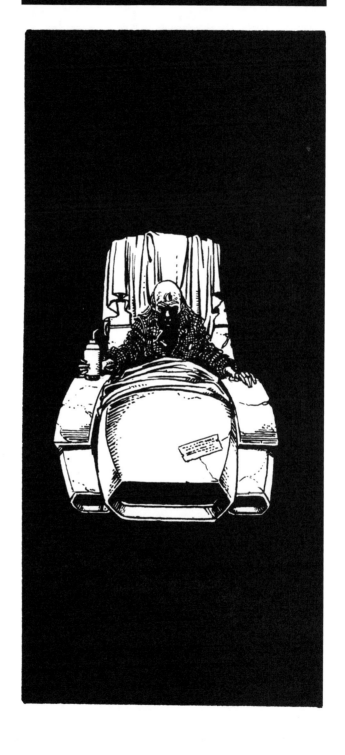

Chapter 21

He had no legs.

A face, yes, that he had. One that once had a certain boyish charm to it, but was now older and infinitely sadder. A vicious scar cut across the left side where he had lost an eye. He never did have the wherewithal for a replacement, and had settled for squinting a lot.

And arms he had, long and gangly, operating the controls of the device that was his way of getting around. A torso, slightly concave, a waist and hips, working "plumbing," as he called it. All this was intact.

But legs? Long gone.

Instead his truncated body was affixed to a small, square go-cart, which was surprisingly maneuverable. He hung out mostly around one particular street corner in a seedier side of Dystopia, and he had nothing to offer anyone except a prodigious memory. He was a storyteller, and for those who were fairly well off or simply feeling up for a diversion, he could spin a fascinating yarn of times gone by. No one ever knew how much truth there was to them. Ultimately, it didn't matter. They were good stories, and that was all that mattered.

Actually, it was remarkably ironic that his means of locomotion had reached such a state, considering that it matched his name.

"Skooter."

Skooter looked up at a large, imposing form that stood over him. He squinted and said, "Yeah? You want to pop me who you are?"

The large form heaved a sigh. "My God, look what they've done to you."

"We in the know of each other?" he asked suspiciously. "You sound awful chumly-like."

The newcomer squatted down, glanced right and left, and then said in a low voice, "This is going to be hard for you to under-stand—or even believe—but I'm here to help."

"Help?"

"I know about you and the Outlaws. About Janis. Pizfiz. Gram-pa Rick. All of them."

At this, Skooter went dead white. He quickly shifted the con-trols of his rolling cart. It sped backward and he whipped it around, trying to put as much distance between himself and this new, threatening individual.

And to his shock, the newcomer vaulted over him and landed squarely in front of him. He snagged the rolling cart before Skooter could back up.

"I have no reason to lie to you," he said urgently. "All my checking around turned up exactly one name: yours. And your location: this one right here."

"Get away from me!"

"I know how it used to be, Skooter! In another time—in another place—I was one of you."

Skooter looked at him askance. "What?" He stared hard at the newcomer and then said, with obvious curiosity, "Lemme scan your mug."

"All right, but . . . promise not to panic."

"What, you muted?" scoffed Skooter. "Nukem burns? Rads do you a treat? Hey . . . nothing you can flash to Skooter gonna knock him for a loop."

The newcomer pulled back his hood slightly.

Skooter took one look into that green face and promptly fainted dead away.

With a sigh, the Hulk picked up Skooter, cart and all, and disappeared into a nearby building.

It took some time, and a good deal of patience, to explain it all to Skooter. Ultimately, the Hulk wasn't sure if Skooter fully understood, or fully believed. But Skooter came to the realization that he had nothing to lose by taking the story at face value—particularly since he wasn't in a position to betray anyone or get himself in even greater trouble.

"Ain't in the know of this time machine you're talking about," Skooter said.

"I know. I didn't think you were. As I said, you never found it . . . and considering that Janis never told me where you people did dig it up, I wouldn't have a clue where to start looking myself." In the dimness of the empty room he'd found, the Hulk leaned closer in to Skooter and said, "I know it's painful . . . but tell me. What happened?"

"Maestro's what happened," Skooter said. "We'd been staying one step ahead of 'im, but you can only do that for so long. He found us. Found our hidey hole. Nailed us before we could relocate. It was a flarkin' slaughter."

"How? How did he find you?"

The tears started to well in Skooter's eyes, and he looked away. And in that instant, the Hulk knew.

"You told him."

Skooter nodded. "I slided him the info. I was bagged, brought to his fortress . . ."

"He used a mind scanner, didn't he?" Bruce had heard from Janis about the insidious devices at the Maestro's command. Machines that probed the mind, drew images out from them and displayed them. The harder you fought back, the deeper the machine would drill and with greater effort. The information would come regardless, and all that resistance got you was a brain incapable of functioning any further.

Again Skooter nodded. "I shoulda fought him better . . . I shoulda . . . woulda buyed them more time, they coulda got away maybe . . . but it hurt so much . . . the Maestro . . . he promised he'd let me go if I made it easy . . . and I didn't want to make it easy . . . but I . . . it hurt . . ."

"I know, Skooter," the Hulk said softly. "I know. Then what happened?"

"The Maestro . . . he came back to the Fortress . . . and he had . . ." He closed his eyes against the recollection. "He had this bag, and the bottom was red with blood. He opened it for me, made me scan it. There were . . . there were heads in it. Janis was there, and Dakord and . . ."

The Hulk couldn't even say it. "Rick?"

"No. He left him there. He said . . . he said he was standing over Grampa Rick, with the blood of the others on his fists, and he told Rick to beg . . . that if he begged, then the Maestro would let 'im live. And Rick, he said, 'Get stuffed.' And the Maestro . . . he said he left Rick alone, but he kinda grinned when he said it. And after he came back to the Fortress, he . . . he made me into this." He indicated his lack of legs, forcing his trembling voice to even out. "And then he threw me out. Like I was nothing. Which . . . I am."

"Skooter, do you know how to get back down below? I don't know my way around the city . . . I can't recall where Janis showed me the one entrance I . . ."

Slowly Skooter nodded, even smiling slightly. "I know one. They thought they closed 'em all off, but I know where there's one still." His eyes looked dead as he said, "I . . . never had the nerve to go down. To scan what's left."

"Do you want me to take you down there with me?"

And Skooter slowly shook his head. "Heroes died there," he said simply. "I'm not good enough. Not good enough . . ." and he looked at his ruined body ". . . by half."

No one had cleaned up afterward. They had left the Outlaws, the rebels, to rot where they lay.

When Banner had last been in the tunnels, they were polished, gleaming. Now they were thick with dust.

Once they had been teeming with life, with all the residents of the down under huddling wherever they could for safety. He had strode down the catwalks and walkways, and because of the obvious resemblance to their oppressor, they had looked up at him with fearful eyes.

Now they simply looked up at him with dead eyes.

It had been twenty years since the massacre. Rick Jones was already ancient, even back then. There was simply no way in hell that he could possibly still be alive, and yet . . . Rick was the single most resourceful human that Bruce Banner had ever met. If any-one—if *anyone*—could have pulled it off, it would be Rick.

The bodies had been picked clean by vermin long ago. Skeletons clad in rags lay everywhere. He tried to close off his mind to it, not to let it horrify him beyond his ability to cope. He kept remind-ing himself that his earlier efforts had not been in vain. That in an alternate timeline, the Maestro was but a memory. All these people were alive and free, free of his tyranny, free to exist in an atmosphere of . . .

He saw the skeletons of two children, their bony fingers interlaced. He leaned against a wall and vomited. When there was nothing more in his stomach, he continued with dry heaves until he was finally able to continue on his way.

With each step his fury grew. With each body, with each set of skeletal remains, he chalked that off to another atrocity that the Maestro would be made to pay for.

And with the evidence of every new death, there was still that nagging, nauseating voice in his head that reminded him of the simple, awful truth: he was the cause for this. It didn't matter that it was his future self, a self whose actions he was repulsed by. The bottom line was that if the Hulk had never existed, the Maestro would never have existed. Far, far above, on the surface, Skooter was sobbing over his inability to protect his friends. And the being to whom he had vented his misery was the one who was genuinely responsible.

And he could never make it right.

Never.

He wandered the tunnels for some time before he had finally familiarized himself sufficiently with his surroundings to get his bearings. Once he had, he headed unerringly for the Trophy Room. The Trophy Room, where a wizened Rick Jones had sat like a giggling, harmonica-playing gnome in a high-tech wheelchair.

The Hulk stopped.

Lying in front of him was a skeleton wearing Janis's clothes. Its head was gone. Several other headless bodies were scattered nearby.

To the right was the entranceway to the Trophy Room.

It was clear enough what had happened. They had fallen back

as far as they could, made a last stand defending Janis's great-grandfather. Defending Rick Jones who, in one reality, was the valiant savior of the people of Dystopia. And here, he was . . .

"Rick?" the Hulk called softly.

No answer. Then again, could he possibly have expected one?

He entered the Trophy Room. He would never forget the feeling that first time, seeing it crammed with relics of an age long gone. Capes, photographs, Captain America's shield, Thor's hammer, Wolverine's adamantium skeleton. Supposedly indestructible items such as the Silver Surfer's board or Iron Man's armor, shattered. Objects offering mute testimony to final battles that no one survived.

No one but Rick Jones, the ultimate survivor.

All of that, the Hulk had been faced with that first time. But this time . . . this time . . .

There was nothing.

The room was empty. Picked clean of all the treasures therein.

No. Not empty.

In the dimness of the room, he saw one thing. He saw a chair.

Rick's chair.

And in it was Rick.

Alive.

As ancient as the Hulk had remembered him from last time. Bald except for a few strands of white hair clinging forlornly to the side of his head. Wearing a red flannel shirt, with that same cocka-mamie harmonica clutched in his right hand. He was staring straight at the Hulk as if he'd been expecting him at any moment.

"Rick!" he said in astonishment.

He ran across the room, kicking up dust. It was absolutely impossible that after all this time, Rick was still here. But he'd done it again, accomplished that which could not *be* accomplished. Then again, that was standard procedure for Rick Jones.

He dropped to one knee, words spilling over each other as he said, "Rick, damn, I don't know how you did it, but you did! It's me, Bruce! I'm here to help! If we work together, perhaps we can find Doom's time machine and . . ."

That was when, even in the dim light, he noticed that Rick wasn't breathing.

He passed a hand in front of Rick's face. Nothing. No eyeblink. Nothing at all.

But it couldn't be. He couldn't have died that day twenty years ago. He'd have rotted away like the others. Could he have *just* died only moments earlier? Waited twenty years in this hellhole, and expired just before help had arrived? Could that possibly be?

He touched Rick's skin. It was rock hard.

And then he saw it, although his mind couldn't completely grasp it at first. He looked closely, very closely into Rick's eyes.

They were glass.

Get stuffed, Rick had told the Maestro.

No.

And the Maestro kinda grinned. . . .

"No," said the Hulk in a voice he didn't even recognize as his. His chest began to shudder and he backed away, stumbling, unable to tear away his gaze . . . wanting to rip out his own eyes. The stuffed body of Rick Jones stared at him with passive accusation.

The Hulk started to sob, although no tears came to him at first, nor air to his lungs. And then, finally, there were tears, and great racking sobs, and a voice that screamed and echoed and re-echoed through the corridors as he howled, cursing the Maestro, cursing himself, "You son of a bitch! You *son of a bitch!*"

And his cries fell on deaf ears.

Chapter 22

The daily bacchanal was in full swing.

The higher-ranking nobles of Dystopia were partying wildly. The sounds of strummed music filled the air, along with laughter and merrymaking. It was hard for anyone to hear each other, and so people were pushed in fairly closely together, which certainly suited the mood and spirit of the evening.

Various members of the Hulkbusters were in attendance as well, enjoying the revelries, the women, and the copious food and drink that had been brought in from raided city-states hundreds of miles away. Such raids were possible through the auspices of the Hulkbusters, and all within the great hall were ecstatic to be part of the privileged and deserving membership of the Maestro's court.

Brett lay back on a curtained bed. He had a woman on either shoulder, one snoring contentedly, the other running her fingers through his gray-black hair.

"What can I do for you, my lord?" cooed the one who was still awake.

"You can stop calling me 'my lord,' " Brett said amiably. He studied her for a long moment. Then he reached toward her . . .

And she flinched. Ever so slightly, but it was there. She smiled quickly and almost managed to cover it.

"Are you afraid of me?" he asked.

"Yes, Brett," she said.

"Why?"

"Because . . ." She hesitated, and then shrugged. He'd asked. "Because you could kill me."

"I wouldn't. Why would I do that?"

"Because you could."

"Just because you *can* do something doesn't necessarily mean that you will."

"Forgive me, Brett, but . . . in my experience . . . it usually does."

He frowned, and then rose from the bed and stepped out into the main hall. His appearance was greeted with a chorus of cheers from those members of the nobility or the Hulkbusters who happened to spot him. He waved briefly, bobbed his head, and then walked out of the main hall, scratching his chin thoughtfully.

Slowly he paced a corridor, his hands behind his back. Various members of the Hulkbusters went past him. He greeted them by name, which was fairly easy, since they were all called "Hulk."

There was a great deal going through his mind that he was having trouble articulating. All this business with the Great Conquest, and the spread of fear. It all made such sense. And yet . . .

"Excuse me."

He turned. One of the Hulkbusters was standing behind him.

"Ah. You're one of the articulate ones," said Brett.

"That's right," said the Hulk, smiling lopsidedly. He gripped Brett's hand firmly. "I'm Robert Bruce Banner."

"Aren't they all." Brett grinned. Then he frowned slightly. "Are you new? When did you arrive? I don't remember you."

"Several days ago. I've been out looking around . . . getting myself acquainted with the era and the area. It's amazing."

"It is, isn't it?" said Brett.

The sounds of the partying were still fairly loud. "Can we chat for a few minutes?" asked the Hulk, gesturing for Brett to walk with him. Brett nodded amiably and they started off down the corridor at a very leisurely pace.

"I'm still a little unclear about this plan of your father's," said the Hulk.

"The Great Conquest? Well, it's fairly straightforward, really. Cross the dimensions back to the 1990s and ravage the Earth. Simple." He beamed. "It's going to be an epic battle! I can't wait!"

"Neither can I," agreed the Hulk. "The joy of cracking human heads—crushing your enemies beneath your feet—we're entitled. After years of deprivation and betrayal, we're entitled."

"That's exactly what Father says. He says only the strong survive. We're the strongest. So we should survive."

"Yes, I know. He said as much to me."

Brett nodded approvingly.

They got toward the end of the corridor, turned a corner. "I must admit, I'm curious," said the Hulk. "Where'd your father get that time-traveling gem of his?"

"Oh, that? It's a mystic artifact. It used to belong to a guy named Strange . . . and then somehow it wound up in an underground room belonging to some old man named Dick Jones. . . ."

The Hulk refrained from correcting him.

"A couple of other magic talismans, some books, plus a ton of other weapons and such. Jones died, so of course he had no more use for it. So my father took all the stuff and moved it out. And the Minister, he managed to decipher the books and use those to figure out how the talismans work. Well . . . how some of them work, at any rate." He shook his head, chuckling. "One he managed to get open, and my father swears this big eye came out of it and just floated away. Kept right on going, up and up, and the amulet it was in just went dead. But the interdimensional thing, that they got working perfectly."

"As I'm very well aware," agreed the Hulk. "You . . . wouldn't know where your father keeps it, would you?"

"Not really. I think he keeps it locked. . . ." Then he stopped walking and regarded the Hulk suspiciously. "Why do you ask?"

"Me? Just curious."

"Yes. Yes, real curious." Suddenly he started firing questions at the Hulk. "What era are you from, precisely? How did my father recruit you? When did . . . ?"

In that instant, the Hulk knew he had absolutely no choice as to his next actions.

He hauled off and slugged Brett as hard as he could.

It wasn't quite hard enough.

Word had spread quickly throughout the fortress. The Maestro wanted to see everybody—and that meant *every*body—in the Hulk-busters. Ranger troops had quickly been recalled, and different Hulks throughout the castle were promptly herded into the main hall.

This was not a decision that sat particularly well with them. It was a testimony to the Maestro's personal command and charisma that he had managed to hold the other Hulks in check through sheer force of will. Although it had not hurt matters that on two different occasions he had fought and killed recalcitrant Hulks who had been giving him excessive lip or else had actually had designs on leadership themselves.

They had learned their lessons and had come to appreciate the opportunities of this world that had not existed in their own. Nevertheless, when the Maestro ordered them to come running, there was a whiff of resentment. Not much. But a little.

"You're sure about this, Minister?" he demanded in a low voice as he faced a sea of green.

"Absolutely, Maestro," the Minister told him. "You can ask them yourselves."

"I will," he said, and then spoke more loudly. "Listen to me carefully. What began as a casual inquiry has turned into something of a minor mystery. No one will be punished or even remonstrated. We simply need to know for security purposes. Were any of you visiting the Survivalist encampment on the Wastelands early this morning?"

There were blank expressions, exchanged looks, scratching of heads.

"No one? No one was there and came leaping back here?"

Again, nothing.

A cyborg Hulk looked questioningly at a water-breathing Hulk. An extremely hairy Hulk exchanged glances with a Hulk who was missing an arm. Hulks from five dozen dimensions and realities, and they were all clueless.

For a long while no one said anything.

"I do not like that one of you is lying to me," said the Maestro dangerously. "The Minister saw it clearly."

"Perhaps it was Brett he saw?" suggested one of the Hulks.

"No, impossible," the Minister said immediately. "Brett was with me."

"That being the case, Son, were you able to . . ." The Maestro's voice trailed off. He looked around. "Where the hell is Brett?"

Answers to this question came no more quickly.

He spun, faced the Minister. "Where is my son?"

"I'm afraid I don't . . ."

And the Maestro bellowed so loudly that the walls of the great hall shook, *"Bring me my son!"*

Brett staggered, went down to one knee, but he did not go out. "You've got one *hell of a nerve!*" he snarled and charged.

The Hulk leaped, slamming a foot forward and kicking Brett hard in the face. The actions he was taking were killing him; this was his son, *his son*. And the legacy of violence and strife that he'd bequeathed him dictated that the first thing he had to do upon their reunion was try and knock him out.

Of primary importance was getting him the hell out of the fortress. Because if the two of them were still going toe-to-toe as a squadron of ersatz Hulks showed up, then Bruce was well and truly finished.

The one break he had caught was that he had gotten Brett within range of where he wanted to take him.

Brett was momentarily stunned, but he'd shake it off fast. Moving quickly, Bruce charged forward, wrapping one arm around Brett's middle and clamping his free hand securely over Brett's mouth. Brett struggled, tried to make some sort of noise, to sound an alarm, anything . . .

And then it was too late, for they had gone out a window at the end of the corridor.

It was a long drop, but not one that would present any sort of problem for either of them. Ten stories below they hit the ground, landing on an incline and tumbling down the side, rolling one over the other, struggling, slugging. When they skidded to a halt, it was Brett who was on top. He delivered several furious blows to the Hulk's head before the Hulk swung his legs up, crisscrossed his powerful calves across Brett's neck, and twisted like a wrestler. He slammed Brett to the ground and then, while the youth was stunned, slugged him repeatedly as hard as he could. Harder than he would have liked to. Perhaps harder than he should have.

Brett stopped moving, his head lolling to one side. For a hideous moment the Hulk feared that he might have killed him. But then he saw that Brett was still breathing.

It was at that moment that he heard a roar from within the castle. It sounded very much like the Maestro. And what he had shouted sounded very much like "Bring me my son!" bellowed at many decibels above safe zones for human hearing.

The Hulk wasted no time. He slung Brett over his shoulder and made for the hidden entranceway to the underground as fast as his legs would take him.

And he wondered, not for the first time, just what he was going to do when his son woke up.

Chapter 23

The castle had been searched from top to bottom, and there was no sign of Brett.

The Maestro paced his inner sanctum, the Minister watching passively as he moved back and forth. "One of them is lying to me," the Maestro growled. "Lying to me, covering up some sort of little scheme."

"You think one or more of the Hulkbusters plots against you?"

"Isn't it obvious? I should have anticipated this. Indeed, I *did* anticipate this. Made an example of a couple of them, if you recall."

"Oh, I recall indeed, although I thought the heads on a pike in the center square were a bit much."

"Well, apparently it wasn't 'much' enough. And . . ."

He paused, which was a rare enough occurrence in the Maestro's speech pattern to garner the Minister's immediate attention. "And what, sir?"

"And what I'm most concerned about," the Maestro said, "is . . . what if Brett is a part of this . . . this whatever it is? What if he's off scheming somewhere? Who knows what he's up to?"

Brett slowly became aware of a pressure on his chest. With a low moan he forced his eyes open.

The Hulk was sitting on him. He was perched atop his chest, looking down at him with a combination of anger and sadness.

Immediately Brett began to struggle, wordlessly trying to force the Hulk off him. "Don't bother," the Hulk told him. "I'm not moving, and you're not making me move, so we might as well both get used to that."

"Who are you?" demanded Brett.

"Funny you should ask that," the Hulk replied. "Ever think of asking that of yourself?"

"I don't know what you're talking about!"

The Hulk sighed. "Yes, I know you don't. That's the pity of it, really."

"Get off me! I don't know who you are, but get . . . off . . . *me!*" He slammed his hands against the Hulk's arms, tried to shove him away, tried to adjust for leverage. And he was starting to make headway.

Bruce rose and stepped away from him.

Brett immediately got to his feet and stood there, fists cocked, poised for battle. He was expecting his kidnapper to charge, to challenge him, to . . . something.

What he wasn't expecting was for the Hulk to turn his back and simply walk away.

"Wait a minute . . . what do you think you're doing?" demanded Brett. "What's going on here? You drag me away, to . . . what? Kill me? Hold me for ransom? Use me as leverage against my father?" He folded his arms and looked smug. "If that's your plan, you don't know my father."

The Hulk regarded him with pity. "I *am* your father, you moron."

At that point he stopped walking, waiting for Brett's response. That response was a disdainful snort. "Oh, I suppose you consider yourself as such . . . my father being the ultimate incarnation of creatures such as yourself. But . . ."

Bruce turned to face him and, in a very quiet voice, said, "Tell me about your mother."

Brett didn't seem to follow the question. Nor did it seem worth his while to respond. Instead he looked around the tunnels where the Hulk had brought him. "This is the old shelter, isn't it? The place under the city, where those outlaws and that Dick Jones . . ."

"*Rick* . . . Jones. And yes, this is the place." His eyes hardened. "This is the place where the Maestro slaughtered those good and brave people."

"They would have killed him if they'd had the chance. It was a great and epic battle."

The Hulk stepped in close, but Brett didn't back down. Instead he met the Hulk's angry stare with a steady, even gaze. "I can take you to the bodies if you'd like. People denied proper burial. Left to rot where they fell, their bones picked clean, their bodies mutilated. It was a massacre."

"Whatever he did, he had his reasons," Brett said firmly. "Isn't that what they always used to say about God? If it was good enough for Him . . ."

"Yes, Brett . . . they 'used to' say that. And we rationalized it by saying that God was unknowable. But the Maestro . . . he's all too well known. Monsters like him have been commonplace enough in history. What he did down here was nothing short of butchery. The sadistic actions of a grotesque, demented mind . . ."

Brett slapped him. It sounded as if a small bomb had dropped, and the Hulk rocked slightly on his heels. He shook it off, smiled for a moment, and slapped him back. The impact knocked Brett on his ass.

"Respect," the Hulk admonished him. "A very important commodity. Maintain it at all times, please. Your mother wouldn't approve of anything less."

Brett worked on straightening his jaw. "Why do you keep bringing her up? She died years ago."

"Well, that can't be argued, I suppose. And who was she?"

"Why do you keep asking me th—?"

"*Who was she?*"

Brett was taken aback by the intensity of emotion in this renegade Hulkbuster's voice. He had no idea of what to make of this insane situation. The only conclusion that he could draw was that this particular Hulk incarnation had completely lost his mind. But Brett's father had taught him that, when confronted with an opponent who was inclined to chat or boast, it was best to try to draw him out. Let him keep on chattering. There was always more than enough time to kill a foe, but valuable information could be had from one who was overconfident. Or, as was apparently the case here, just kind of nuts.

"She was one of my father's chumlies," Brett said with a shrug, while running a finger casually along the dust-covered wall. "He never told me her name. He said it didn't matter. She died giving birth to me."

"No," said the Hulk. "A part of her died, perhaps, when you were taken from her . . . from her and me. But she was still alive when I left her. And she'll be alive when I bring you back to her."

Brett laughed uncertainly. "You're insane. You know that, don't you?"

The Hulk stepped toward him and extended one finger. Brett didn't flinch, but regarded him suspiciously as the Hulk put the finger to Brett's chin and tilted his head back slightly, studying his face.

"You have her eyes. Her eyes, and the general shape of her nose."

"What are you talking about?" Brett asked for what seemed to him the umpteenth time.

"Your mom," and he wasn't quite able to keep his voice even. "Your mom was Betty Banner. She was brave, and kind, and deserved better than to have her son snatched away by the Maestro. But that's what happened, and I came here to make it right, as best I can. We're going to find a way to stop the Maestro so that he does no further harm, and then I'm going to bring you home. And we'll live happily ever after."

The Minister regarded the Maestro with astonishment. "You don't truly think that Brett is out to undercut your authority, do you?"

"I don't know what to think!" said the Maestro in exasperation. "All I know is that Brett is gone, and one of my Hulkbusters is lying to me! What other sort of conclusion am I to dr—"

And then his eyes widened as another possibility suddenly burst into his mind. "Damn me," he whispered, and then he fairly bellowed, "Damn me, *of course!* It's him! He's come! Of all the times, and of all the gall!"

"Maestro, I regret to say I'm not following. What 'him' are you . . ."

"Him! Me! Banner!"

Then the Minister comprehended. "You mean . . . *that* Hulk? The one who . . ."

"Brett's father, yes. Exactly." He slammed an open palm on the table and this time the legs snapped. "I should have known. I should have *known.*" He paced the room, wagging a finger. "The first year after I brought Brett here, I was completely on my guard. Wary for any sign that he had shown up, had somehow managed to track me. I was certain that it was impossible; not with all the directions I could have taken along the byways of infinity. But still I was vigilant, as I said, that entire first year. The following five or so, I relaxed that vigilance ever so slightly. And as each year passed, and as Brett grew taller, and more powerful . . . Blast him, Minister, I became smug and overconfident."

"But I don't understand," said the Minister. "Could he have been searching for twenty years, nonstop? Tracking down every Crossroad through an infinity of possibilities? What sort of creature would—"

"Be that obsessive and determined? I would. And he would. And he's taken Brett, that much I'm certain of now. Brett didn't go willingly." He turned to face the Maestro. "You saw him coming from the direction of the Wasteland Survivalists? Boz's people?" The Minister nodded. "All right. All right, then. Minister . . . bring me Hulkbusters number . . ." he paused and thought, "number twenty-three and number forty-seven."

"That would be the Cyborg and the Barbarian."

"Correct. Bring them to me immediately. I have a son to find," and he added darkly, "and a Hulk to bust."

Brett stared into the glass eyes of Rick Jones. The Hulk stood nearby, having to make a serious effort not to choke just looking at the ghastly corpse.

"I don't see the problem here," Brett said after lengthy consideration.

Banner couldn't quite believe he'd heard right. "You're . . . you're not serious . . ."

"Well, look at him, for God's sake. He was at death's door as it was. For all we know, he died of natural causes." Brett glanced at Rick's bald head and wiped off some dust.

"He performed *taxidermy* on him, for God's sake!" the Hulk cried out, appalled.

"So? It's just a corpse." Brett looked at the Hulk pityingly. "Perhaps in your time, you didn't have to deal with a significant number of dead bodies. In my time, they're much more commonplace. I'm just not as fainthearted about these things as you are."

Bruce was staring at Brett as if his son had come from another planet.

Brett tapped the side of Rick's face, that hollow sound making Bruce wince. "In a way, my father was honoring him. Making him into a permanent tribute to the bravery of those who fell here. What would be more appropriate than that?"

"It's *barbaric!*"

"What would have been better?" demanded Brett. "If he was dead . . . to bury him? Cremate him? Where's the tribute in that? If he was alive . . . then what? Leave him here with the dead? Make him a prisoner, so he could die in a dungeon? Set him free, so he could die homeless in the streets? Even if . . . Rick," he took care to get the name right, "wasn't already dead . . . even if my father did kill him, which I'm not conceding happened, but if he did . . . it could easily be viewed as exercising mercy."

"I don't believe it." The Hulk was shaking his head in astonishment. "I don't believe it. I mean, I know people say they have trouble talking to their kids. But this is ridiculous."

"I wish you wouldn't refer to me as 'your kid,' " said Brett uncomfortably. "I don't accept this claim that you're my father . . . that my mother was the long-dead 'Betty' that the Maestro has spoken of from time to time, usually in words of contempt."

"Yeah, well . . . I'm not too sure I believe she's your mother either, at this point." And he walked out of the final resting place of Rick Jones.

Brett quickly followed him out. He casually stepped over the skeletons, not giving any indication that he even noticed they were there. "What do you mean by that? Are you now changing your nonsensical story?"

"I mean," said the Hulk, unable even to look at him, "that Betty is so benevolent—so giving—that she would be as horrified as I over what was done to these people, and to Rick. She wouldn't have to have it explained to her, or outlined to her, or defined in words of one syllable. She'd know in her heart—in her gut—that what we see here is nothing less than the remains of something truly abominable. These people didn't battle against the Maestro because they were power seekers, or hungry for some great glorious battle. They were fighting for their lives! Fighting against his oppression, his incursions, his callous and insensitive treatment. . . ."

"Indeed," said Brett calmly. "In my history lessons, I was taught that American settlers treated the natives in pretty much the same way."

"They taught you that, huh?"

"Yes."

"Did they also teach you that two wrongs don't make a right?"

"They did indeed . . . when we got to the section on 'trite sayings.' Look . . ." he gestured helplessly, "I don't know what you expected. That you'd show me examples of my father's handiwork and I'd turn against him? That I'd be repulsed by him because you paint him as a monster? Here you come to our time . . . you kidnap me . . . you slander the being to whom I owe everything . . ." His eyes narrowed. "And you want me to take your word that there's someone in Dystopia who's a greater monster than you yourself? I don't think so."

Cyborg Hulk was the twenty-third that the Maestro had "harvested." In his particular alternate dimension, he had been plucked from the year 2047. The Maestro had come upon him after he had barely managed to avoid an all-out effort to wipe him off the face of the Earth. A near miss with a 200-kiloton nuclear warhead had left him a genuine basket case, with arms and legs reduced to shriveled stumps. The Maestro had salvaged him, gotten him away from that world as his enemies had closed in on him. The circumstances of the rescue, and the Maestro's subsequent restoration of number twenty-three to fighting status through mechanical grafts, had made the cyborg one of the more unrelentingly faithful to him. His arms and legs were gleaming, segmented columns of silver, not quite up to the strength levels of the original limbs, but fairly indestructible.

Number forty-seven, Barbarian Hulk, was an even more interesting case. Barbarian Hulk had spent many, many years in a subatomic world, the consort of an empress named Jarella. While there he had possessed the full intellect of Bruce Banner. That, combined with the love of Jarella, and the occasional battles with ill-advised invaders, had combined to give him a complete and happy life. Jarella had lived to a fine old age and, eventually, died.

The tragedy of this was that, as always, the gamma radiation that granted the Hulk his phenomenal healing power had reduced his own aging rate to a crawl. He had had to watch his beloved Jarella grow old and die, while he remained young and vital. The exercise in extended loss had nearly driven him mad with grief, and upon her passing he had left Jarella's subatomic universe and had returned to his nominal "home."

Because of his extended foray there, he maintained much of the intellect he possessed there. But his personality had changed dramatically, although he didn't quite realize it or acknowledge it. He was darker, angrier, burning with resentment. He sought out battles, arenas of conquest. He had brought back with him a broadsword that Jarella had once given him—an ebony blade that could cut through anything—and this weapon never left his side. He didn't truly need it. His arms were weapons, after all. But he was never seen without it, and when he did choose to employ it, it was with lethal force.

The greatest tragedy was that the world he returned to was one that had somehow not been plagued by any of the mid-twentieth-century strife that had afflicted other dimensional incarnations of Earth. A golden age of peace was dawning, and it was an age into which a sword-wielding, gamma-spawned behemoth simply did not fit—and would not be allowed to remain.

The persecution grew to intolerable levels. Friendless, hopeless, the Hulk had been on the verge of lopping off his own head and ending it all when the Maestro had interceded, offering him more battle than he would ever need. The forty-seventh addition to the Hulkbusters could not have been happier.

These two fearsome incarnations of the Hulk now faced the Maestro in his war room, taking in his instructions as to how they should proceed.

"There are three likely possibilities," he said, ticking them off on his fingers. "The first is that Banner has taken Brett and returned to his own time. If that's the case, then I'll simply find him when we embark on the Great Conquest. The second is that he's returned to the encampment of old Boz. I want you to go there," he said pointing at the barbarian. "I have no way of proving how closely tied in with him they are. Then again, I don't have to prove anything to anyone. Besides, the Minister spotted him wearing garments of those people. That's enough of a connection for me. I am *extremely* angry with them for this duplicity. You will discern as much information as you can, and then you will express to them just precisely how angry I am. In this endeavor, leave no stone unturned."

The barbarian nodded in understanding. The Maestro then turned to the cyborg. "A third possibility is that he's gone to ground. That he's in the tunnels below. Take however many of the others you think you require to do a thorough search, and go through the tunnels. Be prepared; he's an extremely crafty and vicious fighter."

"We gonna try and recruit him?" asked the cyborg.

"No. We're going to try and obliterate him."

"You want him alive?"

The Maestro gave it a moment's thought. "If it's at all convenient, yes. But I'm not married to the idea. If he dies . . ." He smiled ruthlessly. "I won't shed any tears."

Chapter 24

Things were not going as the Hulk had hoped.

He'd been speaking to Brett for many hours. In fact, he had completely lost track of how much time had passed, or what the hour was up above. He had told him of the circumstances of his birth, of how he'd saved his life with the gamma gun . . . even the battle with Talbot, just for the additional drama of it. Of his kidnapping by the Maestro. All of it . . .

Except Ross. He hadn't mentioned Ross. He wasn't sure why, but something had made him hold it back. Perhaps it was because the pain of his loss was so recent, so numbing, that he could not bring himself to speak of Brett's lost twin.

Bottom line: He had found the entire business an exercise in frustration.

After hours of going in circles, he had finally said in exasperation, "This was a mistake. This was a waste of time. Go back to the Maestro. Go back to that creature that you call father. I wash my hands of you. But this isn't over, I swear. I'll find a way to stop him, even if I have to start all over again."

He turned and stalked away from Brett, kicking up clouds of dust in his wake. The skeletons of the lost rebels looked on.

Brett followed him quickly, which should have pleased him.

But in his present state of mind it only angered him all the more. "What are you, deaf?" demanded the Hulk as he kept walking.

"*You* started this," pointed out Brett. "Don't blame me because it's not going the way you wish."

"You're right. I started this. And I'm ending it. Even if you wanted to go back and meet Betty, whom you still seem intent on denying was your mother, it would be crazy for me to do that."

"Crazy? Why?"

The Hulk stopped and turned to face him. "Because you're utterly amoral," he said. "Better that she never knew. Better that she thought you died. That way she can mourn you and then go on with her life. But if she met you as you are—if she spoke with you at any length—she'd be completely repulsed by what you've become. And she'd probably hate me for it, because the Maestro turned you into this, and the Maestro is a future incarnation of me. I can't tell her what you've become. I can't."

"You can't tell her that I've grown into a strong, confident individual who has the courage of his convictions?"

"*Convictions!* What convictions? That the strong shall inherit the earth and the meek will be crushed underfoot? That mercy is for the weak?"

" 'The sick are the greatest danger for the healthy; it is not from the strongest that harm comes to the strong, but from the weakest.' Nietzsche said that," Brett said smugly.

"Indeed. He also said, 'Whoever fights monsters should see to it that in the process he does not become a monster. And when you look long into the abyss, the abyss also looks into you.' That would also apply, I think, to people who were raised by monsters. He also said, 'Distrust all in whom the impulse to punish is powerful.' This Great Conquest that the Maestro has planned . . . it's a revenge trip. Oh, he may try to paint it as some great and glorious adventure. But it's really just payback on a vast scale. He wants to go back and put paid to everyone who ever did him dirt or mistreated him."

"And what's wrong with that?" demanded Brett, but in a voice that sounded, ever so slightly, hesitant.

"Because power without compassion is wrong! It's an affront against God and man, two things that the Maestro cares nothing for! To use power merely in the service of destruction is a waste! That's what this has been all about!"

"This? This what? I don't—"

"This! Me!" And he thumped his chest with his fist. "That's the lesson that was driven home to me that day the gamma bomb went off! Talking to you, talking until I'm blue-green in the face, has finally made it clear to me. I've spent all these years wondering what the point of my suffering was, and now I understand. I can't believe it didn't occur to me before."

"I'm not following you."

The Hulk circled Brett. "All my knowledge, all my skill, all my scientific wisdom that I could have used to better humanity . . . and what did I do with it?" he asked with an ironic, bitter laugh. "I used it to build a bomb! A bomb! As if people didn't have sufficient means of turning themselves into piles of ash, I took joy and pride in finding some brand-new way to kill them! What was I thinking? What, not good enough that we could obliterate, oh, five square miles in a tenth of a second? No, no, my friends. Now, thanks to Dr. Robert Bruce Banner, we can obliterate five and a half square miles in a hundredth of a second! There's progress for you!

"My intellect, my wisdom, was nothing less than a gift from God, and I squandered it! I don't know what my gift was genuinely intended for. Something great, something fabulous. It must have been. Because when somebody Up There saw the use that I was putting it to, He must have gotten pretty pissed. And He looked down and said, 'Banner, you blew it! I gave you scientific aptitude,

I gave you a brain, and look at what you've done with it. Well, buddy, if you're going to squander it, then I'm going to show you what it's like not to have it at all. You can experience firsthand what it's like to be a brainless, unthinking brute. A flesh-and-blood incarnation of the destruction you've taken such pains to build. A bomb on legs. That's what you are, that's what you'll be.' And by gosh, that's what He did. He not only punished me, but He made me an example for all the world to see. An example of the dangers of intellect without wisdom, of power without pity. People could look at me and revile me, and maybe see something of that in themselves so they could know the sort of behavior to avoid."

He was silent for a short time after that. And then Brett stepped close to him and said in a low, withering tone, "Haven't you heard? Nietzsche said 'God is dead.' "

The Hulk said tiredly, "Do you really believe the things you're saying? How the strong must reign over the meek, with no regard to humanity?"

" 'Humanity' persecuted you and hounded you your entire life, and laid waste to this world. Humanity is overrated," Brett said blithely.

"I don't know how much of you is saying that, and how much of it is what the Maestro drummed into you. But I'll point out to you that the greatly despised 'humanity' gave birth to you, Brett. As inhuman, as monstrous as I may appear, your mother is—was— is very human. Very mortal. Where would she fit into the plans for world conquest, eh? When a green tidal wave stampedes across the face of old Earth, balancing the scales for every transgression com- mitted against Hulks everywhere, does it matter to you if Betty's trampled underfoot as well?"

"Not this again . . . not this ridiculous story about—"

And the Hulk grabbed him by the arms, yanked him forward

so hard that his head almost snapped off. He wanted to be able to keep talking calmly, to try to make rational, logical points. To deal with this in a detached, intelligent manner. But his frustration boiled over.

"It's not ridiculous, and you know it's not ridiculous. You just haven't admitted it to yourself yet. And the fact is that humanity *isn't* the great swarming pool of depravity that the Maestro has painted it to be. Yes, there's been persecution and betrayal and all the other ills that people can visit on each other. But there's also been love and caring and tenderness, all those things that the Maestro holds in contempt. All those things which separate him from humanity, and he would take pride in that separation, but you can't! You mustn't! Whatever it is I've become, whatever it is my genes mutated into, you're still half human, and you owe allegiance to that!"

"I owe allegiance to my father," said Brett angrily, pulling away.

"Yes, that's right. You do," the Hulk agreed readily. And then, in an ugly voice, he said, "The Maestro's going to find Betty, you know. He'll hunt her down, bet on that. He hates her with a passion because she knew him back when he was me. Back when he still had the spark of benevolence that he finds so distasteful now. He won't suffer her continued existence."

"This is of no interest to m—"

"What do you think he'll do to her, huh?" He gestured toward the corpses. "Oh, she'll beg for mercy, most likely. Won't get it. There's no mercy in him. I doubt he'd kill her quickly. Maybe he'd crush her, one limb at a time. Left arm, then right . . . then left leg, then right leg."

"Stop it," said Brett tightly.

"Each limb becoming a bloody pulp as she screams and

screams," the Hulk continued relentlessly. "Then maybe he'll crush her hips . . . collapse her rib cage and finally end it by grinding *your mother's* skull between his fingers before he rips it off her—"

"*Stop it!*" he shouted, and this time he struck the Hulk. The Hulk went down, but gave no sign that he'd even felt the blow. From the ground he sneered, "Or maybe he won't do that at all! Maybe he'll just snap her neck like a rotting tree branch, and then have her stuffed! Honor her like he honored Rick! Give her a permanent place at the breakfast table, so you can greet your glassy-eyed mom each morning and ask her how she slept."

He wouldn't stop. He was down, and Brett started kicking him in fury. The Hulk rolled with the impacts and came to his feet.

"The one thing you can count on, Brett, is that he'll give her pain. Agony surpassing anything she felt during the labor pains of you and your brother."

Brett froze. "B-brother . . . ?"

The Hulk stopped dead. For a moment he felt guilty; now, after all this, he'd finally slipped and mentioned Ross. And it wound up being an emotional club. But then, mentally, he shrugged. He was tired, so tired, and part of him just wanted to hurt Brett. To make him feel some of the pain that he himself was feeling. "Oh, did I forget to mention him? Yes. Your brother. Your twin brother, Ross, who died hours after you were born. Siamese twins, joined at the head. I never thought that Betty could suffer more than she did with his loss, but I bet the Maestro will prove me wrong. He's very inventive. I bet he's got plans for her that haven't even occurred to me. But don't worry, Brett. I betcha he'll let you watch. In fact, he'll probably insist on it."

In a hoarse whisper, Brett said, "You're . . . you're an evil creature."

"Me?" The Hulk laughed a laugh that sounded very much like

the Maestro's. "Kiddo, compared to your alleged father, I'm an amateur."

Brett spit at him. It landed at his feet.

The Hulk stared down at it, then looked back up at his son. In a voice almost too low for Brett to hear, he said, "All I wanted . . . all I wanted was not to be the monster my father was. Not to turn into him. And in many ways, I think I'm worse." Then, a bit louder, he said to Brett, "I had these dreams . . . dreams of what fatherhood would be like. Dreams of how we would be. And it's all ashes now, Brett. Just . . . ashes."

Suddenly the ground around them started to shake. Brett knew instantly what it was. Certainly he had been there enough times when the Hulkbusters had gone somewhere in force. Subtlety was not exactly their strong suit.

"They're coming," he said tersely. "The Hulkbusters are coming." And now he turned to the Hulk and said, "Your only choice is surrender. You can't escape."

"You'll pardon me if I don't take your word for that."

He started to move . . . and froze.

Coming from around the corner were three Hulks. The one in the lead had gleaming arms and legs. He took one look at Banner and clenched his fists. Curved metal claws popped out of the backs. He spoke quickly into what appeared to be some sort of comm unit on his wrist as he said, "We've got him sighted. Track my signal and converge."

The second Hulk was the rocky-skinned one the Hulk had spotted from a distance. He was carrying a trident, which he was wielding now with deadly intent in his face.

The third was greenish gray. He was smaller than the others but looked exceedingly crafty. A chain, attached to a heavy iron ball, was wrapped around his hand.

Banner recognized the implements they wielded immediately. They had all been artifacts from Rick's trophy room.

He started to move, and Brett blocked his path. The Hulk slammed into him as the others pounded toward him, and for a moment father and son were struggling, toe to toe.

They looked deeply into each other's eyes—and suddenly Brett was off his feet, the Hulk tossing him aside. But even as Banner did so, he was positive that he had not been the driving force in the throw. Brett had pushed off from the balls of his feet ever so slightly, aiding the Hulk in the throw. That was the Hulk's impression, at any rate. For all he knew, Brett had simply slipped.

For whatever reason, Brett crashed into the wall, leaving a huge dent in it. His path momentarily unobstructed, Banner took the opportunity to bolt down it.

The others slowed as they got to Brett. "Are you all right?" the cyborg demanded.

Brett nodded, looking slightly dazed.

"Converge!" the cyborg barked into his comm unit once more. "Converge! Don't let him get away!"

Banner rounded a corner, heading for one exit, and almost crashed squarely into a Hulk who was covered with thick, matted hair. Banner smashed a fist into him, and it was like hitting a mattress.

The hairy Hulk snarled at him and lunged. Banner spun out of the way and, while the hairy Hulk was momentarily off balance, slugged him as hard as he could on the thick muscles behind his head. The hairy Hulk went down and then, before he could get to his feet, Banner grabbed huge handfuls of his hair and hurled him in the direction of his pursuers.

The cyborg saw it coming and flattened. The hairy Hulk arced over his head and slammed into the rocky and green-gray Hulk.

The cyborg kept on going, not waiting for them to recover their wits.

He moved at high speed and, seconds later, was within range of the quickly moving Banner. He extended his fingers and a jet of thick black liquid spurted out.

It pooled under Banner's feet before he could break his forward motion. He skidded, waving his arms, trying to recover his balance and failing. He hit the floor hard.

The cyborg leaped, claws extended, slashing downward. Banner barely got out of the way and the cyborg clawed up a huge section of the floor with the sweep of his arm.

Banner lashed out with a foot, connecting with the cyborg's chin. It snapped his head around but wasn't enough to stop him from slicing out again with the claws. This time he had more luck, cutting across Banner's right shoulder, three ribbons of green blood welling up, accompanied by Banner's scream of outrage.

The cyborg drove both arms forward, and Banner barely caught them in time. They staggered, the oil now getting under both their feet as they slipped and slid, losing traction. Banner heard the pounding of feet, more of them pursuing him. He had run out of time, and the cyborg was trying to drive the claws down and through the Hulk. . . .

Banner twisted, shoving the cyborg's arms back and up, and then both of them slipped once more. They both went down, and there was a sickening sound of something thick being punctured, like a wooden stake being jabbed through a balloon filled with blood. Banner felt warmth jetting onto him, and for a moment he thought he was bleeding profusely. Then he pushed the cyborg back and saw what had happened. The cyborg had slipped and fallen on his own claws before he'd been able to retract them. They had perforated his face, through his forehead, the bridge of his nose, and his upper lip, and gone through and out the other side. Brain matter and gore decorated the tips of the claws.

Horrified and disgusted, Banner shoved the corpse aside and continued to run. Then he skidded to a halt, placing his palm against a section of wall. It rotated open, revealing a hidden exit. It had been the way he'd gotten in, and now it was the way he got out. By the time the other Hulks converged, Robert Bruce Banner was gone.

The Maestro's infuriated roar could be heard from outside his sanctum.

"You let him get away?!"

The Maestro's hand moved so quickly that the green-gray Hulk had no time at all to dodge it. He went down from the vicious smash. With a growl he started to get up, but the Maestro kicked him in the head with such force that only a minimal amount more would have been required to send his skull scudding across the floor.

"Stay down," the rocky Hulk advised his compatriot.

At that moment the Minister entered, moving with his typical eerie silence. Immediately he saw the tension in the room and stopped where he was, waiting for whatever was happening to run its course.

The green-gray Hulk looked balefully at the Maestro. He realized he was taking his life in his hands, but at that moment he didn't care overmuch. "We'd have had a better shot at him if your son had managed to hold on to him."

The Maestro stood over him, fists trembling in fury, and then raised them above his head as if to smash them downward. The green-gray Hulk, no match for the Maestro in strength, nevertheless did nothing to try to get out of the way.

Slowly, slowly, the Maestro lowered his arms.

"You're a brave one," said the Maestro. "Foolish, but brave. And I have no desire to lose a second Hulkbuster today." He extended a hand to the green-gray Hulk and helped him up . . .

And broke his arm.

The green-gray Hulk let out a startled shriek of pain and staggered, but did not fall. The Maestro watched impassively, and then nodded. "Stout fellow. It's a clean break and will heal within a fairly short time. Go attend to it." And as the green-gray Hulk staggered off, the Maestro's coarse laughter followed him.

But then his laughter trailed off under the level gaze of the rocky-skinned Hulk. "Orders, sir?" asked the latter.

"Orders? Status quo. Everyone on alert. Any irregularities, report to me immediately."

The rocky-skinned Hulk bobbed his head in acknowledgment and left the room, the Minister stepping slightly to the side to get out of his way. The Minister waited until he was gone, and then said to the Maestro, "Number forty-seven has reported back."

"And was forty-seven able to extract any information?"

"Oh yes, he's quite proficient at that. It seems our intruder simply appeared, out of the blue. No one knew or understood much about his background. Boz accorded him some small aid in the way of food and clothing before the intruder went on his way."

"Did he?" the Maestro said darkly. "And were Boz and his people aware of the treasonous designs that the newcomer had upon me?"

"Boz denied that he did at first, but after continued questioning, he confessed that he did."

"I see. I hope our barbarian made clear the extent of our displeasure when it comes to aiding and abetting potential troublemakers."

"Oh yes. He's very thorough."

"In that case," said the Maestro, rising from his huge chair. "Only one other thing remains for the moment. The thing I look forward to least, I must admit. I must have a chat with Brett. I am most concerned about things that the good doctor might have said to *my* son during the time they were together."

"Of course, sir. You're concerned that he may have filled the boy's mind with lies about you."

The Maestro looked at him as if he'd grown a second nose. "Of course not, you fool. I'm concerned he told him the truth."

"Ah. I see. And . . . if he did? How will you handle it, if I may be so bold as to ask."

"I'm not quite sure." He tugged his beard thoughtfully. "Dissembling might do me more harm than good at this point. As unorthodox as it sounds . . . I may genuinely fall back on the truth."

The Minister couldn't cover his surprise. "The *truth*, sir?"

"What can I say, Minister?" The Maestro shrugged blandly. "Desperate times call for desperate measures."

Brett paced his room, trying to sort out what had happened over the past hours.

All the things that this . . . this "Hulk" had said—could they be true? Could it be that everything he knew about himself was a falsehood?

The Maestro had been the only father he had ever known. His earliest memories were being at his father's side. Or clambering on his lap and pulling on his beard, an activity that always prompted bursts of hearty laughter from his giant sire.

He remembered the frustration of not taking to leaping the way that his father wanted—and the pure joy of discovering the remarkable fleetness of foot his powerful legs provided.

His father had always been there for him, applauding his achievements and constantly pushing him to do more, ever more. To test his strength, to push it as far as he could and then beyond. To dare anything, to be confident in his power. To take whatever he wanted, care nothing for the concerns of the weak except in those instances where they could be of value to the strong. To . . . To . . .

There Brett had faltered, as much as he hated to admit it. Every so often, in his secret shame, there would be slight moments of doubt or hesitancy. Oh, he had always overcome that hesitancy. And his father had been there to applaud his first battle . . . his first blood . . . his first ravishment . . .

He remembered her, that first girl. She'd been much older, having been a chumly for quite a few years. She was long past her prime. Her name had been Char. She had had thick, curly brown hair, and that same eager-to-please look that they all wore like a shield.

Brett had killed her.

It wasn't on purpose, of course. It wasn't even by his hand. It was simply that after that first time, he had felt—he wasn't sure— as if he wanted there to be some connection with her. As if she were special somehow, perhaps because she was his first. Although the Maestro had taken no steps to prevent it, he had nevertheless advised against it. He was right to do so, as it turned out. Brett's attempts to actually get to *know* the girl had seemed to make her more unhappy rather than less. As if his well-intentioned endeavors cracked through mental barriers that she had erected to cope with the life she led. (Although what was wrong with that life? That was something that Brett had never been quite able to figure out.)

In any event, they had eventually found the poor woman with her wrists open and a simple note saying, "I'm sorry, Father." Brett asked who her father might be. The Maestro couldn't recall. There were, after all, so many chumlies.

His father . . .

His mother . . .

The Hulk had claimed that he had her eyes. Was it nonsense? It had to be. And yet . . .

Brett placed his hands over his forehead and over his nose, leaving just his eyes visible. He stared into a mirror, trying to separate his eyes from the rest of his face. Trying to imagine them in someone else's face, and what that face would look like . . .

This was nonsense.

They looked like his eyes, and nothing more. There was nothing feminine or soft in them. They were just . . . him . . .

All lies . . .

And yet . . .

There was one thing he could not ignore.

Slowly he pulled back the hair that hung low over his forehead. He peered intently at his left temple.

Considering the remarkable healing prowess of both himself and his father, the continued presence—throughout his entire life—of the odd circular scar he bore had always been a source of mystery to him. The Maestro had simply said it was a birthmark and never seemed interested in discussing it beyond that. For what was there to say?

And yet . . .

A twin.

Every so often—lying there at night, in the silence that was occasionally punctuated by laughter or screams—Brett would lie there and feel . . .

Incomplete.

That was the word. It was never something that he'd ever been able to quantify before.

Or was he now simply being fanciful? Ascribing emotions retroactively to the simple fact that he lived in a world where he was utterly unique? There was the Maestro, and there were the earlier incarnations—but there was exactly one son.

It would make sense that there was a feeling of isolation. The notion that he was somehow "incomplete" was probably just an extension of that.

That sort of . . . ghost feeling . . . the notion that there was someone near him whom he could sense but not see. It couldn't have been real. It couldn't have been.

And yet . . .

No.

It couldn't be.

The door to his room creaked open. He saw the Maestro's reflection in the mirror. He turned and they stared at each other for a long moment.

"It's true," said the Maestro.

Robert Bruce Banner, the incredible Hulk, stood in the midst of the Survivalist encampment.

There were no survivors.

As the sun crept over the horizon line, more and more details of the disaster were evident. Something had come through there like a hurricane. The small homes, meager as they were, had been destroyed. The crops had been torn up. And the rubble . . .

Everywhere there was rubble. Rocks, debris, all from the cliffsides. Except there were no cliffsides anymore. The dimensional gate through which the Hulk had entered was gone, the cliffsides reduced to a massive pile of boulders that had been strewn throughout the encampment.

It was clear what had happened. Someone—one of the Hulkbusters, no doubt, for the Maestro probably would delegate such work—had ripped up the cliffside one huge armful at a time. And he had hurled each massive rock down upon the people. . . .

The people . . .

They had tried to run. There were bodies everywhere, beneath boulders, under collapsed houses . . . everywhere. The ground was darker than it had been the last time the Hulk had been there. Dark with all the blood that it had had to absorb.

His mind started to shut down. It was more guilt, more horror than he could readily take in. He tried to turn away, find something that he could look at that wouldn't shrivel his soul.

He saw Boz's head sticking out from under a particularly large boulder, the rest of his body crushed. One arm was outstretched from under it as well. It seemed to be reaching toward the Hulk in supplication, for help that would never arrive.

Doc Samson wasn't going to come now. He hadn't even been sure if Samson *could* have come. Would he have been able to get through the bizarre temporal fluxes of the interworld? Would he also have wound up facing two possible exits . . . or more? A million questions, and for all he knew Samson was already lost. Another life, another loss to be added to the tally that was accruing on his shoulders.

Nor was the Hulk leaving. The entranceway had been through the rock of the cliffside. The rock was gone, pulverized.

And it was at that point that he knew. He knew, beyond any question, what he was going to do now. He had begun to formulate the plan even while he'd been with Brett. It had been somewhat haphazard, maybe even unlikely . . . no, *definitely* unlikely.

He had developed the first part of the plan. Indeed, he hadn't known that a second part was required. But with the ghosts of Boz and the Survivalists howling at him—with the indelible vision of the corpses strewn throughout the tunnels—and Rick, God help him, Rick, sitting there as an eternal overseer of lost souls . . .

Yes indeed. A two-part plan was required.

The first part was that he would find a way to take all of them—the Maestro, the Hulkbusters, all of them—and turn them into puny humans. That would have been a wonderful irony.

But it was no longer enough. Hence, part two of the plan, after he'd turned them into puny humans.

He would smash them.

Smash them until there was nothing left.

Smash them all.

They had spoken through much of the night.

"So you see . . . you became my greatest enemy," the Maestro said. "In my timeline—the time that leads to this world—moments after you were born, the government came in. They had been spying on me. Betty and I were trying to live anonymously, but it's not easy when you're seven feet and green. But they learned Betty was pregnant, and decided not to make their move immediately. No, no . . . the bastards waited until Betty gave birth. Almost seconds after you were born, they made their move."

"Who were 'they'?"

The Maestro paced the room, his hands behind his back. "I never found out what agency it was . . . something that no one knew of, or at least spoke of. They stole you away, absconded with you deep into the recesses of the hidden places. You were so ill, so sickly at birth, that I thought you had died. But no, they saved you, for their own nefarious purposes. They . . . did things to you. Made you into a guinea pig, to forge you into some sort of . . . of super weapon.

"Eventually, you found me—came after me—an operative of the beloved United States government, trained to do their dirty work. Part of a strike force composed of genetically engineered, irradiated beings called the Gamma Quadrant. I was one of their targets.

"Eventually it came down to a final confrontation between the two of us. By that point I already had a grasp of my ultimate destiny. I saw what humanity was doing to itself. I knew that all I had to do was wait them out. And still they came after me . . . sent you after me. I . . ."

His voice trailed off. Brett prompted, "What happened? That 'final confrontation' you mentioned . . ."

The Maestro looked at him levelly. "I killed you."

Brett's voice was barely above a whisper. "You . . . you killed me?"

"I had no choice. You were like a stranger to me. Hell, you *were* a stranger to me."

"You *killed* me?"

The Maestro threw up his arms in exasperation. "What would you have had me do, Brett? Sacrifice myself? Embrace oblivion for the sake of someone else? Have you remembered nothing I've taught you?"

"Yes, I . . . remember."

"You're hurt," grunted the Maestro.

"Well, what do you *expect* from me, Father? You stand there, you tell me you killed me . . ."

"And look what I've done to rectify the situation! When I discovered the dimension-crossing abilities of the Timeond, look at the first thing I did with it! I went back in time! Sought out Dr. Trotter, disposed of him, and took over his identity. You should have seen me, Brett. Shifted back to my old Banner identity. No one recognized me. Not Samson. Not Banner himself. Although I suspected Betty might, the bitch.

"I used a century's worth of technology to 'cure' Banner. By doing that, we managed to keep a lower profile, giving the government and the mysterious agency less time to mobilize. And shortly after you were born, I came to get you and bring you here." He frowned. "Banner had changed back into the Hulk at that point . . . I wasn't anticipating that. Still not sure why that happened. Didn't stop me, though. Nothing can."

"And you raised me. . . ."

"Yes! Raised you and made up for the barbaric behavior of others! And we will have our revenge, Brett. We will return to the era that abused us, and we will make them feel the anguish that we felt! It will be wonderful! Glorious!"

Brett was quiet for a long time. The Maestro waited for him to say something, and eventually his impatience began to be more evident.

"If you'd left me," he said finally, "what would have happened?"

"The same thing. What would have been the point of that?"

"You don't know that." Brett rose and went to the window, looking to the distance. "It might have turned out differently. Isn't that part of the whole notion of alternate dimensions? I . . . I might have grown up in my own time, my own world. I might have known my mother. . . ."

"I knew your mother. You didn't miss a damned thing."

"He saved my life. My father—my other father—my . . ." He rubbed his forehead in confusion. "He used a gamma ray gun . . . helped stabilize me . . ."

The Maestro made a dismissive wave. "I knew he would do that. If he hadn't, I'd have attended to it. . . ."

"He almost got *killed* doing it!" said Brett. "Some army guy tried to stop him."

"So what!" the Maestro shot back. "So he risked his life! People risk their lives every day. *I reordered reality!* Do you understand the magnitude of that accomplishment?" In a voice louder than he would have liked, he bellowed, *"Do you!?"*

Brett looked down shamefacedly. "Yes, sir."

"Well, *good!*" He drummed his fingers impatiently, still unable to put aside the annoyance he felt with his ingrate of a son. "After all the time, all the sacrifice, all the investment I've made in raising you . . . to think that Banner could show up after all this time and supplant me."

"That hasn't happened, sir," Brett said sincerely. "It never could."

"Well, good," the Maestro said again, this time slightly mollified. "I just wish I knew what he was up to. What he was planning. He'd have to be insane to make another run at the fortress. We're on guard this time, and outnumber him sixty to one."

"I have no idea, sir."

"Did he say anything?"

"Nothing specific. He just said that he's going to stop you . . ." He frowned, trying to remember. Banner had said so much. He seemed incapable of shutting up. ". . . uhm . . . stop you even if he had to start all over again."

The Maestro nodded and gave a curt laugh. "Yes, I'm sure if he had it to do all over again, he'd . . ."

And then he stopped. His eyes widened.

Brett looked at him curiously. "Father . . . ?"

"Of course," he whispered, and then fairly shouted, "*Of course! Start all over! Go back to the beginning!*" And excitedly he grabbed Brett by the shoulders and said fiercely, "We've got him. Thanks to you . . . we've got him."

He headed for the door of the room as Brett stood up. "I don't understand . . . how have we got him?"

"Because," said the Maestro, "I know where he's going. And we're going to go after him, and bring him down. And then, Brett, the Great Conquest begins . . . and we'll bear the corpse of the incredible Hulk in front of us."

Chapter 25

It always seemed to end up back there.

No matter how far the Hulk came . . . no matter how much he endured, no matter whatever experiences he encountered . . .

It always seemed to end up back there.

Gamma Base in New Mexico. The place where a naive scientist named Robert Bruce Banner had overseen the test of his invention, the gamma bomb. A test that would have tremendously far-reaching consequences, both for Banner and for the world. A test that would result in the creation of the Hulk.

And there had been something about that place that had made it more than just a place. The Hulk had a connection to it that bordered on the psychic. No matter where he was, if he simply put his mind to it, he could make his way back to that spot. He needed no compass, nor map. No landmarks were required. All he needed was the power of his legs and enough time to make the journey, and he could always return to that place. A place of blackened ground and blackened dreams.

It was shortly after that explosion—shortly after his double life had begun—that Banner had discovered a large cave out in the desert. Rick Jones, ever-influenced by comic books, had dubbed it the Gamma Cave.

It had served a twofold purpose. First, it had presented a place where the Hulk could be penned up during some of his more uncontrollable rages. And second, it was a secret laboratory. It was there that he first constructed the larger, more powerful gamma-projection machine. He'd used it to regulate the transformations.

He had come to suspect that those early changes had, in fact, not been effected by the gamma machine at all. He had *thought* the machine was executing the changes, and the thought alone was enough to accomplish the deed. It was a crutch. The transformations were a result of his Multiple Personality Disorder, the gamma machine itself a convenient tool to avoid the realization that he himself was causing the transfiguration of man into monster and back again.

After all, he'd changed perfectly adequately many a time without the use of additional gamma rays. For that matter—although he had not questioned it at the time—how had flooding him with gamma particles managed to change him *back* to human form? No, no . . . it had never made any sense, except to a strained and ill mind that wasn't ready to accept the reality of the situation.

Nevertheless . . .

The equipment had been perfectly functional. It hadn't done what it was supposed to do, but it was functional nonetheless.

And now he was going to try to provide it with a different function.

The problem was, it was a tremendous gamble.

As the Hulk leaped through the air in vast, mile-consuming jumps, he was too painfully aware that his leaps were symbolic. They were leaps of faith.

The last time he had been in the cave, it had blown up, the equipment trashed. What he was banking on now was the intervening years being fruitful. Because the fact was that it had been over a century since he'd last been in the Gamma Cave. There was every chance that *sometime* during all those years, he'd been back to the place. And there was a further chance that he had done more work, built more equipment.

Of course, there was a chance he hadn't. There was a chance that after jumping all that way, he would arrive at his old haunts and discover nothing except a few hunks of rotted-out machinery. In which event he had wasted his time.

Not that there was much else for a time-tossed fugitive Hulk to do with his time. As far as the concept of waste went, it was pretty much relative.

The ideal situation was that he would arrive there, find equipment that he had created in the intervening time that could be modified, or even used as it was, to drain the gamma radiation from the Maestro. A weak, human Maestro against an enraged Hulk. It would be, without question, a slaughter.

Slaughter.

An ugly word, that.

As he descended toward the ground, only to bounce off it once more and hurtle skyward again, he thought of the bodies. The murders. The atrocities.

His heart hardened.

He wondered if, in contemplating the murder of a helpless opponent, he was embarking on the first step in the long path that led, unerringly, to his becoming the Maestro? In trying to eliminate the Maestro's evil, was he, in fact, guaranteeing the Maestro's existence?

He didn't care.

When it came down to it, with the dead eyes of all those innocent victims staring back at him, he simply didn't care.

A cold fury burned within him as he kept going, going. After a while his brain effectively shut down. He fell into a steady rhythm, leap, land, leap, land. That and the snarling mental picture of the Maestro were all that mattered to him.

And as it had so many times before, the Hulk's unconscious mind—with accuracy bordering on the supernatural—guided him. Exactly as he had feared, the topography had changed substantially. The fact that landmarks such as major airports were gone didn't surprise him. But good Lord, there were entire *mountain ranges* that had been replaced by craters. What the *hell* kind of weapon could do that?

Cities lay in ruins. In some areas there were actually signs of civilization. Lights in some of the buildings, or thriving encampments. The farther away he got from Dystopia, the more he saw it. It was becoming more and more apparent what had happened: Dystopia had served as a drain for the area. All resources, from the essentials to the luxuries, had been siphoned off by the Maestro and made to serve his interests.

But these places were living under a cloud. Who knew when the Maestro might turn his attention to them?

He wondered what sort of weapons had been used in the century since he'd walked the earth. The amount of ingenuity and inventiveness that humanity had displayed in its endeavors to obliterate itself were nothing short of astounding. If the human race had put as much work into elevating itself as it had into destroying itself, the entire solar system would have been colonized and thriving before the start of the twentieth century.

He thought of Brett.

He had blown it. He had completely blown it.

There had been moments when he thought he might be getting through. Indeed, when he'd make his break for freedom, he'd even fancied that Brett had "let" him go somehow. But the more he thought about their time together—his impassioned speeches that had not penetrated, the complacent and cold amusement in Brett's face as he contemplated the notions of compassion and mercy—the more frustrated he became.

It was a truism that, to some degree, sons always rejected their fathers sooner or later. It was a part of the maturation process, a way of declaring that the child was now going to forge his own path in life.

But he had been rejected by his son and the boy had never even really had the chance to know him. And it wasn't just he himself. It had been everything that he had brought with him. All the noble qualities of humanity, all the higher emotions and respectable attributes that so many of the people the Hulk had encountered *had* displayed.

Always within him there had been a growing resentment of mankind. Humans had hounded him, pursued him, tried to kill him time and again. But there were those who mattered. Individuals who had helped him, or supported him, or loved him. People who had tried to make a difference in his life, as he had in theirs.

If somehow, in some way, the Hulk had managed to impress his memories of those people upon Brett, then their contributions and basic goodness of heart and spirit would have had lasting impact. He had spoken to Brett of them, described them in detail. But it had not seemed to matter. There was an air of cynicism around Brett. His soul dwelt in a castle, with pessimism as a moat and misanthropy as the barricade walls.

He should have known. He had tried to undo in hours what the Maestro had built over a period of two decades. It was an effort doomed to failure from the beginning. The only way it could possibly have succeeded would have been if some sort of ephemeral quality of his mother had made its way to Brett's heart.

For Betty Banner loved people more than anyone Bruce had ever seen. She valued their souls, treasured the spark of life that fired them and the uniqueness of every living being. Faced with the greatest ugliness, she was capable of searching and searching until she found some worthwhile quality. She had seen too much to be an incurable optimist. But her capacity for pure, undiluted hope remained unstinting and undiminished. And Bruce had been praying that some of that had gone to her son, the only inheritance she had been able to give him.

Like so many of his prayers lately, the answer he'd received was less than inspirational.

The sun passed overhead, and shadows had already begun to lengthen as the Hulk approached The Place. By this point he was ravenously hungry, and his thirst was such that he felt as if he could have drained one of the Great Lakes. He'd brought a small amount of food and water with him, which he'd taken from the encampment, along with a few other essentials—all the while trying not to feel like a grave robber. The contents were slung in a bag lashed to his shoulder. He left them untouched, however, for he had no idea how long he would have to make them last. So he forced himself through the physical distress. At this moment nothing mattered more to him than finding the cave, seeing if there was any equipment available—and learning whether there was any hope of this miserable business having any sort of positive ending.

The Hulkbusters stood in the courtyard of the Fortress. They were there in full number and full strength. The Maestro walked among them, murmuring brief words of encouragement to key members of the troops.

He paused longest with his son. His gaze went deep into Brett's eyes, as if trying to read his mind. Had anything that Banner had said gotten through to him? Was Brett now a danger to the Maestro? And if that was the case, then what actions would the Maestro be willing to take?

The answer, of course, was: whatever actions were necessary.

It did not, however, appear that it was going to come down to that. For Brett met his scrutiny with no hint of trepidation. Clearly the young man felt he had nothing to hide. No thought crossing his mind that could be considered treasonous, no scheme unfolding to plot the Maestro's downfall in favor of the weak-minded, weak-kneed, mawkish Bruce Banner.

He nodded approvingly, then stepped back and faced them.

"Hulkbusters," he said, "we stand on the brink of the Great Conquest. But first there is a matter to be attended to. A loose end to be tied off. His name will likely be familiar to you: Dr. Robert Bruce Banner. I have reason to suspect that, even now, he plots our downfall. The odds of him accomplishing that are extremely slim. But, as you all know all too well, those odds have never daunted us before. So there is no reason to expect that he would feel any trepidation over them.

"I am certain that he has returned to our birthplace. He has a considerable head start. But I am not concerned, nor should you be. We are many. We are mighty. We are unstoppable. We are a green wave of irresistible force, against which no object is unmovable. We will find him, and make certain that he cannot harm us ever again. And then . . ." He held up the Timeond. "Then we will cross the dimensional barrier and begin our great and epic adventure. I do not know when, or even if, we shall return to this place. In truth," he looked at the Fortress in mild annoyance, "I have grown bored with it. Perhaps even complacent. We—all of us—are meant for greater things than languishing in emerald towers." And suddenly he roared, "*We deserve battle!*"

"Yes!" they shouted as one.

"*We deserve to wade through the pulped remains of our enemies!*"

"Yes!" they chorused again.

"*We deserve conquest!*"

"*Yes!*"

"And my son," and he clapped Brett on the shoulder, "who has never known the true joy of conquest—the true exhilaration of being the strongest one there is—we'll show him a hell of a time, won't we?!"

"*Yes!*"

He gestured in the general direction of New Mexico, thousands of miles away. "Consider this little side trip a prologue before our true story of magnificence begins. Hulkbusters . . . *are you ready?*"

There was a chorus of cheers and affirmations. The Maestro adjusted the shoulder straps that held a piece of equipment to his back. Then he gripped Brett firmly by the forearm, prepared to provide his son with the extra lift and power he was going to need to keep up.

"Father" and "son" leaped heavenward, and a sea of green roared after them.

The people of Dystopia watched them go and looked at each other in puzzlement. They weren't exactly sure what had just happened. Where had the Maestro and his great army gone? They'd never moved out en masse in that fashion. What was the purpose?

And from his street corner, Skooter saw them leave. And he had a feeling. A feeling that they would not be coming back.

This was his moment. He would rally the people. Organize a revolt. They would charge the castle, take it back, take over. Dystopia would enter a new golden age.

"Down with the Maestro! Let's storm the castle!" he shouted.

A passerby snickered disdainfully and tossed him a very small gem as he went. It made a clinking sound as it landed in Skooter's cart.

"No! I'm not looking for your charity! I'm serious! Let's storm the castle! The Maestro's gone! We can do this!"

WHAT SAVAGE BEAST

He continued to shout that for the rest of the day until his voice was raw. And after that, he went home and sobbed himself to sleep.

The Hulk found the cave immediately, as he had known he would. What he had not expected to find was a genuine entranceway. It had, after all, been blown up rather thoroughly last time he'd been there, and the hope that anything had been done with the cave in the intervening time was just that, hope. A faint hope, really, although one that he was zealously clinging to.

But when he discovered the cave, the faint hope began to burn more brightly. For wedged into the mouth of the cave was a sizable boulder. It might be that he was imagining it, but it certainly seemed to him as if the boulder had been placed there by design. Oh, it was possible some sort of landslide had put it there, but it didn't seem terribly likely.

If it was coincidence, then it meant nothing.

But in terms of a "door," if that's what it was, it was rather effective. After all, it wouldn't occur to the casual observer that there was something *inside* the cave that was being protected. So they wouldn't have any reason to show up with the sort of heavy-duty tools that would be required to demolish the thing. And it weighed a few tons, so it wasn't as if just anyone could show up and roll it out of the way.

Fortunately enough, of course, he wasn't just anyone.

He placed his hands on either side of the boulder and pulled.

It didn't budge at first, and he was momentarily concerned he was losing his touch. But then it did, rolling out of the mouth of the cave and, as it so happened, over his foot. He didn't even feel it, much less care about it.

The inside of the cave was dark. He reached into his bag and pulled out an electric torch, which looked sort of like a wand with a lengthy light bar on the end. He didn't know what powered it exactly, but whatever it was, he hoped it lasted.

He switched it on and it glowed pale green.

"Figures," he muttered, and entered the cave.

As he moved through it, he thought briefly and wistfully about that time-travel movie about the two gonzo teenagers wherein, every time they needed something to get out of a situation, they just decided that they would go to some point in the past and leave it handy for themselves. And lo and behold, there it was.

Unfortunately, the Hulk wasn't in his own reality, so that entire strategy—as temporally debatable as it was—wasn't any sort of option in any event. He was counting entirely on capitalizing on whatever the Maestro might have done in his own past, back when he was merely the humble Hulk.

Still, just for kicks, he said, "I know! I'll leave a lighting system in place!"

And he almost jumped when the lights snapped on before he had even completed the sentence.

He looked around in confusion, his eyes narrowing. "And . . . I'll leave a box of cookies right . . . there," and he pointed to the floor.

No cookies were forthcoming.

He then realized what had happened. At some point in the intervening years, the Maestro (Hulk, whoever) had built in some sort of lights to replace the series of lanterns that Banner had used. And they were voice-activated.

He passed a large generator that had likewise been put in, studying it carefully. The technology was like nothing he'd seen before. He had no clue what was powering it. It was purring softly, like a square red cat, and now lights and devices were flickering to life all over the cave. He turned left and right, not knowing where to look first.

"Oh my God," he whispered.

He'd come back there, all right. Come back with a vengeance.

The cave was lined with equipment. What had been a crude laboratory by earlier standards was beyond what was available in top twentieth-century laboratories. The Gamma Cave was, quite simply, high tech.

"I don't believe it," he murmured. "All I need is the Batmobile and I'm all set."

Not only that, but there were cans of food, bottled water, all manner of sustenance that might be required for a lengthy stay. It made him wonder, in a rather morbid frame of mind, what set of circumstances had arisen that had prompted him to turn a temporary shelter into something more permanent. Had he been on the run? In hiding? What had gone wrong?

He had no idea. The thought that he might someday find out was rather sickening to him, and so he tried his best to put it completely out of his mind.

He backed up, looking around, and bumped into something. He was slightly startled as he turned around quickly, and then he saw it. It was a gamma-ray gun.

It was big. Damned big. It looked like about ten bazookas all welded together.

It was thick with dust, as was everything else in the cave. Nevertheless, it too was humming with electronic life. The level monitors lined the base of the gun, and were in "warm-up" mode. After who-knew-how-long a period of inactivity, it was impossible for him to guess how long it was going to take for the gun to reach full power. The wave readings were on their way to a steady buildup, but it was clearly going to take a while.

Already his mind was racing with the amount of work he was going to have to do. To a degree, it was like reinventing the wheel. The gamma-ray gun, as near as he could tell, was still designed for firing gamma rays, not absorbing them. Indeed, if he'd ever found a way to do that very thing, his own problems would have been over a lot faster.

But he was in a different time now and, looking around, he saw more equipment and technology that was new to him. It was entirely possible that he could retool the gamma-ray gun to make it work that way. But the first thing he was going to have to do was fully grasp the purpose and use for all of this . . . stuff. It was like a seventeenth-century cabinetmaker being shoved into a twentieth-century workshop and told to produce some furniture. There were things there that he was able to grasp the basic function of, but figuring out how to use all of it, and what to use it for, was going to take him some time.

He wondered how much he had.

Chapter 26

Once, buffalo had wandered the plains.

They had traveled in great herds, and to see them move was nothing short of awe-inspiring. The ground would thunder beneath them as they migrated, confident in their power, unstoppable in whatever direction they chose to go.

Americans had not seen anything like it in centuries. In fact, most people had never even heard of buffalo. Of the few who had, most of them had never seen a picture of one. And of the few who had seen pictures, they still were not capable of grasping just what it was like to be witness to such raw, unyielding force.

Until the green wave.

It swept across the middle of America, its advent announced by thunder that rippled through the air from a distance, and seismic waves that spread for miles. Five dozen gamma-spawned behemoths landing, not all together, but in rapid sequence like a series of hailstones the size and heft of meteors. And then they would take off again, pushing themselves off like so many divers, laughing off the planet's gravity, continuing on their way.

Most people knew of the Maestro. Few had seen him, but all trembled at the mention of his name, and even used threats of him to scare recalcitrant children. And there had been rumors that the

Maestro was gearing up for some great offensive. Mutterings from highly unreliable sources reported that the Maestro was creating more creatures like himself for some diabolical purpose. But no one truly believed it, or at least didn't want to believe it.

Now, though, came the indisputable proof.

They could be seen coming, swarming through the skies, like jade locusts. People would hide in their homes, seek shelter any-where they could, as the horde would approach. Then it would land, staccato, a barrage of rapid-fire tremblings, and the people would cry out or pray and know beyond any question that this was it, this was the end.

And then the horde would leave again. Without slowing down, without even bothering to pay attention to its surroundings, it would continue on its way. Not believing what had just happened—not believing their narrow escape—the people would watch as the green wave would recede into the horizon. A horizon that was dark-ening, clouds moving in and pale, odd colors swirling across it. A storm was gathering.

And they would give praise to whatever deity they felt was watching over them, and breathe great sighs of relief that whoever was going to feel the force of that armada, it was not going to be them.

Still and all, no one who witnessed that migration ever slept soundly again. And any loud noise would be enough to startle them into screaming wakefulness.

Bruce Banner was in trouble.

He needed a pencil, and in all this wonderful, high-tech envi-ronment, there wasn't a single damned pencil to be had.

He'd been working on the gamma-ray gun for some hours, moving as quickly as he could. The size of his fingers had been something of an impediment, as had his unfamiliarity with much of the equipment.

What had been a godsend (which was nice, since he felt that God certainly owed him a few) was some manner of particle phase rechanneler that he had found—insanely—propping up a table. It was precisely what he needed, and he had been spending much of the last hour trying to wire the damned thing into the gamma-ray gun.

Some of this equipment, the more he studied it, looked as if it had origins that were not quite of this world. Had there been some sort of bizarre alliance forged with extraterrestrials? Just what *had* gone on?

And furthermore, if he'd actually possessed the equipment to rid himself of the gamma radiation that had cursed his life, then why hadn't he just gone ahead and done it already?

He suspected he was beginning to piece together the answer. When he'd been holed up in this cave, he must have already been the Maestro. The Maestro would not be remotely interested in finding a way of removing his gamma-spawned power. Furthermore, Banner was well aware that the Maestro was fully capable of willing himself into the mortal form of Bruce Banner (albeit a remarkably old-looking Bruce Banner, keeping with the Maestro's own advanced age). So if he wanted to move around inconspicuously, he would easily be able to do so without artificial means.

None of which answered the question of where he could find a pencil. He wanted to be able to make some notations as he monitored the flux couplings. There wasn't going to be a lot of margin for error.

Finally he found one stuck in a corner. Now all he needed was a piece of paper.

There was none.

He started digging around in his pockets, hoping to find a scrap there. He found some old crinkled receipts . . .

And a photograph.

A Polaroid, to be specific. He had completely forgotten he stuck it in there.

Looking slightly flustered and embarrassed in the photo was Betty, in her hospital gown, seated and with Brett in her lap. She was holding the bottle to his mouth and she was caught in mid-motion of trying to shoo Bruce away.

"I'm sorry, Betty," he said softly. "I really screwed up."

He laid the picture down on a counter and went back to the gun to make a few more notations.

Then he felt the distant rumblings.

For a second he thought it was an earthquake, but he quickly realized the error. No, he knew now without question exactly what it was.

He was completely out of time, and he'd had no opportunity to test any of his hurried reworking of the gamma-ray gun.

"Guess we'll have to field-test it," he muttered. His eye caught the photo on the counter and he called to it, "Wish me luck, hon'. And don't wait up."

The photo didn't reply.

The Hulk was waiting for them when they arrived.

They filled the sky like the flying monkeys descending on Dorothy, which somehow seemed appropriate to the Hulk. It kept with the *Wizard of Oz* motif.

He was standing outside the cave, the massive gun at his side.

He would want them to get as close as possible, of course. He knew that. And they would know that. The question was, were they going to begin with a full frontal assault? Zoom in toward him like so many guided missiles? If they did, he'd have to fire in as wide a beam as possible. That might dilute the effectiveness. Could he really take out that many of them, that quickly?

He was still busy running mental calculations when the Hulkbusters descended.

As one, they landed half a mile away. Naturally Banner saw them go to ground before he heard the vibrations of their landing.

And then they stood there.

Unrushed.

Unperturbed.

And for quite some time.

The only move they made was slowly to spread in a line stretching across the desert, almost shoulder to shoulder. For one giddy moment Banner expected them to link arms and form a kickline.

Dead center of the line was the Maestro. To his immediate right was Brett, watching impassively.

Rolling in from the distance, the sky was darkening, as if someone had spilled a bottle of ink on it and it was slowly washing in their direction, obliterating all light as it went.

Then, moving at a relaxed stroll, the Maestro started toward him. He was clearly unarmed, his hands hanging at his sides. His arms swung in leisurely fashion. If he was at all concerned by the threat that the Hulk posed to him, he certainly didn't let on.

The Hulk cast a quick glance over his own shoulder, in the event that someone was coming up behind him by way of ambush. But no, there was no one moving in from the rear. The Maestro's entire forces were concentrated directly in front of him. Squarely in the path of the gamma gun.

Slowly the Maestro drew closer and closer. The Hulk waited, his fingers poised over the triggering devices, waiting for the Maestro to make his inevitable charge. Certainly he wouldn't simply stand there and let the Hulk . . .

"Fire," said the Maestro calmly. He had stopped about thirty yards away. Close enough for the gun to work excellently, but too far for him to charge and get within proximity to destroy it. Even an attempt to slam his hands together and generate a sonic wave could be headed off by a quick blast of the gamma-ray gun.

But he was making no such move. He didn't even seem to be considering it. Instead he was regarding the Hulk with undisguised disdain.

"Oh, I'm sorry," amended the Maestro. "Perhaps the word you're waiting for is 'draw.' That *is* what this feels like, you know. A spaghetti Western. Perhaps I should be wearing a duster to flap in the breeze. Or a serape. Either way, a Stetson would certainly be in order, don't you think?" He whistled a five-note theme that floated away in the gentle breeze blowing across the desert.

Banner waited.

"Go ahead. Fire," urged the Maestro. "That's what you intend to do, isn't it? That's what this little," and he gestured vaguely, "showdown is all about, isn't it? You think you can shoot me with your popgun and drain the gamma energy from me. Correct?"

"Yes," said the Hulk evenly.

"Are you waiting for me to make some sort of 'move'?" The Maestro shrugged his wide shoulders. "Why should I? That would imply that I have something to be afraid of."

"Don't you?"

"Nothing that you have to offer, certainly." His lips curled back, revealing his yellow teeth. "So . . . did you enjoy some quality time with my son?"

"My son," corrected the Hulk.

"Tell me, my dear doctor, what did you think you would accomplish? With the kidnapping, and now this display that wouldn't win first prize in a high-school science fair. I haven't been back here in years, and looking at that thing, I'm appalled by how shoddy the workmanship was. Aren't you embarrassed?"

As if the Maestro hadn't spoken, the Hulk repeated, "He's *my* son."

"Yes, well . . . it doesn't seem like you'll be entering the father/son potato sack race anytime soon, does it? I'm afraid that whatever you told him didn't make much of an impression. Then again, you know kids. How does the song go? Oh yes . . . why can't they be like we were? Perfect in every way."

"Give me the Timeond," said the Hulk evenly, fighting to keep the revulsion from his voice. "Give me the Timeond . . . and Brett. We'll leave, and that will be that."

"There's several problems with that," the Maestro told him, sounding almost apologetic. "Number one, you don't know how to operate the Timeond."

"I'm a fairly clever fellow. I'll figure it out."

"Ah, but that leaves us with number two: I don't trust you."

"That makes us even."

The Maestro's eyes widened, and he looked mortified. "You don't trust *me*? I don't *have* to lie. I can do whatever I want, and I never have to apologize for anything. So what reason would I have to lie? Tell you what: I'll prove it to you. I have so much faith in myself, and so little in you, that I'm simply going to stand here and let you shoot me. Hell . . . even better," and he raised his voice so that it carried to the waiting line of Hulkbusters, spread across the horizon. "*Gentlemen, if Dr. Banner's little device here defeats me, you are to leave the field of battle and go back home, never to darken anyone's doorway again! That is my direct order! Is that understood?*"

Like an army regiment, they chorused, "*Yes, sir!*"

The Maestro stood with his arms behind his back, one leg slightly bent at the knee. He might have been leaning against a bar waiting for a drink to be served. "Go ahead, Doctor. Do your worst."

It was a trick. Banner was positive it was a trick.

Was the gun booby-trapped somehow? Was that it? But he'd found nothing to indicate it. Everything seemed normal. Was the Maestro going to try to leap out of the way? But his legs weren't coiled to spring.

The Hulk's finger was frozen over the trigger as his mind raced, trying to anticipate, trying to figure out the angles.

And the Maestro sneered, "You pathetic punk. You come here, thinking you can be a match for me? A father to my son? A conqueror of great foes? You coward! You nothing! Fire, if you've got the guts! I'm not afraid of you! I'm not afraid of anything! *Fire and be damned!*"

The Hulk's finger stabbed the trigger.

And the instant it did, the Maestro whirled.

In the fading light, a disk of red and white glinted on his back.

In another time, in another place, the proud shield of the long-dead Captain America had proven a momentary salvation for Rick Jones from the Maestro's wrath. It was a different time, a different dimension, and a different Maestro. Nevertheless, a Maestro in any timeline would have appreciated the irony of that masterful weapon now providing protection for the Maestro himself.

The gamma-ray beam ripped out of the gun and struck the shield. It happened in a split instant, before it even had time to fully register on the Hulk what had just happened.

Captain America had been legendary, his shield no less so. It was renowned, even feared, for its impenetrability. That reputation was well-deserved.

The beam ricocheted straight toward Bruce Banner.

Still unable to grasp what had just happened, the Hulk's reflexes were the only thing that saved him. He hit the dirt as the beam crackled over his head.

The Maestro spun, the entire maneuver taking just under a

second, as he whirled out of the path of the beam. The deadly ric-
ochet ceased, but before the Hulk could scramble to his feet, the
Maestro had unslung the shield from his back and hurled it with all
his might. It hurled through the air with the speed and accuracy of
a cruise missile, and smashed squarely into the gamma-ray gun.
The shield sliced through the gun like a buzz saw.

The gamma-ray gun sputtered, and then flame leaped from it.
The Hulk lunged toward it, his heart sinking, and there was nothing, absolutely nothing he could do except shield his eyes as the
gun exploded into a million pieces.

And before he had the chance to lower his arm, the Maestro
was upon him.

He slammed into the Hulk, driving him back. But the Hulk
grabbed a toehold in the dry ground and was moved only a few
feet before skidding to a halt.

"Fighting back. Good for you," grunted the Maestro.

The ground was rumbling. The Hulkbusters were charging at
full strength and at full speed. Within seconds he was going to be
outnumbered sixty to one.

In his mind, he saw Betty's face crying to him, shouting, begging for him to do something. . . .

He saw the faces of millions of innocent people who would fall
beneath the unstoppable power of an army of Hulks. Women, children, all of them . . .

He saw the face of Brett looking at him with disdain . . .

And he saw the Maestro. But not in his mind's eye, not in his
recollections. It was right here, right now, that sneering, twisted,
evil distortion of himself, shouting something at him that he
couldn't even hear because the blood was pounding in his ears and
the fury was building.

With an animal roar, the Hulk lifted the Maestro over his head and hurled him in the direction of the Gamma Cave. He hadn't intended for him to go there; it was just the direction the Hulk happened to be facing at the time.

The Maestro smashed into it, rubble from the cliffside falling on him, and then the Hulk was there, moving faster than he'd ever moved before. The Maestro, off balance, nevertheless delivered several furious blows, any of which could have reduced a giant sequoia to splinters. The Hulk's skin quivered beneath each punch, but he had sent the pain to a very faraway place, and he returned each slam with equal ferocity.

The Maestro hadn't quite been prepared for it. He had allowed his personal disdain for the civilized, humanitarian mind-set of Dr. Robert Bruce Banner to undermine his estimation of the Hulk's capacity for sheer brutality. In short, he had been overly confident . . . and now it was on the verge of costing him.

The Hulk struck again and again, a blur of punches that left the Maestro reeling. He jammed his fingers into the Maestro's eyes, his fingers crushing against the base of the Maestro's skull with such force that it cut off circulation of blood to the Maestro's brain.

The Maestro couldn't believe it. He was pounding on Banner, but the blows were having no effect. A black haze was covering his eyes, and at that moment the Maestro was closer to death than he had ever been.

And a gray form charged into the Hulk from the side, knocking him clear of the Maestro. The Maestro lay there, gasping, clutching at his throat, unable to believe how quickly he had almost tossed away everything.

Brett slugged his father as hard as he could. The Hulk staggered, still slightly confused. He'd been so focused on the Maestro that he was having trouble readjusting his targets. It was getting increasingly hard for him to think—a warning sign, but he was too deep in the midst of combat to think about it.

Brett's desperate blows drove the Hulk back, back toward the cave. But then he swung wide, the Hulk ducking under the round-house, and the Hulk came in fast, aiming several quick and vicious blows at Brett's belly. It was rock hard, but even rocks crumble under steady pressure.

Driven, angry, his fury mounting, the pressure and stress of the last several days was finally catching up with him. The Hulk was completely losing control, and this time Brett was the recipient of his undiluted rage.

He smashed Brett into the ground, creating a crater three feet deep. The world seem to spin around Brett. He tried to twist away, but the Hulk had slid his arms in and around, his hands clasping on the back of Brett's neck, shoving his head forward and down toward his chest. The Hulk started to twist, apply all his strength. Within five seconds he would break Brett's neck . . . ten and he'd rip his head clean off his shoulders.

And in a strangled voice barely recognizable as his own, Brett gasped, "*Father . . . don't . . . please don't . . .*"

The words cut to the core of the mind of Bruce Banner. And he heard his own voice uttering those words, heard his own pleas to his own father, pleas that had gone unanswered as Brian Banner had beaten him, savaged him, done things so hideous they were buried and locked away . . . the child-voice of Bruce Banner, begging for mercy that never came.

The Hulk hurled him away.

Brett tumbled, out of control, hurtled into the depths of the Gamma Cave.

The Hulk whirled just as the Maestro slugged him in the jaw. He heard a loud crack like a rifle shot as his jaw shattered under the impact. He staggered, the pain so great that even he was unable to blow it off.

Instantly the broken bones of his jaw began to heal, but then it was too late, for the Hulkbusters were upon him.

In the Gamma Cave, Brett got to his feet, sucking air into his grateful lungs. Thankfully, the world had stopped spinning.

He heard the sounds of struggle outside. Obviously the Hulkbusters had converged on Banner, and if that was the case, then certainly the fight would not go on for very long.

He took a deep breath and started to head out again when he noticed something out the corner of his eye. Something small, with the edges slightly curled, lying on a counter. He reached for it and stared at it.

A woman looked back at him. A woman in some simple white outfit, and she was holding an infant.

An infant with gray skin.

He continued to stare at it. It started to shake and he wondered why, until he realized that his hand was trembling. He forced his hand to remain still as he continued to regard the picture with fascination.

Emotions tumbled through him. He tried to sort them out but they were moving too quickly for him to grasp. She was staring at him, right *at* him, as if looking through the lens of time. What was that in her face? Embarrassment? Chagrin? In a flight of fancy, he imagined that she was examining him across a century and was mortified to see what he was. What he had become . . .

It was ridiculous.

He was ridiculous.

He threw the picture to the ground. This woman was a stranger to him. So . . . all right. So, biologically she had spawned him. Him and his brother, his long-dead brother who had haunted him . . .

"He didn't! He didn't haunt me and she didn't haunt me and I'm not being haunted!" he shouted to no one. He turned and bellowed at the picture that lay on the floor, "I don't know you! You mean nothing to me! *Nothing!* I don't need you! I don't need anybody! I was *happy* until he came along, spouting at me about humanity and conscience and all the weaknesses I spent my whole life despising! Get out of my head! Get *out* of my *life!*"

And without realizing it, he had sunk to his knees, his face becoming wet with tears. He wiped them away so fiercely that his entire face almost went with them. He picked up the photo again and pleaded, "Please . . . get out of my life."

She looked back at him, frozen in time, for all time . . .

And he thought, *Oh God . . . I have her eyes . . .*

At first the Hulk thought he might actually have a chance.

This notion lasted for about five seconds. They came at him from all sides, an unrelenting, unstopping force. Everywhere he turned there were fists in his face, in his gut . . . everywhere. He couldn't even begin to build up a defense.

This didn't stop him from trying.

He chose a direction at random and charged that way like a locomotive. He crashed directly into Barbarian Hulk with such force that the barbarian dropped his sword. The barbarian went down as Banner grabbed the sword up. But before he could bring it to bear, the rocky-skinned Hulk had slammed into him. They staggered, weight against weight, power against power, the rocky-skinned Hulk trying to wrestle the sword away, Banner struggling to hold on to it. The others held back, trying to find an opening to get in, wary of the sword. The ebony blade whipped back and forth as they vied for control of it.

The barbarian, from behind, tried to jump in and grab at it. And the rocky-skinned Hulk, not seeing him, picked that moment to get the upper hand on Banner. Banner staggered, and the sword whistled to the right.

It sliced cleanly through the barbarian's throat.

He wobbled a moment, looking extremely befuddled, and then his head slid off his shoulders. His lifeless body joined his head on the ground a moment later.

From a distance, the Maestro saw. And he howled in fury, "Get him! *Get him!*"

And now the battle was truly joined. They pounded on him relentlessly.

And he fought back.

He didn't yield. He was beyond fear for his life, beyond regrets for what he had not accomplished. Beyond anything except a ceaseless determination to take as many of them with him as he could.

There was no plan to his pounding, no art, no strategy. He flailed away, faster, angrier, his strength escalating. The others matched him for ferocity, his struggles on par with those of Sisyphus. But he kept on going, kept on pounding, kept on fighting, everything except his need to destroy washed away in a haze of green fury. . . .

And then the blows started to hurt. Really hurt.

He was too far gone by that point to realize what was happening. That's the way it always was at these moments. Each time he swore it wasn't going to happen again. Each time he didn't realize it when it was happening. And each time it happened, he was helpless.

The pain was jarring, disconcerting, and angered him all the more. The anger fed into it, speeding up the process and the transformation.

The Maestro, watching from a distance, saw it happening. He remembered when he himself had gone through that stage—a necessary developmental one that he'd been damned lucky to survive.

The incredible Hulk shrank away, his skin turning from green to pinkish white, his mass disappearing, his musculature becoming soft and undefined. The only thing that was growing was his rage, and a fat lot of good that was going to do him.

"*Hulk will smash fake Hulks!*" he bellowed in a raging but reedy voice.

This generated a roar of laughter from several, and a half-dozen green fists drew back for the purpose of turning Bruce Banner's head into something resembling a bowl of cherry gelatin.

"*Wait!*" shouted the Maestro. "Let's see him!"

Banner was hauled to his feet—all 120 pounds of him. He ranted. He roared. He did everything except impress anybody.

"He's yours to kill, Maestro," said the hairy Hulk.

And the Maestro laughed. "Ohhh . . . I've got a much better idea than that."

While overhead, the sky turned black. . . .

Chapter 27

The Minister understood. At long last—as he looked to the skies, as he looked to his soul—he understood.

He had been drowsing uneasily, falling asleep while working on translating one of the arcane verses on the "true nature" of the universe. And in his state of semiwakefulness, there had been a sudden flash of insight. Whether it came from within or without he could not be sure, but the point was, he had had it.

And so he understood . . .

There are two great powers in the universe—Order and Chaos—constantly at war with each other, each recruiting their unwitting agents, each acting to outdo the other. . . .

And Chaos had chosen the Maestro, and he, who thought that he ruled over all, was their unwitting servant, rampaging through the dimensions, through the timelines, the embodiment of chaos. . . .

And the Great Conquest had within it the seeds of even greater destruction than the Maestro would or could understand. . . .

And Order was fighting back. . . .

"He has to be stopped," whispered the Minister. "He has to be, or it . . . it could be the end of everything. . . . He has to be stopped. . . ."

The Minister went quickly to his closet and removed one of the mystic artifacts that he had spent twenty long years studying and understanding. It was a long red cloak with yellow trim.

He wrapped it around himself and launched himself toward the window. The mystic cloak of levitation raised him off his feet, propelling him toward the balcony and off it.

His arms outstretched, the cape fluttering behind him, he swooped down toward Dystopia, then started to arc upward toward the sky. He wasn't sure how he was going to be able to follow the Maestro, but he knew he had to try . . . he had to endeavor to stop him . . . he had to . . .

He never heard the blast that struck him. The laser scissored through his head, bisecting his skull.

Without his will to give it direction, the cloak of levitation slowed to a halt. The Minister hung there, lifeless, and then slowly, very slowly, drifted toward the ground.

Far below, peering out through the window of his hovel, Skooter pumped his arm in triumph. Every night now he'd sat there, vigilant, laser rifle next to him, hoping that somehow, someday, he'd get a crack at the Minister.

For it had been the Minister who had suggested cutting Skooter's legs off. The Maestro hadn't cared one way or the other. It had been the Minister who had recommended it . . .

. . . just to see how much pain Skooter could take before passing out.

. . . just for an experiment.

. . . just for fun.

"Got you, you bastard," Skooter crowed. He put down his rifle and leaned his head back, rocking on the stumps of his legs in triumph. Stumps which would shortly be irrelevant when Skooter's new red-and-yellow-trimmed acquisition made him, henceforth, the most mobile man in Dystopia . . .

* * *

They stormed through the dimensions, an unstoppable tidal wave of green.

The Maestro led the way, and he carried in front of him an X-shaped cross made from metal bars.

Tied to them, at the hands and feet, was the battered form of Bruce Banner.

They'd worked him over a little, just for fun. Blackened his eyes, bruised his skin, cracked at least one rib. And then they'd made him into their masthead, their standard, their insignia.

The Maestro marched, shouting at Banner, "When humanity sees us coming, there will be the devastated remains of the being who tried to save them. The living symbol of what we once were, held in contempt for all to see! You're our flag! No . . . even better, and more appropriate! You're our Banner!"

At the Maestro's side was Brett, marching in lockstep. The howls of laughter and glee from the others rang in his ears.

Bruce was trying to pull free of his bonds, still fired by the rage burning within him.

All around them the temporal winds were howling. The roads that ribboned around them were shuddering under the gusts.

Although the Maestro said nothing to his army, the truth was that there was something in the air he didn't like. He had traveled the interdimensional pathways many a time, but had never encountered anything quite like this before. It was as if the very environment was . . . fighting him. It seemed a bit harder to push through, and the road was that much more unsteady. It was as if all the Hulks, in their collective presence, had garnered the attention of something beyond the senses. Something that was angry. Something that was resisting.

He clutched at the Timeond, on an iron chain around his neck, focusing his will through it, battling the churning surroundings.

The Hulkbusters were confident, fierce and prepared, unaware of the potential danger.

And, preoccupied as he was, the Maestro was paying no attention to Brett at all.

Brett, whose mind was racing ahead to what they would find when they came out the other side.

Brett, who was looking up at the struggling, helpless form of Bruce Banner, and remembering him in his savage state of a short time ago—a point where he held Brett's life in his hands . . . and had spared him . . .

It was an action for which the Maestro would have had nothing but disdain. The act of a weakling. A coward. It was a puny human thing to do.

And Brett was alive because of it.

Brett, who was unable to get the flood of words out of his head. The words that Banner had tossed around which Brett flinched at. *Compassion. Humanity. Sympathy. Mercy.*

There was no place for such things in the Maestro's world. In the real world. In Brett's world . . .

Brett . . .

. . . who touched his pocket, felt the photograph in there that he'd jammed in like a guilty secret. The woman with the soulful eyes . . .

A stranger! She's a stranger to you!

"This way!" shouted the Maestro to the Hulkbusters as the road trembled beneath them. The temporal winds were roaring ever louder, and the Hulkbusters were starting to feel a slight bit of trepidation.

Brett looked at the Maestro, really looked at him as if for the first time—and suddenly wasn't sure who the stranger was. . . .

The Maestro passed the Crossroads of reality. On one or two occasions he had spotted an old incarnation of the Hulk there, but he had generally managed to avoid him. There was no sign of him this time. With the way that time was in flux around them, they were either at a point where he had not yet arrived, or perhaps had already left. Either way, there was no need to worry about him. Hell, if they ran into him, he'd probably even join them.

What he did need to worry about was the very passageway itself. The Timeond was glowing fiercely, starting to become hot in his hand.

He felt as if the entire Crossroads was in danger of being torn apart, shredded to the four corners of unreality by the interdimensional temporal winds. But the Timeond would protect them, would hold them together . . . hold everything together . . .

Banner roared again, struggled against his bonds, and it was a distraction that the Maestro simply didn't need. "Here!" and he shoved Banner into Brett's hands. "Hold him!"

Brett did so, looking up into Banner's face.

Banner returned the gaze, his expression one of anger and . . . . . . betrayal . . .

And Brett stepped around in front of his father, blocking his path. "Father, please don't . . ."

"*Get out of the way!*" snarled the Maestro.

Brett stayed where he was. "You said you were doing this for me. Don't. I don't need it. I don't want it. Let's just . . . let's just go home. . . ."

The Maestro stared at him incredulously. "What? *What?* Are you out of your mind? What do you think this is, a class outing? A picnic? A trip to the beach? *This is war! Us against them!*"

The road rocked under them. To all sides, the ribbons out to infinity were starting to buck.

Bruce Banner didn't notice. His attention had been caught by the argument that was ensuing below him, the words starting to penetrate the haze of his rage.

"It's not right!" said Brett. "It's not necessary! Humanity can't hurt us anymore! There's nothing to be accomplished by—"

And in a white-hot fury, the Maestro stabbed an accusing finger at Banner and shouted at Brett, "He did this to you! He ruined you! Two decades of training and preparation, and this fool comes along and destroys it in two days! I won't have it! *I won't have it!*"

He lunged for Banner, whom Brett was still holding over his head.

Desperately Brett kicked out, knocked the Maestro back. The Maestro fell and almost skidded off the edge of the road. He caught himself as the other Hulks, who were lined up two by two, fell back.

Infinity yawned around them.

With a roar the Maestro rushed Brett. Desperately, Brett dropped the crucified Banner to the road and braced himself for the Maestro's charge.

The Maestro lunged, consumed with fury and trying to get to Banner. Brett ducked under it and came up with his shoulder catching the Maestro squarely in the pit of his stomach. His legs propelling him forward, Brett drove the Maestro back, slamming him into the Hulkbusters.

There was an immediate domino effect, and two of the Hulkbusters were knocked clean off the road. They tried to find something to grab on to, but there was nothing but temporal winds that picked them up and hurled them away. They bellowed protest, but there was nothing to be done for them as they spiraled away, out of sight, into infinity.

The Maestro couldn't believe it. He saw them fall, saw that he was helpless, and he turned the full fury of his malignant glare onto Brett. "You . . . *imbecile* . . ."

"Don't," Brett warned.

"You think to cross me? *Me?* Without me, you'd be nothing! Without me, you'd be dead!"

"I'm dead inside already! What's the difference?"

"You want to know the difference?" howled the Maestro above the roar of the temporal winds. *"Here's the damned difference!"*

The Maestro bore him backward, pounding furiously at him, giving him no chance to mount any sort of counterattack.

Punctuating each sentence with a cruel punch, the Maestro shouted, "You're *soft!* You're *weak!* You're *puny!*"

And as Brett went down, the Maestro gave a vicious kick that knocked him off the road.

But before he'd fallen any distance at all, a powerful green hand lashed out and snagged his wrist. In one smooth motion the incredible Hulk swung his son back up onto the road, behind him, acting as a shield between the infuriated Maestro and the dazed young man.

A moment frozen out of time, the Hulk and Maestro faced each other.

"Good. I'm glad you managed to change back," the Maestro told him. "It's better this way." And he closed quickly, swinging a roundhouse punch.

The Hulk chose the exact same moment to make the exact same move.

Both punches missed their targets, but their elbows interlocked. They were joined, arm in arm, like dancers.

The winds became more and more fierce, the Timeond glowing ever brighter. And now the howls of confused and angry Hulkbusters filled the air as the road started to ripple even more fiercely, the Maestro's will distracted by his opponent.

They struggled, the final battle, angling for position, trying to throw each other into the void. Their elbow-locked position brought them face to snarling face, past looking into future, hatred upon hatred—hatred of what one had been, and what one would be.

And the Maestro started to get the upper hand.

He began to bend the Hulk's arm backward, getting the higher leverage. Brett, on his feet, tried to get in to help, but the Hulk's body was between Brett and the Maestro. With a bellow of triumph, the Maestro bent the Hulk farther, farther down. . . .

The Hulk's face was at eye level with the Timeond, gleaming against the Maestro's chest.

He grabbed it with his teeth. And before the Maestro knew what was happening, the Hulk's powerful jaws bit down and shattered the mystic talisman.

The reaction was immediate and overwhelming. The wind, which until that moment had been a muffled roar, was now an earsplitting, overwhelming howl. A million voices from a billion realities, all screaming at once, protesting the incursion of these creatures.

The temporal ruptures that had threatened the Hulk on his original passage through now slammed through the interdimensional gateway with a force that escalated geometrically with every passing second. The Hulkbusters stood no chance at all. The road beneath them cracked, shattered, started dumping them wholesale into the outer reaches of eternity. Each of their confused and angry bellows became nothing more than just one more scream, joining the chorus of voices trapped forever in between.

The winds battered the Crossroads sign, shattering it. Roads of every color cracked apart, blasting into uncountable shards, multicolored rain that made the interdimensional zone seem like the inside of a child's snowflake globe.

And a light cut through. A beam of light, accompanied by a high-pitched, eldritch whine.

As the road cracked and splintered around them, the Hulk saw the ray. Hope, of which he had none, flared with renewed life.

The Hulk twisted in the Maestro's grip and slammed his head into the Maestro's face. The Maestro staggered back, the road crumbling beneath their feet, the nothingness reaching out to them all . . .

And the Hulk leaped upward toward the beam of light, praying that it was what he thought it was. Sure enough, it was more than just light. It was tangible. He snagged it with his right hand. He stretched out his left hand and shouted, "Brett! *Brett!*"

And as the road vanished under him, Brett jumped. He was not, nor would he ever be, on par with his father when it came to jumps.

This time, though, it was enough.

He snagged the Hulk's left hand, his fingers clutching desperately, trying to firm up the hold.

And then another weight jerked on him.

The road was gone. The Hulkbusters were gone.

The Maestro was still there. He was holding on to Brett's ankle.

"Brett! *Hold on!*" shouted the Hulk. But his grip on the beam of light wasn't all that secure. He struggled to reinforce it.

Brett desperately tried to kick the Maestro loose, but the creature's grip was too strong, his rage too towering. The Maestro started to haul himself up, hand over hand. His screeches of fury were drowned out by the howling of the wind.

The light beam started to retract, started to pull all three of them back to the point of origin. Brett slammed his free foot repeatedly into the Maestro's head, but the Maestro kept coming, kept climbing, using Brett to get closer and closer to the Hulk. . . .

And the Hulk's hold started to slide once more on the light beam. The struggle was too violent, the grip nowhere near steady enough.

Brett saw that they weren't going to make it.

He looked up into his father's eyes and at that moment the Hulk knew, knew beyond any question, what was about to happen. "*No!*" he screamed, his words carried away by the winds. "*No! Don't!*"

Brett yanked his wrist free of the Hulk's grasp.

The Hulk grabbed out desperately, but it was too late. Brett and the Maestro plummeted away, falling faster and faster, locked in combat and snarling into each other's face. Within seconds they became specks, twin blobs of gray and green, whirling away into nothingness.

And the winds bore away with them the sounds of a father's grief . . . .

EPILOGUE

For Major Bill Talbot, it had begun and ended in Chicago.

He stood on the curbside of the busy street, looking smart and proud in his full dress uniform, thinking about the battle that had taken place in this very spot many months ago.

There he had battled the Hulk.

There he had had the opportunity to get the job done . . . and had failed to do so.

And when confronting Banner months later, he had failed again. Failed more comprehensively, more thoroughly, than he would have believed possible.

Only two people knew, of course. He himself . . . and the Hulk. The creature who had bedeviled his uncle, defied authority—the creature who was the living incarnation of everything that Talbot stood against—had won. Had beaten him in as complete and profound a way as he could ever be beaten.

He had long dreamed of going up against the Hulk. He had aspired to bring him in. Indeed, he had aspired to greatness. In many ways, the Hulk—and his hatred for the monster—had filled much of his life. Had become one of his great goals.

He could never face the Hulk again.

Because the Hulk would always know. Always. He would always look at him with that mixture of pity and contempt.

He could never face his superiors. For they would consider him an officer, and he would consider himself a lie.

He could never face his subordinates, for who was he to give someone an order?

He faced a life where nothing could ever be as it was. Where someone he hated and despised would always be superior to him. Would always have that hold over him.

He could not allow that.

It simply was not an option.

But no one must ever know. There could be no suspicion. Not the slightest.

That, however, was easily arranged.

He glanced to the left ever so briefly. The white station wagon was hurtling toward the intersection, rushing to make the light before it changed to red. Perfect.

He walked out directly into its path.

He didn't even feel the impact of the front fender as it crumpled against him. Instead he felt free, as if he were flying for the briefest of instants before his body slammed against the windshield. It spiderwebbed, the driver shrieking, the airbag already in the process of inflating and breaking her forward motion.

She slammed on the brakes and Talbot rolled off, moving at roughly thirty miles an hour. He hit the street, rolled, crashing into a lamppost with enough impact to split his skull.

Sylvia leaped out of her car, screeching. The car that she had taken such pride in. The car that Betty, her former coworker, had brought back without a scratch (as Sylvia had begged), albeit with traces of a stench like a sewer that had taken Sylvia fully a month to get out.

"My car! My car!" she kept wailing, still in shock over what had happened and, therefore, oblivious of the dying man on the pavement.

Major Talbot stared up at the gathering pedestrians. And as the light faded from his eyes, his last conscious thought was that maybe Javert wasn't such a freaking moron after all. . . .

It was as if he had never left.

Within moments after Strange had sent the Hulk into the interdimensional zone, he had sensed some sort of temporal collapse. So he had sent the light from the eye of Agamotto back into the portal, as a probe and—if necessary—a lifeline. It had pulled the Hulk back through . . .

And the Hulk had sat there, grief-stricken.

Betty knew. She knew the moment that she'd seen his face. He hadn't needed to say anything. Indeed, when he started to, she had put up a hand and simply said, "Don't."

And she had said nothing further.

That had been several weeks ago.

Betty Thaddeus, for such she was calling herself now, sat on the small balcony on the second floor of her modest rented home in Boulder, Colorado. The street was lined with trees. It was late in the afternoon, the sun a great red ball hanging low in the sky.

Her husband sat nearby at a computer, studying a particularly confusing bit of research.

"Okay," she said.

Bruce turned and peered over the top of his glasses at her. Relief fluttered in his chest. All this time she had been silent. Not a word had she uttered. Leonard had been keeping close tabs on them, and had been sure that sooner or later she would start speaking again. Nevertheless, Bruce's concern had been growing. Now, though . . .

Well . . . now what?

"Okay?" he echoed. "Okay . . . what?"

"Okay, you can tell me what happened."

Slowly he removed his glasses, moved over toward where she was sitting, and began to speak. He tried to keep his voice as even as he could, although there were several points where he almost cracked.

Finally, when he got to the end of the narrative, he simply stopped. And waited.

"His life wasn't wasted," she said after a time. "It wasn't for nothing."

"The Maestro was going to invade our world. Thousands . . . perhaps millions would have died."

"And Brett prevented that."

"Yes. He did."

Tears started to trickle down her face, and she wiped them away, steadying her chin. "You want to know what a bitch I am?"

The word seemed a tremendous obscenity coming from her. "You?" he asked in surprise.

"I am so selfish that part of me doesn't care about millions of faceless people. It just cares about one. Just one face . . . that I won't see again."

"Look in the mirror," Bruce told her. "They say eyes are the window of the soul. He had your eyes. . . . I think he had some of your soul, too."

She looked back out at the sun.

"Hold me," she whispered.

He did so, gently, and they stayed that way until long after the sun had set, and the green of the trees had been swallowed by darkness.